A LADYLIKE RETICENCE

"I really must be going, my lord," Megge managed.

He bent his head toward her. "I don't think so."

In some dim corner of her mind, Megge felt she owed it to the dictates of propriety to make one last desperate stand before she melted like tallow in his arms. "That, sir, must be my decision, not yours."

Sir Olyver looked up at the stars, as though seeking guidance. "Hmmm. You are quite right, my lady." He stepped away and tucked his hands behind his back.

"Oh." She adjusted her cloak.

"Well, then." She backed up a step.

"I'll just…"

She launched herself straight at him.

Other books by Jennie Klassel:

GIRL ON THE RUN
SHE WHO LAUGHS LAST

The Lady Doth Protest

JENNIE KLASSEL

LEISURE BOOKS   NEW YORK CITY

A LEISURE BOOK®

March 2005

Published by

Dorchester Publishing Co., Inc.
200 Madison Avenue
New York, NY 10016

ISBN 0-8439-5392-6

Visit us on the web at www.dorchesterpub.com.

For Marc Ratner and David M. Ratner,
who rode to the rescue.

"Love and war are the same thing, and stratagems
and policy are allowable in the one as in the other."
—Cervantes, *Don Quixote*

'Tis said that when the moon sails full o'er the Great Tower of Castle Rising and the Merry Dancers rule the northern skies, then do the fairest of the Fay slip from the amorous embrace of their lovers' arms, creep from the chamber of love, and venture forth from the half light of the lower realm into the world of men. There, with haunting cries and magic herbs do they send foolish mortals from the place and secure the precinct for their dark design.

Then does the artful Tytania herself ascend the ramparts for all to see, and calls out to the men of the Fay in such wise:

"Grant each of us our heart's desire and we will lie with you once more, and with passion and abandon join with you in love's sweet play. Fail to bestow upon us this boon and you shall suffer the pangs of unfulfilled desire, nor will you find solace in any arms but ours. Hear this, o men of Fay and believe."

And the call goes forth for Auberon, cunning king of the Fay, to come to the aid of those lovesick fools who will not forswear, that he should command the siege of that unassail-

1

able citadel and compel proud Tytania and her company to yield.

Who can foretell the final act of such a comedy? With each new playing the ending differs. Now Tytania, now Auberon, prevails, and we can only wait 'til the next full moon to discover how love makes fools—or wiser men—of us all.

Chapter One

"Betrothed at nine. Betrothed at twelve. At fifteen."

Megge swung around, her green wool gown swishing against the blue carpet figured with tiny birds, and paced from hearth to window, frowning in concentration as she ticked off on each slim finger a suitor who had failed to survive long enough to wed and bed her. "Oh, and let us not forget that paragon of knightly virtue, Sir Crispin," she exclaimed. "That makes four."

She glowered at Lady Orabella as though that plump, kindly person might very well be the author of the evils she was now recounting. "Accidents will happen, dear," the good lady replied as she stared thoughtfully at the delicate little cornflowers she had just embroidered around the neckline of a pale blue silk bliaut. "We cannot know the mind of the Lord in these matters. We are all but instruments of His will."

"Accidents? *Accidents?*" cried Megge. "Perhaps in the first three instances—I will include a fatal malady as an accident of fate in the case of that snotty-nosed

Jennie Klassel

little Arthur person when I was but nine—but Baron Broward suffering a heart seizure in the arms of a harlot only hours before our betrothal contract was to be signed certainly cannot be consigned to the realm of the accidental."

Lady Orabella smiled. "No, I suppose not. But if you will consider it from a different perspective, Megge, is it not fortunate that he expired during his moment of supreme joy in her arms rather than in yours?"

Little Lady Sybille giggled. Delicate as a china doll, she would be as dim at seventy as she was at seventeen. Since she had nary a thought of her own and could scarce follow the thoughts of others, she was inclined to giggle, titter, and nod her pretty little head yes or no according to what she thought was expected of her.

Everyone loved Sybille, for she never gave or took offense, and her new husband was well pleased to have secured so obliging and malleable a young woman, not to mention her large dowry. Barely five months after the consummation of her marriage Lady Sybille was already with child and was uncertain what supreme joy Lady Orabella referred to. She herself paid the marriage debt dutifully, and her young husband usually finished up his part of the transaction so quickly that it was difficult to ascertain if his shout of completion was of supreme joy or merely relief that he had done his duty and could now return to the arms of his mistress.

Megge was not to be mollified. "Well, I can tell you what the Lord has in mind for me," she announced. "Perpetual virginity, that's what." She threw up her hands in disgust. "I am four and twenty and still a maid and likely to remain so.

"Which," she added with an impatient toss of the head that sent curly dark brown hair tumbling down her back, "brings me to my 'marriages,' which, to date, number three. Thrice have I stood before the church door, thrice has the king placed my hand in the hand of the suitor of his choice or his representative—*his* choice, I should like to emphasize—thrice has the marriage bed been prepared—"

"Once," Lady Orabella corrected. "You really must curb this tendency to exaggerate matters, my dear. It was most unfortunate that Sir Wallwit could not take the time to bone the mackerel before taking such a large bite at the marriage feast, and the second and third times, if you will recall, you were married by proxy. You could not very well expect Lord Ardleigh to bed you in his nephew's stead now, could you?

"Nor, I suspect, would you have wished it so if such a thing were possible," she continued as she selected a skein of creamy yellow thread with the intent of replacing the cornflowers with primroses. "It cannot be at all pleasant to kiss a man with but two or three teeth left in his mouth."

Mistress Gilly, comfortably ensconced upon the scarlet-striped cushions in the window seat, let out a loud guffaw. "Snuff out the candle and one man's as good as another so long as he possesses a lance bigger than his thumb and can find the mark."

Megge plopped down on the padded bench opposite Lady Orabella, and sighed. "I wouldn't know. Perhaps if Lord St. Mihiel hadn't stopped off at every brothel between Constantinople and Rome on his way home from Palestine he might not have died of the pox on the crossing to Dover."

"Just as well, my dear," Lady Orabella opined.

"They say he was quite mad by the time they departed Harfleur. I don't believe he would have been at all agreeable to live with. And I can tell you his skin was not pleasant to behold," she added, as though the pox and blotchy skin carried equal weight when it came to imperfections in one's husband.

"I never even met the man," Megge grumbled. "But you're missing the point, Lady Orabella. The bald fact of the matter is that I am six times betrothed—no, seven if we include Sir Crispin—and thrice widowed before once bedded. It is fortunate, I suppose, that my marriages were unconsummated, as I am still in possession of my fortune. Yet I am one of the wealthiest women in all England and cannot put my finger upon one penny of it without the king's leave. I possess vast holdings from St. Michael's Mount to the northern marches, yet I must live beneath another's roof. Not," she added hastily, "that I am not grateful to be Sir Humphrey's ward and live here with you at Flete, but—"

"It is not home." Lady Orabella completed Megge's thought with a sympathetic nod. "I understand, my dear. You have been passed around like a platter of sweet wafers from one hand to another. You possess the finest castle in the south of England—"

Megge took up her embroidery hoop. "In name only," she interjected with a little sniff. "I have little memory of having lived at Castle Rising at all. Papa died when I was but eight and I went to live at court at Westminster. Then to Winchester," she recited, "Dover, Chester, Ardleigh. Bordeaux, Bayonne—"

"And Exeter," Lady Orabella finished, hoping to put an end to Megge's litany of complaints. "Finally

6

you came to us here at Flete. And what joy you brought to us, Megge when the king, before leaving on Crusade, settled upon Humphrey as your guardian."

Yes, Megge thought, it had been a happy day when she came to live at Flete Castle after being shuttled about for a good portion of her twenty-four years. But now the king was considering yet another husband for her, and the man of his choice might very well be none other than the awful Sir Walter, Lord Humphrey's own brother, nearly as old as he and as mean–spirited and sour in his disposition as Lord Humphrey was generous and amiable. Perhaps the lot of younger sons, possessed of no property or standing in the world save what they could earn through their skill in the tournament and on the battlefield, would curdle or harden even the most agreeab'e disposition.

If Sir Walter was an example of the former—as acerbic a man as Megge had ever met—then the fearsome and cold-hearted Sir Olyver of Mannyngs stood as a prime example of the latter, as Megge had reason to know all too well. She had met Lord Humphrey's "right arm," as he called Sir Olyver, only once, on the occasion of his investiture at Westminster when she was but thirteen. It hadn't gone well. It hadn't been her fault.

"Sir Olyver of Mannyngs, my lady."

"Lady Margaret de Languetot, my lord."

He would have bowed and she would have curtsied had the circumstances allowed, but as she was cradled in his arms, disheveled and sopping wet, the introduction would have to do and proper etiquette be set aside.

Megge scrambled for something to say. Since he had just scooped her out of a snowdrift the weather seemed a safe enough topic. "It has been a rather cold winter."

"It has, my lady. Perhaps you should consider wearing a cloak when you are out of doors."

Megge hadn't intended to be out of doors this day. If that snob Beatrice had kept her hateful opinions to herself, Megge wouldn't have had to chase her into the garden and stuff snow down her neck to teach her a lesson, and she wouldn't have ended up tripping over the hem of her pretty new pink gown and falling flat on her face in a snowdrift.

As she had been defending Sir Olyver's honor at the time and hoped he had not heard their conversation, she replied only that she was forever forgetting her mantle and should probably acquire a maid whose sole duty would be to see that she never went out without one.

What else could she talk about? Of course! The man had just been knighted, for heaven's sake. "I congratulate you, Sir Olyver, on receiving your spurs."

"Thank you, my lady."

It had been the first time Megge had witnessed an investiture first-hand, and she had found the ceremony oddly moving.

"Olyver of Mannyngs," King Henry had intoned, "is it your desire to become my man and serve me faithfully?"

The kneeling man placed his hand upon the gold and jewel-encrusted repository containing the relics of Edward the Confessor himself, and bowed his head.

"I so wish, my liege."

"Speak then your oath."

"Henry of England, I become thy man, to bear thee faith of life and member and earthly worship against all men who live and can die, saving the faith of my lord Henry, King of England and his heirs, and of my other lords—if other lords

there be. I swear this without reservation or deception before this company and upon these sacred relics."

"Arise, Sir Olyver of Mannyngs."

The kiss was bestowed; the chamberlain handed the king his jeweled ceremonial sword; and Henry struck the ritual blow upon Sir Olyver's right shoulder.

"Ooohhh," the ladies in the gallery cooed. The initiates who had preceded Sir Olyver had staggered beneath the blow, but he stood firm, quite as though he had felt nothing at all.

"Who was that?" Lady Beatrice inquired as the little group glided along a sheltered arcade on its way toward the banquet hall for the celebratory feast. "He looks so stern and cold. Positively barbaric. Don't you agree, Megge?"

Megge, who had been considering what to name her beautiful new peregrine—a gift from the king to celebrate her betrothal to Crispin of Ely—and had been listening to the chatter around her with only half an ear, frowned. "Who?"

"Sir Olyver."

Lady Enid made it her business to know everything about everybody. "His father is Baron Willard of Mannyngs, but he's the fifth son. He has no property and is not to be enfeoffed. He is Lord Humphrey's man, and will command his soldiers."

Lady Beatrice sniffed. "A mercenary, you mean. Most likely he will die in battle or perish of some vile malady in the Holy Land. Of what use can such a man be?"

Megge, whose own father had met just such an end, took instant exception. "That is the most cold-blooded thing I have ever heard you say, Beatrice. It is not the circumstance of a man's birth but what he makes of his life that shows his true character."

"Oh pooh, Megge. Would you think to marry a fifth son? Or a bastard? Of course you wouldn't. You are a descendant of a king."

Megge bristled. "William of Normandy, I would have you know, was a bastard. He did very well for himself. Perhaps this Sir Olyver will, too."

Lady Beatrice let her jealousy of Megge's high station and noble ancestry get the better of her. "Then why don't you marry him if you are so very concerned for his future?" she sneered. "It would be quite a feather in his cap."

It was at that point that things had gotten out of hand and landed Megge in the care of the very man she'd been defending.

"Thank you, my lord," Megge said, returning to the moment and feeling utterly ridiculous in her ruined gown with her circlet askew and her dripping hair in disarray. "There was no need to bring me all the way to my chamber door."

"It was my honor, my lady."

Megge hesitated. "Well, good day, then." She could not help wondering if he had overheard Beatrice's cruel remarks, since he had been close by.

"I do not wear a cap, Lady Margaret."

"I beg your pardon?"

"I do not wear a cap, therefore I would have nowhere to put my feather."

He had heard, then. Megge felt terrible. "I am so very sorry, my lord."

"That I wear no cap and have no hope of a feather?"

"I don't know," she mumbled, uncomfortable with the thought that she might be the feather under discussion.

"Do not distress yourself, my lady. Your friend is quite right. A younger son must make his way in the world as best he can. It is the way of things."

Megge did not know what to say, so she said nothing.

Sir Olyver bowed. "Farewell, Lady Margaret."

She would never know what prompted it, but she sank

into a deep formal curtsy as she might before the king him-
self. "Farewell, Sir Olyver."

"My lord," she called as he walked away.

"My lady?"

"I hope you don't. Die in battle or perish from some vile
malady."

Lady Orabella plucked out her cornflowers and prepared to plant primroses on her niece's new gown.
Megge glared at her own poorly executed effort. She
took a deep breath.

"I shan't."

She had been leading up to this announcement
ever since the ladies of Flete Castle had settled in
Lady Orabella's solar for the morning. From without
the high walls of the castle could be heard a distant
boom of thunder, heralding yet another day of dis-
mal rain and storms, a day quite suitable, Megge
imagined, for the storm her own announcement was
about to unleash.

"Shan't what, my dear?" queried Lady Orabella,
biting off a thread.

"Shan't marry Sir Walter," Megge replied in as off-
hand a tone of voice as she could manage.

Four pairs of eyes, two blue, one hazel, one brown,
swung in her direction. Megge feigned ignorance of
the astonishment and consternation her announcement occasioned, and bent to her work.

"Surely you don't mean—"

"Really, Megge, what a foolish notion—"

Giggle, giggle.

"Have you lost your wits, girl?"

Megge tossed aside her hoop, leaped up, and resumed her pacing. "I do mean, my lady. And it's not a

foolish notion, Lady Agnes. For heaven's sake, Sybille, will you never stop giggling? And no, I have not lost my wits, Mistress Gilly. In fact, I feel as though I have only just found them.

"I have," she declared, assuming a defiant stance, "decided that I shall not marry again unless the man be of my own choosing. Furthermore, I intend to take up residence at Castle Rising, as is my right under the king's law and in the eyes of God, and make it my home. No man shall have control of my inheritance even if I do choose to marry." She finished up her little tirade even more melodramatically with a wide sweep of her arm. "*Je suis Castle Rising et Castle Rising c'est moi!*"

Too shocked even to giggle, Sybille stared openmouthed at the madwoman who had been vivacious Megge but moments ago. Lady Agnes tut-tutted. Mistress Gilly, Lady Orabella's longtime companion, appeared bewildered and not a little apprehensive, as though Lord Humphrey's ward had just sprouted horns and a tail.

"Calm yourself, my dear," Lady Orabella said. "You don't want to incite that rash that comes upon you when you are unduly agitated. Agnes, Gilly, Sybille, you will please excuse us. I wish to speak with Megge alone. Gilly, please have cook bring a tonic for Megge's nerves. She is overwrought."

"There is absolutely nothing wrong with my nerves," Megge declared as the door closed behind the three women. "Nor my wits. I have given this much thought, my lady, and I have come to the conclusion that it is the only way for me to assume control of my own life. Do you not think it unfair," Megge cried, "that a woman's happiness in this life hangs upon the whim of a father, a brother, her husband, a guardian?"

"Well, as to a whim—" Lady Orabella began.

"Why cannot I choose my own husband? Why cannot I see to the business of my own estates, see to the welfare of my people?"

"A woman does not—"

"Who better to know my heart than I?" Megge demanded of the world.

"Perhaps—"

"No one, that's who!" Megge answered her own question with a stomp of her foot.

"Megge, my dear, it is not so much a matter of the heart as of the mind," Lady Orabella managed to interject, as Megge had for the moment run out of breath. "A woman does not marry for love but for advantage—her own and that of her family. Yes, yes," she continued before Megge could open her mouth to object, "when we are young we may dream of the handsome knight who has eyes for no one but ourselves. And if God so wills it, He will send such a man to us. Alas, He rarely does, so we must be content with what we are given and find our happiness in fulfilling our duty. Perhaps someday. . . ."

Megge stared out the narrow window at the gathering clouds as Lady Orabella meandered on, imagining she could almost see the towers of Castle Rising forty miles to the southwest, high above the broad estuary of the River Lis where it flowed into the sea. She had few memories of her early years there and had only returned on three or four occasions when the old king or Edward had stopped in on one of their endless tours of their realm. Yet that magnificent, unassailable edifice, renovated less than a decade earlier by Master James of St. George himself, had ever been in her heart, had ever been her true home. There in the lovely little family chapel rested the mother she could barely recall save for an elusive memory of soft breath upon her cheek and the faintest scent of rosemary, and the handsome brass memorial plaque for her father, as tall and strong as a great oak in her child's eye, who had fallen sick and died during the siege of Anamur.

Yes, she thought, she was the mistress of Castle Rising. She would claim what was hers by right, make it her home. Its great walls would shield her, create an impregnable refuge where she would no longer be a pawn to be married now to this lord, now to that, at the king's pleasure and for his own political and financial advantage.

" 'Tis madness, Megge, even to contemplate such a rash course of action," Lady Orabella was saying, "not to mention treason. You are subject to His Majesty's command, as are we all, even the greatest of lords. If he bid you marry again, so you shall as your honor demands. Edward dotes upon you and has shown you every kindness since your poor father's death. Never once has he disparaged you by choosing a husband beneath your station. Will you now repay him with disloyalty and disaffection?"

Just such remorseful reflection had plagued Megge in the days since the message arrived from Lord Humphrey in France that his own brother, Walter, had offered for Megge and that Edward had taken the offer under serious consideration. Sir Walter was the last man on earth Megge wanted to marry, nor would she consent *were* he the last man on earth. Canon law might require a woman's consent to wed, but secular power—King Edward—was such that through subtle pressure or outright intimidation few women possessed the courage to object, no matter how reprehensible the man or how dreadful the life she might expect by such a union.

Megge had no need to hear Lady Orabella's present discourse on the duty to marry well and advantageously. She had long ago let go her romantic, girlish dreams and well understood that marriages were arranged with either family connection or material advantage in mind, preferably both. Love had nothing to do with it. She had never expected it. Perhaps a small spark of hope still sputtered somewhere deep in her heart that the Good Lord would indeed send her a handsome knight whom she could love, who would love her, but it lay buried so deep that she herself had no inkling that it lived still.

"So you see, my dear, we must trust our menfolk to decide what is best for us. Of course," Lady Orabella added with a frown, "they do not always know. My Humphrey will never understand that a woman may not desire yet another babe, having birthed five already and provided a strapping young heir and four to spare. He is now partial to the idea of pretty little daughters and mentioned before he left for the games at Coucy that he hoped I would provide him a daughter upon his return." She sighed. "Unfortunately, he shall have another babe soon. Lord help me if it is not a girl, for I shall have to try again."

Megge practically bounced across the room. "There, you see!" she cried. "You are an excellent example of what I'm talking about. You do not wish another stint in childbed, yet he tells you it is *his* desire, it is *his* will. He knows nothing of the matter, of the toll each child takes upon its mother's body. He does not consult you, whether you wish it or no. *He* wishes it, so it must be done! My lady," she said earnestly, "have you never thought to gainsay him?"

Lady Orabella stared at Megge. "Of course not, my dear, he—"

"*He*," cried Megge. "He! He! He! What do you think he would do, could do, if you told him you did not want to bear another babe?"

"I've never thought about it," Lady Orabella admitted. "He comes to my bed, we pay our marriage debt, and off he goes to settle some spat in Spain or joust at the spring fairs, and I bear the child he leaves behind."

"You could say no," Megge insisted. "Or at the very least discuss the matter with him."

"I could?"

"Yes. You could. He is not the kind of man who would force you."

Lady Orabella pinkened. "But I rather enjoy Humphrey's, um, husbandly attentions. We both find it most—"

Now it was Megge's turn to blush. "I am sure you do, my lady," she interjected before Lady Orabella could launch into a description of Lord Humphrey's skill in the marriage bed. "But would it not be possible to deny him until he is willing to listen to your thoughts on the matter of childbearing?"

The very idea shocked Lady Orabella to the core. "Deny him? Tell him he cannot come to my bed?"

"No, my lady, you are missing the point again. You

can keep him from your bed by the simple expedient of not being in it!"

Now came the moment Megge had been waiting for. "Come to Castle Rising with me, my lady," she entreated. "We shall take the keep and hold it until such time as Lord Humphrey and whoever else he brings with him to lay siege will negotiate with us to grant each of us what we desire—no, not just desire but *need* in order to be happy, or at the very least, content with our lot in life. Have you never heard the old story of the women of Athens who barricaded themselves atop the Acropolis and would not grant their favors or yield until their men made peace with Sparta?

"We could be those women!" Megge declared with shining eyes. "We will take Castle Rising by guile, since we cannot do so by force as men would do. We will make known our determination to have a say in matters that most closely concern us."

Her mind whirled with possibilities. "Even silly little Sybille would profit: She could demand of Sir Frederick that he teach her the way to take her own pleasure in his arms. Why should he achieve that supreme joy and not she? And Lady Agnes could demand of that rogue Sir Siward that he cease frittering away her inheritance, gambling and whoring and outfitting himself and his men with no respect for economy. They will be quite undone if he continues so.

"And the maids, the cooks, all the women of your hall and the village of Rising," Megge enthused as she envisioned in her mind's eye a veritable army of women upon the ramparts of Castle Rising, their eyes

17

afire with the righteousness of their cause, their hearts and minds implacable, their victory inevitable.

"We shall have our say!" she promised women everywhere. "Men will have no choice but to listen or suffer the pangs of unfulfilled desire until they are forced to their knees to beg for relief. Nor shall they have it until each woman has made known her desire. We will unite! We will create a new world of our own making!"

"Oh my," said Lady Orabella.

Chapter Two

A sennight later, when the heady warmth of late spring had finally settled upon England's southwest coast, Megge aimed a dramatic finger at the base of a blossoming pear tree close by the high wall that enclosed Flete's orchard, and declared, "There you have it."

Lady Orabella leaned forward as much as her expanding girth would allow and peered dubiously at the small, neat mound of dirt. "What do I have, dear?"

"Why, ants, of course," Megge replied.

"Ants?"

"Look there. No, over there in that clump of grass. See that little ant trying to drag that long stalk toward the anthill? It must seem like miles away, but the ant can't give up—will not give up—until it drags that succulent leaf to her babes that they may thrive. With each step the burden becomes heavier. The ant tires, falls to her knees, her tiny heart filled with regret that she has failed. But behold! Other ants are coming to her rescue. Look how they help her to cut up the leaf of grass so that it will be easier to get it back to the nest. That," Megge concluded happily, "is exactly what we are going to do."

Lady Orabella straightened up. "I for one have no intention of eating grass when there is such a wonderful crop of spinach and early lettuce in the kitchen garden. The leeks are coming along nicely too. I so enjoy leek pie. Really, Megge, you do come up with the most curious notions."

"I am not suggesting, my lady, that we eat grass," Megge began, then abandoned the idea of using such a simple analogy to make her point. It had been such a happy thought—illustrating to the ladies of Flete Castle that by acting in concert for the good of all, the goal of each of them might be more easily achieved. Perhaps she should take a more direct approach, Megge reflected, as she and Lady Orabella settled down on a wooden bench near the arch that separated the orchard proper from the extensive flower gardens.

"What I am trying to say, my lady, is that I have come to the conclusion that it is easier for a woman to win her point with her lord if she joins with other women who find themselves in similar circumstances."

Lady Orabella plucked a stray peach blossom from Megge's dark curls. "Oh dear, you're not going to start that business of seizing Castle Rising again, are you, my dear? I had hoped you'd put that foolish notion right out of your mind."

"Oh no! I have thought long and hard upon it these past days, and if you and the others will just hear me out, my lady, I am sure you will see the wisdom of the thing." She jumped up, strode to the arch, threw up her hands, and plopped back down onto the bench beside Lady Orabella. "Wherever can they be? I sent the boy for them past half an hour ago.

"Why is it that women are always late when summoned?" she continued crossly. "There is always some excuse. 'My lord had need of my company in his chamber'—we know what *that* means—or, 'The children had need of me in the nursery'—or they want to change their gowns or fuss with their hair or see to any number of other menial tasks that could easily be put off to another time."

"For one thing," Lady Orabella replied, "a woman is not a hound to be whistled for or summoned like some lowly serf. And," she added, "a proper woman is about her duties as wife, mother, and mistress of her hall at this hour of the morning, not stirring up mischief in the orchard, like someone I could name."

The words had been delivered in the mildest of tones, as was Lady Orabella's wont, but a reprimand it was, nonetheless. "I'm sorry, my lady, you are quite right. I'm only anxious to get this under way."

Voices could now be heard approaching through the flower garden, and soon the ladies Sybille and Agnes passed beneath the stone arch, followed by Mistress Gilly, with the formidable twins, Gunnilda and Gunreda, known as Gunny One and Gunny Two, head cook and laundress, respectively, lumbering along behind.

When everyone had settled on the benches or the warm new grass, Megge rose, and clasping her hands behind her back, paced up and down the pebbled path like a commander before her troops.

"I expect you are all wondering why I summoned—requested—you to come here to the orchard today—" she began.

"I'm starving," declared Lady Sybille. "Did anyone bring anything to eat?"

Mistress Gilly reached into the deep pocket of her linen apron and brought forth a small sack. "Gingered nuts," she announced.

"Oooh," cooed Sybille as she reached for it. When Mistress Gilly had passed round the bag and everyone was munching happily, Megge commenced her little speech with an affronted snort. "As I was saying when I was so rudely interrupted, we are gathered here today to embark upon a great crusade—"

"We're going on Crusade, my lady?" said Gunny One. "Like the Knights Templar?"

"No—"

"It is not the place of a woman to go on Crusade," Lady Agnes reminded everyone. "One does not hear of the Ladies Templar, does one?"

"Of course not," Megge began, but was interrupted by the indignant bray of Gunny Two. "Aye, they do."

"They most certainly do not," Lady Agnes retorted.

"Ladies, please, if you would just allow Megge to—" Lady Orabella entreated.

"What about Queen Eleanor?" Gunny Two demanded. "She traveled to the very gates of the Holy City itself. All decked out like a warrior queen she was, and her ladies riding astride clad in hauberks and tabards bearing the white Crusader's Cross on a field of red."

"Most unladylike. And uncomfortable, I should think," observed Lady Agnes with a sniff. "I'm surprised King Henry allowed it."

Megge pounced. "There," she exclaimed in a voice sufficiently loud to silence the chatter, "that is exactly why I asked you to come here today."

"Because Queen Eleanor wore armor?" Lady Sybille said, a tiny frown marring her lovely white brow.

Megge prayed for patience. "No, not because Queen Eleanor wore armor, Sybille. Because Queen Eleanor needed Henry's permission to go on Crusade. Why could she not simply say, 'Henry, I'm leaving for Jerusalem in the morning. I expect to return in a year or two. I'll be sure to write.'"

"Well?" she demanded, well satisfied with the confusion, incomprehension, and alarmed concern on the faces around her. She answered her own question with a sweep of her arm. "There *is* no reason, that's why."

"We're going to Jerusalem, my lady?" inquired Gunny One.

Megge closed her eyes and with a sigh answered through clenched teeth, "No, Gunny. Not to Jerusalem. To Castle Rising."

"We're going on Crusade to Castle Rising?" piped up Sybille around a mouthful of nuts.

"I don't recall hearing that Saracens had taken Castle Rising," Lady Agnes interjected. "Is it not in Devon? I thought they preferred a southern clime."

"Devils, they are," opined Mistress Gilly. "Can't trust a one of them Infidels. Big brutes, take a woman, willing or not, wreak their wicked will on her in ways no decent Christian man would think of. Why, I heard tell they got three ballocks, big ones that hang near to their knees, and their lances—"

"I think we need not go into the, er, attributes of the Infidels," Lady Orabella said hastily. "We are gathered here at Megge's request because she has something of great import she wishes to discuss with us. If you will hold your tongues and do her the courtesy of giving her your undivided attention, she can do so, and we can all return to our duties."

"Thank you, my lady," said Megge, grateful for Lady Orabella's intervention, since she herself wanted to scream in frustration. "I should like to ask each of you what she most desires in the world. Let us begin with you, Sybille."

"Rose-colored silk shifts," came the girl's prompt reply. "Linen is all very well, but it doesn't take dye all that well, and I do so like pink. One gets so weary of white and ivory."

"No, no, that's wrong," Megge interrupted. "You desire a moment of supreme joy."

"I do?"

"Yes, you do."

"But, but," stammered Lady Sybille, "is it allowed? Father Boniface instructed me as to my marital duties and he never once mentioned supreme joy. 'You are but a vessel,'" she quoted like a dutiful child, "'created by God for the pleasure of your lord. He may do with you as he will in fulfillment of the marriage debt, and you are bound by your most holy vows to accede to his every desire, as repugnant and coarse as it may appear to you, and to receive his treasured seed with humility and gratitude.'"

"Treasured seed?" Gunny One snickered.

"Gratitude?" Gunny Two hooted.

Lady Sybille tossed her head. "Well, that's what he said. He's a priest, so he must know."

"And a man," Mistress Gilly said darkly. "And we all

know what's uppermost in a man's mind from morn to night."

"And lowermost in a man's—"

"That is quite enough, Gilly," said Lady Orabella. "Really, ladies, we shall be here until prime if you go on like this. Please allow Megge to continue."

Megge fixed her eyes upon Lady Agnes. "What of you, my lady, what is your heart's desire?"

Lady Agnes deliberated for a moment. "I think I should like a manor of my own. Not that it is not delightful living here at Flete, especially with Siward away so much of the time, but a woman wants her own hall. Of course," she added with a sigh, "it is most unlikely to ever come to pass. Even if Lord Humphrey would grant Siward such a boon, he is, I must admit, somewhat of a spendthrift; always from home travelling from one tournament to the next, more often losing horse and armor than winning it."

Megge jumped to her feet. "You shall have your hall, Agnes, and Sir Siward will not be gallivanting about unless you give him leave to do so."

"I will? How is that to come to pass?"

"You'll see," Megge promised. "But first, let us discover what the others have to say."

Mistress Gilly admitted that she wanted nothing more than to be rid of her husband's mother, who had come to visit them in their small cottage in the village and had never once made mention of departing in the nine years since the day she arrived. Gunny One would have her man eschew garlic and other foods that left a foul odor in the mouth and bathe more than twice a year.

Gunny Two complained that her Magnus was so

wedded to the pleasures of the table—most especially tripe, kidney, and the offal of swine—that the measure of his girth far exceeded that of his height, with the unhappy result that he was unable to wield his lance effectively in the performance of the conjugal debt, indeed could not reach the mark at all.

"I am not particularly fond of tripe," said Lady Sybille to no one in particular, having missed the point entirely, "but I do like a nice fatty bit of pork done up in a red sauce of chopped almonds, Corinth raisins, and minced crayfish tails. I have a delicious recipe for calf's brain—"

"I think," Megge interjected hastily, "that we might leave the subject of cookery for some other time and stay with the point that Gunny is trying to make, namely that she would have her husband temper one appetite in favor of another."

Lady Sybille turned to Gunny Two and wagged a delicate finger. "It seems to me that it is you who are at fault in this matter. A man likes his meat, and a wife's duty—"

"Sybille, dear," Lady Orabella said, seizing the girl by the arm and propelling her toward the postern gate that led to the inner ward, "I have need of the privy. I should be delighted if you would accompany me. It is so very uncomfortable when one is with child," she could be heard saying as she marched Sybille away, "to be ever in need of the privy."

"What a silly little goose that girl is," observed Lady Agnes. "I vow she has no more wits than a flea."

Megge once again took up a commanding stance upon the path and gazed down at the three remaining women. "I should like to sum up our various wishes and desires, and then I shall tell you of my plan. I shall begin with myself. I want leave of the king to choose my own husband. Further, I want to take up residence in Castle Rising now and retain control of my own fortune should I choose to marry again.

"I speak for Lady Orabella," she continued, "when I say that she would have Lord Humphrey understand the rigors of childbearing and be willing to consult with her regarding any future offspring he may have in mind. Lady Sybille, though she knows it not, has need of a moment of supreme joy. Lady Agnes would have her own hall and Sir Siward refrain from depleting her fortune at the tournament. Mistress Gilly wishes to see the back of her mother-in-law. Gunny One would have her husband cleaner in his person. Gunny Two wishes her husband to value the obligations of their bed above the pleasures of the table.

"It is within your power, each of you, to have what you desire. You can! You shall!" Megge declared in ringing tones. "Hark now, and I will tell you how it is to be accomplished."

Lady Orabella carefully teased out a tangle in Megge's long hair with a wide-toothed comb. A soft May evening had settled over Flete Castle, and the cries of nightjars and the scent of honeysuckle wafted through the narrow window of Megge's chamber high in the south tower. "I think it best we not tell Sybille of this plan. We shall, of course, take her with us, but she is no more able to keep a secret than a newborn babe is to cease its bawling when it has need of the teat. But what of the others?"

"It took some doing to convince them," Megge confessed, "but ultimately they saw the soundness of the plan. They know full well that physical need will bring even the strongest of men to his knees. It will be but days before your lord and their husbands capitulate."

Lady Orabella set aside the comb and took up the cup of warm sweetened goat milk it was her custom to drink before she retired. "I think I should point out that Gunny Two is not likely to achieve her purpose by denying her Magnus her sexual favors when he has so clearly demonstrated his preference in the matter of his appetites in favor of gluttony over the sanctioned indulgences of the marriage bed."

"I admit I had not thought of it like that," Megge said. "We'll have to think of another way to bring him round."

She spent the next few minutes pacing around the chamber with her hands tucked behind her back and her head bent in pensive mien. "You know, Orabella," she said at last, "it occurs to me that Gluttony is one of the Seven Deadly Sins. If Magnus cannot be seduced by the prospect of physical relief as the other men will be, perhaps he can be frightened into granting Gunny Two her heart's desire. I think I'll just have a word with Father Jerome in the morning."

"And what of the king, Megge?" Lady Orabella continued anxiously. "He will dismantle Castle Rising stone by stone if it suits him."

Megge brushed off the objection with an airy wave of her hand. "Oh, I know Edward can be a bear, but I am sure he has my best interests at heart and will hear my petition. It is not as though I am refusing to marry; only that I wish a say in the matter. As for Castle Rising, my properties, and my plate and jewels, I have more than enough to offer him twice the levy he requires of his vassals each year. His coffers are ever low and he is always borrowing to finance some campaign against the Welsh, the Scots, and more enemies abroad than I could possibly remember. In Ecclesiastes it is written, 'Money answereth all things.' I am counting on money answering Edward's objections. But I cannot only deal from a position of moral and intellectual strength. I must deal from a place of physical strength. What stronger citadel is there than Castle Rising?"

"You have forgotten one thing," Lady Orabella said.

Megge frowned. "I have?"

"Sir Olyver."

"Oh."

"Humphrey will certainly summon him to lay siege to Castle Rising once we have secured it. Sir Olyver is not a man to be trifled with, Megge. What is more, he would have no stake in this matter; he has nothing to gain or lose. He would perform his duty for Humphrey as he has always done. He will care not one whit for you or your desires or demands. And I will tell you, Megge, there is one thing that makes him the most formidable foe on earth."

"And what, pray tell, would that be?" inquired Megge.

"He does not care to lose."

Megge stared into her own dark blue eyes in the silver-backed mirror. "Neither do I, Lady Orabella," said she softly. "Neither do I."

"Oh dear. Whatever will Humphrey say?"

Chapter Three

"Utter flumadiddle!"

"B—but, my lord," the messenger stammered, "I can bear witness with my own eyes as to the truth of the matter. Castle Rising is taken. From within the walls is heard the laughter of demons and strange melodies made by no instrument ever heard in this mortal world. In the fading light of dusk, people of the Fay caper upon the ramparts and rain green and blue fire upon the heads of any man who dares approach."

Lord Humphrey's face bloomed from angry red to enraged purple as the soldier blathered on about fairies and pisgies, derricks and hinky-punks.

"Enough!" Lord Humphrey fixed his bulging eyes upon the men of the garrison of Castle Rising, who had crossed the Channel and ridden hard until they arrived at his manor close by the great castle of his old friend, the Sire de Coucy. He had finally managed to tease out the reason for their sudden appearance at his door from such a skein of nonsense and incoherence as he had ever heard in his lifetime: Persons unknown had seized the precinct of Castle Rising, which many considered to be the best fortified in Christendom and had never before been taken by force of arms or yielded to siege.

"Is there even one among you who can speak in a rational manner?" Lord Humphrey inquired through clenched teeth. "Are you all as simpleminded and superstitious as the lowest scullion that you believe this nonsense of bewitchment and devilry?"

The soldiers arrayed behind their commander shifted uncomfortably. Eyes slid this way and that, looked anywhere but at their glowering liege lord. Feet shuffled, faces paled. An uneasy silence shimmered.

Finally, one young soldier, braver or perhaps more foolish than the rest, ventured, "One thing is known for sure, my lord: The doors are bolted, the great gates lowered in place. We can see smoke from the chimney louvers and the kitchens in the inner bailey, but we have no idea who occupies the place."

"Or what," someone muttered mutinously.

Growling, Lord Humphrey lowered himself into his chair and ordered a page to fill his cup. He drank deeply, motioned again, and drank another. Thus fortified, he sought to make sense of the alarming news that his ward's greatest holding, the supposedly impregnable Castle Rising, was in the hands of villains unknown.

"Send Sir Olyver to me," he barked at his squire.

"I believe Sir Olyver has ridden into the town for the festival of Our Lady, my lord," the lad said.

"Well, find him, and bring him here forthwith,"

Lord Humphrey snapped. "I don't care if he's kneeling at the altar and you have to drag him from the church with the wafer still in his mouth. Bring him."

As the squire scampered away, several servants as well as a number of minor retainers of Lord Humphrey's entourage took the opportunity to slip from the hall and flee the storm that was brewing therein. Their liege, never one to take unwelcome news well, seemed likely to explode without the calming influence of Sir Olyver close by. Heaven only knew if that formidable knight would arrive in time to keep his lordship from flying right through the roof.

"You there." Lord Humphrey motioned to the young guard who had shown at least a modicum of common sense. "Step forward. What is your name?"

"Sir Boys, my lord."

"Boys, Boys," the earl ruminated. "Boys of Leicester?"

"Yes, my lord."

"Knew your father. Well, Boys of Leicester," Lord Humphrey said with a thin smile that dripped sarcasm, "I suppose it would be too much to ask if you bear a message from these fairy beings who have seized Lady Margaret's hall, some demand, perhaps?"

Sir Boys looked to his commander with pleading eyes. He certainly did not wish to be the unlucky fellow to inform their lord that the Queen of the Fay, Tytania herself, had appeared upon the battlements and commanded the displaced garrison to bear a message to Lord Humphrey posthaste.

"You will inform your lord that Castle Rising is taken and will not be yielded up until certain demands are met," she had instructed. "He well knows that not even the legendary Sir Olyver himself can take this keep. Further, tell him that he may lay siege as he will. It will avail him nothing, for the magic of the Fay is infinitely more powerful than force of arms or the silly games of the siege. We may, if it suits us, yield when our terms are met and return to the lower realm. Tell him Tytania, Queen of the Fay, so commands."

Lord Humphrey glared down at the nervous soldier. "Well?"

"Er, we are commanded to inform you, my lord, that—"

"By whom?" Lord Humphrey fumed. "Who dares command me, the Earl of Flete?"

The guard looked as though he wished the wide oaken boards of the floor would open beneath his feet and the earth swallow him whole. "Well, as to her identity, sire—"

The bristles of Lord Humphrey's thick black moustache quivered in disbelief. "She? She? Do you have the ballocks to stand there, man, and tell me that a woman commands the citadel?"

Fearing that his man might shame himself by wetting his hose in full view of the assemblage, the commander stepped forth bravely and faced his liege lord.

"Aye, my lord, a woman it was who spoke to us from the walk above the barbican at sunrise a fortnight past," he said. He wisely omitted the damning detail that she was draped in a filmy moss-green gown, wore a half mask and crown of silvery stars, and sported diaphanous fairy wings that floated gently in the fresh morning breeze.

Lord Humphrey squeezed shut his eyes and lifted a shaking hand. "Not a word, sir. I fear I shall suffer palpitations of the heart if you speak another word." For an interminable minute he moved not a muscle, then ordered all but his closest advisors from the hall and his physician brought to him at once.

Unaware of the unhappy news his lord had just received, that poor unfortunate made bold to suggest that Lord Humphrey's present low spirits most likely resulted from a hardening of the matter within the bowel and would likely be relieved by taking an infusion of anise, wart-wort and spurge.

"Not my bowel, you fool, my heart," Lord Humphrey shouted.

"Oh, that is quite another thing altogether," the physician said hastily. He lay gnarled fingers upon Lord Humphrey's wrist. "I find no unusual rapidity of the pulse, my lord. It is my opinion that you suffer from a disorder of the nerves deriving from lack of, er, congress with your dear lady. It has been some time, has it not, my lord, since—"

"Out," Lord Humphrey snarled.

"Might I suggest several doses of fella bog? It is most efficacious in calming the heat of the loins—"

"Out!" Lord Humphrey thundered.

The physician fled.

Lord Humphrey subsided into brooding silence. His silver-chased cup remained untouched before him; his favorite beef marrow fritters grew cold upon his plate. An apprehensive page lurked near the serving hatch, ready to spring forward to serve his lord if so commanded, and desperately hoped he would not be. Lord Humphrey's sleek hunting dogs slunk into the far corners of the hall, his favorite gyrfalcon ruffled not a feather upon her perch at his left hand, doves in the rafters above ceased their soft cries.

To those who remained it seemed hours had

passed before voices were heard in the bailey and heavy boots sounded upon the wide stone steps that led up to the great hall. Even the mighty crash of tall iron-studded doors being flung open from without was welcome in the unnerving silence that had settled upon the hall.

Framed in the doorway against a roiling sky there stood such a warrior as is rarely imagined outside the legends of the wild men of old. He might have been hewn from stone, so still he stood. His black, ermine-lined cloak, secured at the neck with a plain brooch of gleaming silver in the shape of a charging boar, swirled around him, and long pale hair, loosened by the rising wind from the braided leather cord that held it back, whipped about a stern, hard-planed face. The expression of the deep-set eyes of palest silver blue revealed nothing of the man within.

As two pages struggled to close the massive oaken doors the warrior had flung wide with such casual ease, he crossed the tiled floor of the entry way, descended the steps that led into the great hall itself, and strode its length to stand before the dais upon which Lord Humphrey, who now looked considerably smaller and less important, brooded. He bowed briefly and with remarkable grace for one so large.

"You summoned me, my lord?"

"Thank God you have come, Olyver."

"I am, as ever, yours to command, Lord Humphrey. How may I be of service to you?"

Lord Humphrey surged to his feet. "Calamity, sir!" he pronounced with great dramatic effect. "The unthinkable, the unimaginable, yea the unspeakable has come to pass. The devil is let loose upon the land.

Evil lurks on every hand. Men are struck mad. To think that in my lifetime I should see—"

"My lord," Sir Olyver managed to interrupt in a voice that was quiet yet sufficiently commanding to stop Lord Humphrey's rant dead in mid-sentence, "perhaps we should begin at the beginning. What is this calamity you speak of?"

"Castle Rising is taken!" Lord Humphrey shouted.

Sir Olyver shifted his stance ever so slightly, narrowed his eyes, and tilted his head to consider the astonishing news. His reaction was paramount to that of a lesser man jumping about like a startled hare. "Castle Rising? By whom?"

"The Fay! Or so these fools would have me believe." He glared at the guardsmen.

Sir Olyver turned his head slowly and fixed diamond-hard eyes on the commander of the group. "Speak."

The soldier, now an unbecoming shade of dirty chalk, with many a stutter and stammer repeated his message, and thought it prudent to add that he himself did not believe such nonsense, despite the old tale.

Sir Olyver stepped onto the dais and threw off his cloak. He settled his powerful body into a huge padded chair beside Lord Humphrey and stretched out his long legs beneath the table. He looked at the soldier over the rim of the flagon just handed to him by his alert squire. "Let us hear this tale."

"They say, sir," the soldier began, "that beneath the citadel of Castle Rising lies the great summer hall of the Fay. Queen Tytania reigns there and Castle Rising is under her protection, which is why it stood even against King Stephen himself in his war with Matilda.

"Of course," he continued hastily, "it is only an old wives' tale, perhaps to frighten away those who set their sights upon taking the place."

"It would appear that the tale has failed to deter someone who is admirably sensible from occupying the keep, as it is now in hostile hands," Sir Olyver observed.

"True enough, sir," the commander agreed, hoping that he had portrayed himself as a reasonable man in Sir Olyver's eyes. He blanched again however when the knight inquired in a cool voice how it came to be that the garrison had been ousted from within the walls. There was nothing for it but to speak the truth. Sir Olyver had a way of looking at a man that froze equivocation or an outright lie upon the lips.

"As to that, my lord, we received a message that your good lady had encountered some difficulty upon the road," he began with some trepidation, addressing Lord Humphrey because he could not bear looking at the stern, impassive visage of Sir Olyver. "We departed immediately, of course—"

Lord Humphrey's brows shot up. "My lady? Orabella? Upon the road?"

The commander could feel the earth begin to shift beneath his feet. "Er, yes, sire, as I said, upon the road—"

"And what road would that be?" inquired Lord Humphrey in a voice that had the commander backing away to a prudent distance.

"The road to Trelissick?" he ventured.

"My wife, Lady Orabella, was on the road to Trelissick?"

"Aye, my lord. And your ward, Lady Margaret, and

Lady Sybille and Lady Agnes. To visit with your lady's sick mother, I am told."

Lord Humphrey shot to his feet. "Her mother?"

The commander wanted to weep like a baby. "Um, er, so I was told and, um—"

"Lady Orabella's mother has been dead these five years!" Lord Humphrey shouted.

It was all the commander could do not to fall to his knees and beseech God to take him there and then.

Lord Humphrey dropped back into his chair speechless. Seeing that his liege was unable to continue the interrogation, Sir Olyver set aside his flagon and rose to restore some modicum of order and intelligibility to the proceedings.

"Continue," he ordered.

Anxious to have done with it, the commander blurted out the rest of the story. "As I said, sir, we departed immediately to go to Lady Orabella's assistance. Trelissick is somewhat northwest of Castle Rising, and we had not gone but twenty or so miles before another messenger met us near Movey Ford to inform us that Lady Orabella and her entourage had arrived safely at her mother's dower house—er, at Trelissick, I should say—and that we could return to Castle Rising without further apprehension as to her safety."

He paused, hoping Sir Olyver or even Lord Humphrey, who now wore a ferocious frown upon his broad freckled brow, would say something, anything. Finding no relief in that quarter, he staggered on with his story.

"By the time we approached Castle Rising it was well past dusk. One of my men espied eerie lights dancing amongst the trees about a quarter mile beyond the bridge. Thinking the village people were about some mischief or other, we rode out to investigate, but somehow they always seemed just beyond our reach."

In a valiant attempt to retrieve his dignity and perhaps save his hide, he schooled his shaky voice and tried to finish up on a positive note, if one were to be found in this sorry tale. "I surmised these lights were some ruse or other and ordered my men back to the castle, only to find that the great gate had been lowered and the doors bolted shut. I immediately prepared a plan to scale the—"

Sir Olyver rapped big scarred knuckles on the table. "Enough. In short, you were lured from Castle Rising on a false pretense and during your absence the keep was taken."

The commander bowed his head in shame. "Aye, my lord."

"What of your men on the ramparts?" demanded Lord Humphrey. "Say you that you left the castle unprotected?"

"Oh no, my lord," the soldier assured him. "I know my duty. Thirty men stood watch while the rest of us reconnoitered, but when we returned, twenty of them lay insensible upon the ground at the base of the outer curtain wall. What has become of the remaining ten, we know not."

"Bewitched," the young guard muttered. His eyes widened in terror as Sir Olyver ordered him to step forward.

"You have an opinion you wish to share with us, sir?" the knight inquired softly. "Say you the garrison was bewitched?"

Throwing caution to the winds the young man

burst out, "Aye, my lord. Or," he added with a commendable sense of self–preservation in the face of Sir Olyver's flat stare, "we were made to believe so. Everyone knows that a great cavern does indeed lie beneath the castle. Many believe it is the summer hall of the Fay, ruled over by Tytania herself. The lady upon the barbican wore strange garb and what appeared to be wings upon her shoulders."

"That's quite enough of your nonsense," growled Lord Humphrey.

Sir Olyver held up a huge, callused hand. "Nonsense it may be, my lord, but the fact remains that the castle is taken, be the woman who commands it Queen Tytania herself or some mortal Amazon. I fear she is a wily opponent."

Lord Humphrey spewed wine over his plum velvet tunic. "Woman? Nonsense. Women have not the wits to formulate such a daring ploy. Trust me, it is some man, a coward who thrusts his woman into danger to deliver his demands, who is behind this."

"You are mistaken, my lord," said Sir Olyver. "I suspect we may very well be dealing here with a woman; one of considerable guile and determination. Where a man espouses force, a woman must resort to trickery. After all, even the silliest of women knows how to bring a man to heel, but it takes a very clever woman indeed to enlist the foolish man against himself. Yes, I am certain it is a woman who commands your ward's keep."

"Then it should not require much time or effort to take back Castle Rising if we are merely facing some mad female," Lord Humphrey declared.

"I am not sure," remarked Sir Olyver, "that even I could take the place. I have not seen it with my own eyes, but I have spoken with Master James of St. George about it. Surrounded on three sides by high cliffs with the sea and estuary below, he believes it to be unassailable. Heaven knows, King Henry and Edward spent enough to make it so."

Lord Humphrey looked uncharacteristically glum. "What then are we to do?"

"The citadel of Castle Rising may be invulnerable," Sir Olyver replied, "but the woman who holds it is not. In short, we lay siege. If you will allow, we shall invoke the Conventions of the Siege so that I can negotiate with her and in so doing find some point of vulnerability to exploit. I am very much looking forward to making the lady's acquaintance. I promise the terms of her surrender will not be to her liking. For surrender she shall."

"Excellent, excellent," said Lord Humphrey. "Let us prepare to depart for Flete immediately for reinforcements and provisions. I have need to consort—I mean consult, yes consult—with my dear Lady Orabella, and then we shall ride on to Little Rising and set up camp. By God, I haven't laid siege in years, not since Antioch. I do like a good siege. Provided, of course, that it doesn't last too long and one can obtain decent food and drink from the surrounding villages. Castle Rising is but two days' ride from Flete. I shall be able to visit with Orabella whenever the, er, need arises. Oh, and there is the matter of Megge's betrothal to see to."

"Your ward is to marry yet again?" inquired Sir Olyver.

Lord Humphrey looked at the curious faces around him and suggested Sir Olyver join him for a short stroll. "Yes," he said as they left the demesne and walked toward the town, "Edward is considering my younger brother, Walter, this time. I confess I am not pleased. Megge is a young woman of—how shall I put it?—high spirits. Yes, high spirits, that's it, and is perhaps more intelligent than is to be desired in a woman. She will require a firm but kindly hand in a husband. Walter, I regret to say, is a man of unpredictable temper and licentious ways. He will not find in Megge the obedient wife he has twice secured in the past."

"Lady Margaret appears to be unlucky in the king's choice of suitors and husbands," Olyver observed. "A man might think twice about wedding with her in view of the sad fate of past candidates. But then, a woman of her exalted lineage, leading back to the Conqueror himself, and amongst the wealthiest in England, would be proof against any such apprehensions."

"And lovely," added Lord Humphrey with a fond smile. "Well, perhaps not lovely in the usual sense, but arresting in her looks and most regal in her manner. She is somewhat forthright in stating her opinions, but she is a good, sensible girl and can be charming when it so suits her."

"Is she?" Sir Olyver mused. "Is she, indeed?"

"Megge is as fine a prize as any man could wish," Humphrey continued, "and I must say that it galls me that Edward would even consider handing her off to Walter; he is well aware of my brother's reputation as a tyrant and profligate. Still, we must get her married off, and I imagine Edward sees political advantage in such a match, else he would not entertain the thought."

"Hmmm."

"I only wish there was some other candidate Edward would find acceptable."

Sir Olyver gazed out over the rolling green hills of northern France toward the great citadel of Coucy, whose huge cylindrical towers seemed to pierce heaven itself.

"If you will hear me out, Lord Humphrey," said he, "I think I know just the man."

Chapter Four

The child could not have been above six or seven years, small for his age, almost puny. He stood before his lord with shoulders hunched and chin tucked under, as though expecting a blow from a heavy hand. He had been standing thus for some minutes, managing only to shake his head yes and no as Lord Humphrey flung question after question at him.

The boy was clearly terrified, as was each and every soul in Flete Castle that rainy June night. Well they might be, Sir Olyver thought, as Lord Humphrey appeared possessed by the very devil himself, and had been since the moment the company rode up to the door of the great hall and their lord had been informed by his household steward that the reason Lady Orabella was not upon the steps to greet him as was her custom was that she was not resident in the castle at this time.

Unaware of the maelstrom his words were about to unleash, Master Basil assured his confounded lord that his lady was safely ensconced at Trelissick and hoped to return home within a fortnight, or at such time as she believed her mother to be out of danger and well on the road to recovery.

"That," Lord Humphrey had replied in a strangled voice, "would take a miracle, as the lady in question is quite dead."

"Oh no, my lord," Master Basil assured him brightly, "her malady is not so very dire as . . . dire, er . . ." He faltered as Lord Humphrey's eyes bored into him. "Um. . . . that is to say—"

"If I say the woman is dead, she is dead," roared the lord of Flete Castle.

A film of perspiration popped out across Master Basil's forehead and his knees began to buckle. Though he could expect no hope from that quarter, he looked to the menacing warrior who had yet to dismount from the largest, ugliest war horse he had ever beheld for some slim hope that Lord Humphrey would not draw his sword and behead him on the spot.

Seeing that the steward was on the verge of keeling over and unlikely to provide further intelligence, Sir Olyver had suggested they repair to the hall, take refreshment, and find someone who could. As the stable lads led the horses away and Lord Humphrey's entourage disappeared into the torch-lit hall, Master Basil sank into blessed insensibility.

"Simpletons," snarled Lord Humphrey. "I'm surrounded by simpletons. Is there not one man in this hall who can speak a coherent sentence?" He speared a large chunk of burnt beef, crammed it into his mouth, and chewed ferociously. He threw down his knife and gestured to the platters before him. "This food is unfit for swine. Send the cook to me." He took in the gaping faces around him. "Don't tell me: The cooks are gone, too. Sweet Jesus, I don't believe this."

Sir Olyver, who had given up on the cooked dishes after the first few bites, gestured to his squire to bring the water bowl, and washed the grease from his fingers. "Come here, child," he said to the trembling boy who had retreated to a corner by the serving hatch.

The boy dragged his feet as he climbed the three steps up onto the dais; he might have been ascending the scaffold to be hung by the neck. Had Sir Olyver been standing, the child would not have reached as high as the buckle of his sword belt. The knight pushed his chair back and guided the boy to stand before him between his knees so that he could look into his terrified brown eyes.

"What is your name, boy?"

"L-Lancelot, my lord."

"A fine name. Lancelot was one of Arthur's bravest and most trusted knights; did you know that?"

The boy nodded.

"Since you bear his name, you must be brave, too. Are you?"

"I don't know, sir."

Sir Olyver took a handful of gingered nuts and offered some to the boy. After the briefest hesitation, he scooped some up with grubby fingers and stuffed them into his mouth.

"I believe," the knight continued in a stern voice, "that you know more about what occurred in this castle a fortnight past than some others here. It takes a brave man to speak the truth. Are you brave enough to tell us what you heard the week before Lady Orabella and the others left the castle?"

The boy squared scrawny shoulders. "Yes, sir."

"Speak then."

It transpired that Lancelot had been shirking his

duties in the stables and was snoozing away the morning behind a thick lilac bush in a corner of the orchard when he chanced to overhear a conversation between her ladyship and Lady Megge, who were soon joined by Lady Agnes, Lady Sybille, Mistress Gilly, Gunny One, and Gunny Two.

"And the nature of this conversation?" Sir Olyver prompted, holding the dish of nuts just beyond the boy's reach as further incentive to reveal all he knew.

Lancelot eyed the nuts, understanding that more would be forthcoming if he spoke the truth. "Well, my lord, they were saying as how men were bad and foolish and women had to stand up to them."

"Bad?" echoed Lord Humphrey with a scowl. "Foolish?"

Lancelot wasn't sure, but he thought it might have something to do with what their lords did in the . . . well, when they made the babies, and—

Lord Humphrey's fist hit the table. "What are you saying? They were discussing—?"

"Let him finish," Sir Olyver advised, laying a hand on the boy's shoulder to keep him from bolting. "I begin to see the way of this."

"I didn't understand what they were talking about," little Lancelot admitted, "but Lady Megge said the only way they could get what they want is to make men beg and plead for, er, well I don't know what they're supposed to beg and plead for, but she said men couldn't live without whatever it was."

Lord Humphrey choked on his ale. His squire rushed forward to pummel him upon the back. "M–megge," he sputtered. "I should have known it. That girl is, is . . ."

"Clever, as you said," Sir Olyver mused. "Go on, lad."

Lancelot was beginning to enjoy his newfound status in the unfolding drama. "Well, sir," he continued importantly, "Lady Megge had a plan."

"Always a plan. That girl is far too clever for her own good," muttered Lord Humphrey.

"Lady Megge said what they should do was go to Castle Rising and take it like in a battle and close the gates, and then she wouldn't have to marry Sir Walter and Lord Humphrey wouldn't be able to make more babies and—"

"Aargghh!" Lord Humphrey surged to his feet and hurled his flagon at a point on the far wall, a good thirty feet above the serving table. Pages ducked, stalwart knights of the garrison flinched, dogs scrambled for safety.

Lancelot took a prudent step back.

"Clear the hall," Sir Olyver ordered as Lord Humphrey's bellow echoed from wall to wall. The earl himself was, for the moment, furious beyond intelligible speech, and only an occasional gurgle, wheeze, or burble could be heard from him.

"Stay, lad," Sir Olyver said. Lancelot was poised to flee, but too terrified to take a single step. The poor lad had shrunk once more into a puny little thing, overwhelmed as Olyver himself had been in his own father's hall, by large men of uncertain temper; in his case, a father in his cups long before the midday meal, and four strapping, mean-tempered older brothers. When they were not pounding one another into the hard-packed dirt of the bailey or the filthy rushes on the hall floor, they were harassing him without mercy. Berating and belittling him until Olyver thought himself the very least of boys. Perhaps this young one would be fortunate enough, as had he, to grow up to possess a body and demeanor that struck fear into other men and ease, in some degree, the shame and pain he had suffered as a child.

That Olyver had become such a man was due in great measure to the guidance of Lord Humphrey, Earl of Flete, the man who had fostered him, and who was now sitting in frozen shock to his right, grappling with the humiliating knowledge that the women of his keep, incited by his own ward, had taken leave of their senses and staged an insurrection so that he should be deprived of the pleasures to be found between the plump thighs of his sweet Lady Orabella.

"Lancelot," said Sir Olyver, "where is your mother? Did she travel to Castle Rising with the others?"

The boy seemed to shrink even further. "Got no ma, my lord."

"What of your father?"

"Got no pa either," Lancelot said. "James the saddler found me when I was little. He lets me sleep in the hayloft if I help him muck out the stables. I'm nothin', my lord." He bowed his head.

"No man is nothing," Sir Olyver said. "How do you come to know your name, boy?"

"Don't. James said as I should give myself a name."

"Lancelot. Why did you choose that name?"

"'Cause I want to be brave and be a knight. Everyone laughs at me, but that's what I want."

You're just a runt. Papa hates you because you're a runt and won't ever amount to anything. Olyver the runt, Olyver the runt!

It had been years since those taunts had echoed in Sir Olyver's mind. No boy, however baseborn, should be treated so.

"Lancelot, I want you to gather all the children

whose mothers live or work in the hall. Bring them here at once. The babes, too. Tell the saddler he will have to find another boy to muck out the stables for him. I have work for you."

Lancelot's head snapped up. "Me?" As far as he was concerned, the sun had just risen right there in the great hall of Flete Castle. He felt as though he was ten feet tall.

"You."

"Most of 'em are gone, my lord. The babes, too, with their mas or the wet nurses."

"Whoever remains then, and what women may have stayed behind."

To be entrusted with so important a mission by no less than the legendary Sir Olyver himself sent a thrill of excitement from the top of Lancelot's lice-ridden head to the soles of his filthy bare feet.

"Aye, sir," Lancelot breathed, and scampered away.

"What need have we of children?" Lord Humphrey snarled. "What we need are good fighting men, Welsh archers, the trebuchet, the mangonel, the balista, Greek fire. By God, we'll bring them to their knees." The fire of battle lit Lord Humphrey's normally genial countenance. "We had them fouling their braes at Damietta, puking their guts at Crema, bawling like women—"

"My lord," Sir Olyver managed to interrupt. "If you will recall, Castle Rising is presently occupied by the women of this household, your household, most likely your own children. I am sure you would not countenance the use of such force against your own lady. If you will see the thing clearly and not allow your anger to rule your judgment, you will agree that the usual weapons of the siege will avail us nothing in the face of the most formidable weapon they have at their disposal."

"What is more terrible than Greek fire, I ask you?" Lord Humphrey demanded. "We have an ample supply of nut oils on hand, large banded iron pots, and have only to gather sufficient flax seed—"

Sir Olyver, who had more times than he liked to recall been treated to a treatise on Lord Humphrey's favorite weapons of assault, managed to interrupt his liege lord's misguided strategy for taking Castle Rising. "The children of this keep, my lord," said Sir Olyver, "that is the weapon that gives Lady Margaret— I think we must hereafter consider her the instigator and leader of this mad escapade—the bettermost advantage. Your own sons. The very future of your noble house. You must acknowledge she has chosen her chief weapon of defense well. She knows we cannot launch an assault without endangering the children."

Lord Humphrey surged from his chair, sending it crashing to the floor. The scarlet canopy above the dais jounced with the intensity of the anger he felt at what he perceived as betrayal by those he had heretofore held dearest.

"Snakes in the grass!" he bellowed. "Asps at my breast. Treason, perfidy, sedition! To think that my Orabella. . . ." Here a happy thought struck him. "Wait. No, I am indeed not betrayed. It is as those fools from the garrison said: There is witchery abroad in the land. My Orabella is ensorcered. Yes! For her life she would not keep me from her bed. But Megge. What can she be thinking? What is to be gained from this madness?"

Sir Olyver threw back the last of his ale. "I think we will have to ask her."

Chapter Five

There could not be sufficient yarrow, feverfew, and betony in the shires of Somerset, Devon, and Cornwall taken together to banish the headache that had taken hold the moment Megge, mounted upon her little white palfrey, led the women of Flete Castle and some twenty heavily laden baggage carts across the drawbridge of that pleasant keep and turned west onto the road toward Castle Rising.

Sweet Mary! Had her exalted ancestor, Duke William of Normandy, been forced to contend with such foolishness, pettiness, and discord on the day he set sail from St. Valery on a morning thick with fog with 600 ships and 12,000 men to meet Harold Godwinson at Hastings? Had Richard the Lionhearted when he stood before the gates of Jerusalem? Edward at Lewes?

If so, they had recourse to disciplinary measures Megge could only envy: Cut out a tongue here, lop off a head there, toss a troublemaker overboard. The best Megge could do with a passel of noble ladies, maids, grandmothers, pregnant women, wet nurses, babes at breast, and children of every age—not to mention the menagerie of pets that she had been assured would pine and die if left behind—was to appeal, reason, snap, and more often now, shout until she was hoarse.

The whining, the fussing, the sniping and sniveling; the tears, the puking, the puling of babes; contention, altercation, claim and counterclaim. Megge would never in all her days forget the sight of a rail-thin scullery maid rolling in the dirt locked in mortal combat with the ham-fisted Gunny One over who forgot the little chest of fine salt. There had been enough snits, sulks, and sobs to cause her very teeth to ache.

And that was only the first week. After two, Megge was threatening to put to the sword anyone who so much as harbored a negative thought or uttered an unkind word. Should that fail to bring order to the sixty or so women under her command, she would happily fall upon it herself.

So far as leading an army of crusaders, their eyes afire with the righteousness of their cause was concerned, it was but a fond distant memory now. Some evil, unseen hand had transformed it into a gaggle of ill-tempered, carping, goose-eat-goose geese. With the exception of a few stalwart souls of steady temperament, the rule of the day seemed to be, "Every woman for herself," as when Lady Sybille and the beetle-browed Lady Clarice faced off over the ownership of a little pot of the precious rose powder used to concoct cuckoo paint, an elixir for the complexion. Megge had managed to defuse the situation by drawing Lady Sybille aside and appealing, if not to the goodness of her heart, to her vanity.

"Come, Sybille, you must give over. You have only to look at poor Clarice's complexion, so ill and swarthy and coarse, to see that she cannot do without. You, on the other hand, who are blessed with skin so white and smooth that angels must weep with envy, can surely afford to be magnanimous in the face of her misfortune. Will you not prove yourself infinitely the superior in brains and beauty by deigning to assist her in what little remedy she can hope for?"

"Vanity, vanity, all is vanity," Megge had muttered as she left the two, now the closest of friends, to dabble amongst their pots and vials, potions, unguents, and tinctures.

"Megge, my dear, I need a word with you," Lady Orabella called as Megge trudged up the stairs of the south tower to her chamber above the chapel in search of some much-needed and well-deserved peace and quiet. She hadn't had more than three or four hours of sleep at a time since they'd left Flete Castle.

"Come in, my lady," Megge said as she pushed open the heavy oaken door of the lord's solar that she had appropriated for her own use. She had only a few memories of her mother and father, comfortably seated before the enormous hearth of a winter's evening, Megge at their feet with her dolls, puppets and spinning tops, but they were happy memories of a time when she had had somewhere she truly belonged. It would take Edward's entire army to roust her from this keep, from this spacious room with its painted plaster walls and windows fitted with real glass and the huge bed with its deep-blue velvet canopy and thick curtains embroidered with graceful fleurs-de-lys.

"I really must lie down, Orabella, else I'll fall down."

"Oh dear, I hope you're not taking ill. Clarice seems to have misplaced one of the chests containing the herbs, and I'm afraid we can only afford to become ill with a few maladies, as we have not the herbs to use for any others."

Megge groaned. "I was certain that as Clarice is ever complaining about this ache and that indisposition that she would see that every herb and potion known to man would be in ample supply. What maladies must we abstain from?" she added with a deep sigh as she sank into the delicious softness of her feather mattress.

"There can be no flatulence or blockage of livers, as we have but little bifil," Orabella reported. "And heaven forbid any of us harbor worms in the bowel as we have not a grain of hyssop. Boils are a problem as the supply of pennyroyal is quite low. Anyone suffering apoplexy will have to recover by the grace of God, as Clarice forgot the mallow. And no anise," she thought to add.

"Sweet Lord," Megge groaned. "We must have anise for the colic. There are, what, six babes with three due any day? You would think Clarice would remember the anise, as she herself will deliver in a matter of weeks. Is that the lot of it?"

"The chief of it, yes. On the bright side we are well provided with gillyflower, thank goodness. I should not like to go to the birthing chair without it. Oh, and Bessie brought along a goodly supply of coltsfoot, bittersweet, columbine, and damiana."

"Orabella," Megge said between clenched teeth, "I charge you to see to the disposal of the coltsfoot, bittersweet, and columbine at once. Do you not know the ignorant use them for love potions? As for damiana, it is the very last thing we want about the place. It is a damnable aphrodisiac!"

"Please, Megge, you must calm yourself. I'll see to it immediately."

Lady Orabella cleared her throat delicately. "I fear I have saved the worst for last, my dear."

"Spare me, sweet Lord."

"We have no monk's pepper."

Megge shot off the bed. "No monk's pepper?" she cried. "No monk's pepper?" she repeated, barely able to encompass the thought of a castle full of women, at least half of whom might be awaiting or suffering through their monthly courses at any given time with no monk's pepper to hand.

Orabella nodded in complete understanding. "I know."

Megge shivered from head to toe as though an evil wind smelling of death and decay had blown through the chamber. "We must have monk's pepper. Else we'll be tearing each other to pieces like starving wolves. How could Clarice forget such a thing? How?" she wailed.

"Being with child for nine long months does cloud the unhappy memory of one's monthly courses, my dear. I expect it slipped her mind."

"I must be losing mine," Megge groaned. "Do you realize what this means? Someone will have to go back to Flete to fetch it."

"Not so dire a dilemma as that, my dear. I asked Bessie if old Mistress Annie might have some down in the village, and she said like as not she does. We have only to send someone to down to get it."

Megge plopped down onto the huge oaken chest at the foot of the bed. "I had better go myself."

"You mustn't," Lady Orabella cried. "What would become of us if you were taken? And how are you to find your way there? You cannot simply stroll out through the gate."

"I won't be taken; I shall go in disguise. A peasant girl, I think, dirty and unkempt. As for leaving the castle, my papa told me of a secret stair that leads to the cavern beneath the keep, and some tunnel that leads to the river's edge on the landward side."

"But how ever will you find it, Megge?"

"I shall enlist old Henry's assistance. He was here in my grandfather's day and will know of it."

"If he knows of it, others will as well. Sir Olyver will certainly suspect its existence; even Master James of St. George would not construct a keep, even one as mighty as Castle Rising, without a way out in the event of emergency."

Megge nodded. "Of course not, but I vaguely remember papa laughing about it. Something about the salmon that swims upstream, although I haven't a notion what he meant by it. Anyhow, with Henry's help I shall discover it and all will be well."

"But—"

"It should present no very great difficulty," Megge decided, cheering up considerably at the prospect of spending a few hours away from the madness of the castle.

"But what of Sir Olyver?" Lady Orabella said. "What if you should meet with him? You told me you had had speech with him at Westminster. What if he recognizes you?"

"That's highly unlikely," Megge said airily. "It is above ten years since I saw him at Westminster. In any event, I shall disguise myself well. If we do meet it is unlikely that he will notice me. It is my experience that if you don't expect a person to be in a particular place you are unlikely to see him when he is. No, I have no apprehensions of meeting with the great Sir Olyver."

"Megge, if you will excuse me for speaking bluntly, you are piling madness upon madness, folly upon folly. I fear we can expect no very good outcome from this venture." •

"All will be well, you'll see," Megge assured her. "We cannot fail. I am the great-great-great-great—well I forget just how many 'greats' there are—granddaughter of the Conqueror himself. If he could win the day at Hastings and take the throne of England I see no reason why I should not be able to hold Castle Rising until our demands are satisfied."

Lady Orabella sighed.

Chapter Six

"All's well, my lady," Audrey, the shorter of the two women Megge had stationed at the foot of the stairs leading up to the topmost chamber of the tower, assured Megge as she passed by on her nightly rounds. Ten men of Castle Rising's garrison were confined within—soldiers who no doubt now considered themselves the most fortunate of men. "Bessie's been up, and Fat Alice. Reckon they handled all of them, 'cause they're snoring away fit to wake the dead." She hesitated. "Me and Dulcie here's been thinking, my lady, the guards might be wanting something a bit different, if you know what I mean. Bessie and Alice, being whores and all, well, they're used to serving as many as possible in a day, so they're terrible quick about it. No time to be creative, if you take my meaning."

Megge didn't, but wasn't about to ask for details and hoped Audrey was not about to provide them. "Well, so long as they know what they are about."

"So, you know how a man likes a woman's mouth

on him . . . well, maybe you don't, you still being a maid and all . . . and we were hoping you might let us take care of the business tomorrow night. Just for a change of pace, you understand."

Megge blinked, opened her mouth, and only just managed to get out, "Um, excellent idea, Audrey, yes, excellent. We must have them happy and satisfied if we're to encourage them to assist us in such tasks as require a man's strength and skill. Using your . . . er, employing the methods you suggest would, I am sure, accomplish that nicely."

"Never failed yet, my lady," Dulcie declared.

Megge brushed her hands together as though having just completed a job well done. "There we are then. You may proceed tomorrow night. I really must be about my rounds. Good work, ladies," Megge called back as she hastened away.

Now, well after midnight, Megge stood on the south curtain wall of the outer bailey gazing down upon the siege camp laid out in the meadow beyond the river. Seen from this distance, the figures sprawled around a dozen fire pits might have been puppets. Dogs prowled the camp in search of carelessly discarded bones and bits of fat and gristle; horses nuzzled one another in the temporary paddocks by the river; sentries patrolled the perimeter.

That a wooden palisade had not been erected around the site was proof that the besieging force had no fear of harassing sorties from the castle. Lord Humphrey and Sir Olyver would know by now that women—no doubt "mere women" when they spoke of the occupying force—held Castle Rising and posed no military threat, but until the siege was officially declared—usually accomplished by dispatching such notice affixed to an arrow fired into the door of the outer barbican—Megge intended to maintain the fiction that the Fay held the place. It was rather fun, and to that end, she had sent ten giggling maids clad in fairy garb to caper upon the walls at dusk.

In the flickering light of the campfires Megge could make out the dark shapes of the tents erected for the comfort of Lord Humphrey and his knights. One in particular—square, black and spare where the others were elegant cones of white, blue-striped, and pumpkin-colored cloth and set somewhat apart to the seaward side—drew her careful scrutiny.

The faint hope she had harbored that the formidable siege master, Sir Olyver of Mannyngs, was about his sinister business in some far off corner of the world had vanished that morning as she watched the silver pennant bearing his heraldic device being hoisted above that huge tent: the charging boar—the beast who fights to the death, the implacable foe. God help her, Sir Olyver was about his business right here at Castle Rising, and Megge had no idea how she should, or could, deal with such a formidable opponent.

Most women in the keep held the undeniable bargaining advantage of denying the marriage debt or their sexual favors to the men massed beyond the walls, and holding their own children hostage, as it were. Megge possessed no such advantage.

She had, she decided, three weapons that would have to serve: absolute conviction in the rightness of her cause; the blood of the greatest Viking, Anglo-Saxon, and Norman warriors who ever lived flowing in her veins; and, she told herself, an intellect every bit equal to that of the great Sir Olyver. These should serve her well until she could ascertain some chink in his armor—not literally of course, for she never intended to get close enough to him to see if there was one—but an idiosyncrasy of mind, some flaw in his character that she could use to her own advantage.

Though the tents were but dark silhouettes against the feeble light of dying embers and a sliver of moon, Megge's eye was caught by a shadow detaching itself from the big square tent on the cliff: an enormous man, obvious even at this distance, clad in a long flowing cloak. He could be none other than Sir Olyver himself. He bent to a fire pit to warm his hands, strode to the cliff edge to stare out over the sea for a few moments—and relieve himself, if Megge judged rightly by his stance. He sauntered around the camp perimeter, greeting the sentries as he passed, until he came to the bridge that spanned a narrow channel of the River Lis. There he stopped, braced his legs wide, folded his arms across a massive chest, and stared straight at the spot where Megge leaned against the parapet.

The moment of truth had arrived. Begin as you mean to go on, she counseled herself. Already you have the advantage of a siege: an impregnable, well-provisioned citadel. The women under your command have the advantage of barter: their bodies and the issue of their husbands' loins, both guarantees that the besieging force would not resort to force of arms. Know yourself his equal in every way, but do not let him see that you know.

As bracing as these thoughts might be, Megge could feel prickles of apprehension right down her spine and a certain shakiness about the knees as she returned Sir Olyver's unwavering stare with an appropriately resolute glare of her own. Everything about the man rankled: the arrogant stance, the mocking tilt of the head, the carefully fashioned aura of menace.

So he thought to intimidate her, did he? Well, Sir Olyver of Mannyngs would soon learn that Lady Margaret de Languetot of Rising was not so easily disconcerted. Since they were so distant from one another that a cool look or defiant set of the chin would make such a declaration impossible, Megge wiggled her shoulders to set her gossamer wings fluttering in the brisk breeze, and drew herself up into a regal pose worthy of the queen of the Fay herself. The man would not be taken in by the silly deception, of course, as had a number of gullible soldiers and camp functionaries earlier in the evening, but Megge very much wanted the legendary Sir Olyver to see, and appreciate, the ruse that had gained her possession of Castle Rising. He would understand from the outset that she was no "mere woman," but a force to be reckoned with. It would not deter him one whit, but he would know. Hah!

"My lady," one of the women upon the wall called out, "take care."

Too late. Megge heard the telltale sound of ripping fabric, and despite a remarkably graceful lunge could not grab her left wing before it tore free of her gown in a sudden gust of wind and sailed high over the south tower and out over the estuary. For long moments it floated lazily above the river, then slowly spiraled down to settle into some reeds not twenty feet from Sir Olyver.

Tucking his hands behind his back, the big knight strolled over to the spot to examine the strange object, then up again at the frozen figure upon the rampart.

A decidedly unladylike oath carried clear as a bell across the water, and the proud figure atop the battlement whirled about and stomped away.

The mightiest warrior in Christendom, Scourge of the Saracen, whispered to be the very Limb of Hell itself, threw back his head and laughed long and hard.

"You are feeling quite well, my lord?" Sir Olyver's squire inquired when the knight returned to his tent. His thatch of shocking red hair stood straight out in all directions, as though trying to remember which way it was supposed to grow upon his head. He scrambled up from his pallet at the foot of the long camp cot that served as his master's bed.

"I'm fine, John."

"I apologize, my lord. I didn't hear you go out. I would have accompanied you."

It never ceased to amaze the squire how silently such a big man could move about when he chose. Accustomed as he was to the stern demeanor his lord usually wore, John felt some alarm at the strange set of Sir Olyver's mouth as he assisted him in removing his cloak and boots. Had he been pressed to reveal his private opinion of the matter, John might have confessed that Sir Olyver's lips were twitching in what very well might be a smile. Was his lord even capable of such a thing? John wondered as he set Sir Olyver's sword belt and the magnificent long sword of Damascus steel with reverence upon a chest in the corner of the tent.

"Would you care for wine, my lord? Ale?" Perhaps Sir Olyver was feeling indisposed, although John had never remembered him being so, except for the usual lacerations, punctures, bruises and broken bones to be expected in the tiltyard, the melee, or on the battlefield. Even when every soul in the camp at Damietta had lain paralyzed for days with a cramping sickness of the bowel, Sir Olyver had remained on his feet, although John had detected a telltale pallor beneath the bushy beard his lord sported on that long campaign. He would have willingly gone through trial by fire rather than admit the fact to another soul.

Now he peered at the stubbled face he had shaved only that morning and found it to be deeply tanned as usual. "If the insomnia is upon you, I could wake Master Cuthbert and have him prepare a tonic—"

"Wine will do." Sir Olyver settled himself into the huge padded chair that accompanied him everywhere and studied the stiffened piece of silver netting that had detached itself from the person of the purported fairy upon the wall. Tytania, he was sure, would have no difficulty growing another, but Lady Margaret of Rising would no doubt be forced to abandon once and for all the fiction that had served her well. If the oath that had issued forth from the wall—as emphatic and lewd as any he had ever heard in even the lowest tavern—was any indication of the lady's displeasure at her final unmasking, she was very displeased indeed.

A clever ploy, Sir Olyver was forced to acknowledge, when one added in the effect an ample supply of drugged mead and a bevy of buxom, willing maids would have on the garrison of Castle Rising. As evidenced by the present situation, it was more than enough to deliver the precinct into her hands without so much as an arrow being fitted to the bow.

Chapter Seven

Olyver of Mannyngs, duly sworn representative of Humphrey, Earl of Flete, to Her Ladyship, Margaret de Languetot of Rising:

May the peace and good counsel of our Lord be with you.

Be it known to you, my lady, that my liege lord, Humphrey of Flete, hereby declares that the precinct which you now command, namely Castle Rising, located at Little Rising in the shire of Devon, by the grace of God in the stewardship of His Most Gracious Majesty Edward, shall be from this day forward subject to siege until such time as said precinct and all who reside therein shall be surrendered unto him.

Further understand, your ladyship, that as commander of my liege lord's forces, currently camped without your walls, I order you to cede the holding at once or be prepared for such

remedy or action as I deem shall be necessary
to take possession.

> Your most humble servant,
> Olyver of Mannyngs

Lady Margaret de Languetot of Rising to Edward,
King of England:

Greetings to Your Most Serene Majesty. May
God's grace be upon you.
　My lord, you have ever bestowed upon me
your benevolence, courtesy, and compassion
since the death of my beloved father when I was
but eight years of age, and honored me by receiving me into your household as your ward
and according me every privilege of my station.

[You seized the opportunity, as is your habit, of ap-
propriating the revenues of a loyal subject's estates
for your own purposes by declaring me your ward until such time as you could marry me off, or as happened four years ago, selling my wardship to Lord
Humphrey.]

You will wonder then, sire, that I have taken
such drastic measures, as it must seem to you, to
depart the household of your most loyal subject, Humphrey of Flete, and take up residence
at my principal holding, Castle Rising in the
shire of Devon.

[*My* holding, I might remind you, as willed to me by
my father as his only legitimate living heir, and ac-

knowledged by the laws of inheritance you are purportedly sworn to uphold.]

Although I have done so without your leave, my lord, my action, as others will maintain, is no act of betrayal but simply a statement of my belief that at four and twenty years of age, and having been raised up with a liberal education and a full understanding of the complexity of family alliance, I am capable, and should be granted the courtesy, of taking counsel with you and your ministers as to the choice of my next husband, and the disposition of my properties throughout these islands, Brittany, and Gascony.

[Lord knows you could use my help, as you haven't come up with a candidate who hasn't fallen down the stairs in a drunken stupor, succumbed to disease or old age, choked upon a fish bone, discovered to be well within the degree of consanguinity so as to occasion a petition of annulment before we even left the church, or in the case of Sir Greyford, found to be possessed of two wives already.]

Word has reached my ear, Your Majesty, that you have taken under consideration the suit of Sir Walter of Flete to be my next husband; a man whose reputation and disposition, I am sure you know, reflect no merit upon himself, his family, or you as his liege lord . . .

[He cuckolded your own nephew, for heaven's sake!]

I hereby declare, though I know it will grieve you . . .

[You are going to fly right through the roof.]

. . . that I cannot give my consent, as is my right under the charter King John signed with his barons, to such a union, as it can bring no happiness to myself, benefit to my estate, or honor to my family's name.

[Wild horses couldn't drag my headless corpse into the marriage bed with this man.]

I would have you remember, my lord, that I have ever been obedient to your will and hold you in the very same degree of respect that I would my own father had the Lord not seen fit to take him from me. By the grace of God, you are a good father to all your loyal subjects and hold a care for us ever in your mind and heart.

[Most especially when it profits you.]

My liege, I shall remain with my people in the precinct of Castle Rising until I have received some reply from you, which I trust you will send most expeditiously, and in the meantime will hold parley with Lord Humphrey and his appointed spokesman, Sir Olyver of Mannyngs, on other matters that concern the happiness and well being of my friends and the people of my estates who are present within.

[They'll have to carry me out of here in a wooden coffin 'ere I capitulate.]

May every blessing be upon you, sire, and upon your glorious house.

Sealed by my hand this day, 7th July in the year of Our Lord 1275.

Your most humble servant,
Lady Margaret de Languetot of Rising

Lady Margaret de Languetot of Rising to Humphrey, Earl of Flete:

My lord, may God grant you all blessings.

Herewith I send to you a true copy of a letter I did send four days past to his Most Gracious Majesty Edward at Westminster, which I trust will give you understanding of my reasons for removing to my own holding. In the most general way I have set forth my concerns as to my own future and the welfare of my people here at Rising and the estates, manors, farms, chases, and forests, which are mine by right of direct inheritance and acknowledged custom from the time of my grandfather six times removed, William, Duke of Normandy and King of England.

Herewith also I send you a message, sealed by her own hand, from your dear lady, Orabella of Flete, which sets forth her reasons for joining me in this endeavor, and which I trust will set your mind at rest as to her willing cooperation and well-being.

[I hope you will be sitting down when you read it and have your physician close to hand.]

> Herewith also I send to you a message, which I entreat you to deliver into the hand of Sir Olyver of Mannyngs, whom I understand you have appointed to speak for you concerning your stated intent, received this morning, to lay siege to this precinct until such time as I am forced to yield to him.

[Hell will freeze over before that day.]

> Please know, my lord, that I shall never yield either my own person or my holding to Sir Olyver so long as I remain unsatisfied that the terms of myself or the women who are party to this endeavor are met through fair negotiation.
>
> To this end, I request that you and Sir Olyver honor with me the Conventions of the Siege, as revised by King Henry of revered memory, and grant Sir Olyver leave to negotiate on your behalf. You will understand, from the message I have sent to him, that I enjoin him to negotiate in good faith upon the matters that concern myself only, and that he permit the husbands, sons, fathers, and those most closely concerned to negotiate individually with the women whose names I list below.
>
> God grant that we may come to a speedy meeting of minds on these matters, my lord, for I would not be estranged from you any longer than is necessary. Know that I value and love

you, and that the present matter does not in any way reflect upon the kindness, patience, and good will you have shown me since I came into your household.

Sealed by my hand this day, the 11th July in the year of Our Lord 1275.

Your humble servant,
Margaret de Languetot of Rising

Margaret de Languetot of Rising to Olyver of Mannyngs:

Sir, health and prosperity be yours.

I have received this day your notice of intent to lay siege to this precinct until such time as it is yielded up to you and, as commander of the forces that hold this place, I surrender my own person into your custody.

[The Bey of Constantinople will lie with pigs before that day dawns.]

Know that the gates of Castle Rising will not be raised until such time as each woman whose name appears on the list I have sent to Lord Humphrey has an opportunity to enter into negotiation with the person indicated beside her name, this to be accomplished without apprehension as to her safety and autonomy until she is satisfied that an acceptable resolution as to her chief concern has been reached.

With respect to my own concerns, I entreat

that you join with me in open and honest negotiation conducted under the legally constituted
Conventions of the Siege, wherein you will
speak for Lord Humphrey about matters pertaining to my wardship, as bestowed upon Lord
Humphrey by His Majesty . . .

[I should dearly like to know how many shillings,
sheep, bales of wool and butts of wine I am assessed
at. Am I no better than a heifer to be bought and sold
at market?]

. . . and the disposition of myself in marriage
and of my estates from that day forward.

    You will understand, my lord, that my most
earnest demand is that I remain in the precinct
as the mistress of Castle Rising, seat of my illus-
trious ancestors from the time of Gui de
Languetot, and the rightful mistress of all business pertaining unto it. With that in mind,
know at the outset that you should harbor no
hope or expectation that I will surrender myself
into your care or jurisdiction.

[I should like to see you try to force the issue.]

If after consultation with Lord Humphrey you
agree to this demand, I shall meet with you
come the next Sabbath at noontime upon the
bridge that spans the River Lis below the walls,
so that we may discuss how this negotiation is to
be conducted as quickly as possible and to the
satisfaction of all concerned.

[I vow *you* shall have no satisfaction in it.]

> Your legend precedes you, sir, but it is my earnest hope in this instance that you have been wise enough to exact payment for your services from Lord Humphrey in advance.
> Sealed by my hand this day, 11th July in the year of Our Lord 1275.
>   Your servant,
>   Margaret de Languetot of Rising

Edward, King of England to Lady Margaret de Languetot of Rising:

> God curse all women.

Humphrey, Earl of Flete to Lady Margaret de Languetot of Rising:

> Have you gone quite mad, Megge?

Olyver of Mannyngs to Lady Margaret de Languetot of Rising:

> I thank you for your concern, my lady, but I shall have precisely the payment I desire from this enterprise.

Chapter Eight

'Tis said the gardens within the great cavern bloom throughout the year, and the mountain whereon the mighty castle stands is hewn of crystal pure as the air of heaven. Within it is cunningly adorned with pillars of gold. The people of the Fay capture the sun's golden rays and the moon's silver light in orbs of crystal that they might feast and dance and make sweet love though the winds howl and the rains vex the land and sea without.

"It just goes to show," Megge grumbled as she waved her arm blindly in front of her to sweep aside centuries' worth of thick sticky webs, desiccated insects, bats and small birds, and all manner of lurking crawly things. Her battered half boots crunched over the bones of a thousand generations of mice and other small beasties. Far above she could hear the ominous rustle of bat wings. She was certain she would drop dead of fright if she looked up and saw thousands of little beady eyes reflecting back from the single lantern that old Henry held aloft to guide their way.

"Show what, my lady?" Henry inquired as he led Megge and Fat Alice across the huge expanse of slimy boulder-strewn floor of the cavern beneath Castle Rising.

"Not to believe everything you read," Megge replied. "I could easily believe this dreadful place to be far too wretched to be inhabited by even ogres and trolls of the foulest disposition, much less fairies."

"Ah, but you see—take care here, my lady, it's slippery-like—the Fay picks and chooses as who's to see them and who's not. Who knows but they's watching us right now and laughing at our foolish ways."

At the moment Megge would not have cared if Tytania herself danced about them scattering rose petals as they went. She was not in charity with man, beast, or dwellers in the fairy realm. The rough brown wool of her peasant gown itched abominably; she feared all manner of multi-legged things were even now taking up residence in her long hair; and her scraped knees hurt from the tumble she'd taken down the steep stairs hidden beneath tubs of sour, undrinkable wine in an ancient prison cell far beneath the guard room in the inner barbican.

And all because that ninny Clarice had forgotten the monk's pepper. Megge could of course have sent someone else to the village to fetch it, but the prospect of escaping if only for a few hours the tyranny and tedium of female society was nigh irresistible. Even if it meant risking an encounter with Sir Olyver of Mannyngs, the prospect of which was not half so dreadful as the thought of having to once again traverse this wretched cavern when she had accomplished her mission.

"Here we are, my lady."

Megge peered into the gloom over Henry's bony shoulder at the gaping hole in the rock floor illumined for the first few feet by the paltry light from the lantern and continuing down into stygian blackness. To one side lay a moldering heap of fibers and moss-encrusted wood rungs that might once have been a rope ladder.

"Lucky thing I thought to bring new rope, my lady," Henry said brightly. "Must be above a century since anyone passed this way."

"But I thought there would just be a hole in the rock face and I could crawl out onto the river bank."

"Henry, you old fool, you can't expect Lady Megge to be climbing down that godforthaken hole," Fat Alice lisped.

"You be the fool, Alice," Henry retorted. "An enemy'd find a hole to crawl through in half a minute. This conduit's real clever, it is. First you climb down about twenty-five or so feet on a ladder—"

"Twenty-five feet?" Megge mouthed.

"Thereabouts," Henry replied as he measured out the rope and began tying sturdy knots as he went. "The hole is really a natural funnel in the cliff face, and at the bottom there's a floor fashioned of small fitted boulders. We'll move 'em to the side, and then there's another rope that I let you down on another ten feet to the ground. Once you're on the bank, I pull up that rope and replace the rock floor while's you're out and about. Then when you give the signal I let down the rope, pull you up, and you're safe as churches. Don't know if it's ever been used. It's almost impossible to see from the ground. Even I'd have trouble finding it if I was searching the river side of the castle. If someone did spot it, all the defenders would need to do is plug it with rocks. Besides, who'd think to look on the river side? The enemy would be expecting an escape by sea. But that's what's so clever. This little boat here can be lowered down, and when the tide rushes in up the estuary real fast like it does, you just launch it and make good your escape inland while the enemy is waiting to pounce on the seaward side. There's even a false exit on that side to fool 'em."

"I see," Megge said faintly.

Alice held her rush torch aloft, and surveyed the rotting planks of the ancient dugout. "A fat lot of good thith'd do her ladythip. Thee'd be at the bottom of the river afore thee knew it."

"Well, she won't be needing it today," said Henry. "Tide's going out anyhow. Tomorrow I'll get together with young Peter and we'll work up a nice sturdy craft. Now there's no need to be afeared, my lady," Henry continued. "We'll be right here when you get back. I'll be listening for you and you just call up and I'll come down to fetch you."

No, he wouldn't, thought Megge. Which was why she had come up with the happy thought of bringing along Alice to keep the dear half-deaf old man happily occupied, awake, and alert.

Not suspecting the ruse, Henry had grinned when Megge made the suggestion. "That surely is a kind thought, my lady. Fat Alice be a good one to help a man pass the time of day. That little filly likes a well-hung stallion riding behind her, she does."

Even as the ludicrous image of the ropy little man

stud-like atop the jiggling mass of Alice began to materialize in her mind's eye, Megge ruthlessly blotted it out lest she laugh out loud. It was not as though she had not witnessed the joining of men and women, unavoidable, really, in the far-from-private confines of castle and palace. Only those of the uppermost rank were accorded the privacy of their own apartments; others must make do with dark corners, cupboards, storage rooms, stables, haystacks, and the like. A youngster might very well turn a corner on her way to the garderobe of a night to hear groans and giggles and behold a pale rump draped round with disordered skirts pumping vigorously away.

Truth be told, happening upon such an amorous encounter was not always by way of accident. Megge and her friends would often creep about the palace at night to spy out those spots favored by amorous couples. But Henry and Fat Alice, as odd a couple as she had ever seen, was too comical to contemplate. She did, however, wish them a pleasant hour or so, and trusted they would not be still so engaged when the time came for her to summon Henry to assist her back up to the cavern. Given the quick lick of his lips and wag of his brows as he grinned at Alice, Megge felt certain he would complete the business rather quickly.

To Megge's relief, Henry insisted on reconnoitering before he allowed his lady to descend. Having secured the knotted rope around an enormous boulder, Henry disappeared down the dark flume and emerged some time later draped with cobwebs and looking even dirtier than he had when he descended.

"I've moved the stones, my lady, and let myself all the way down. There's been a fall of rock from the cliff face outside and you might have to wiggle through a bit to get out, but I've cleared the way for you. All you need to do is poke your head around to make sure the coast is clear. If not, just bide your time there 'til it's safe to go on."

The ensuing descent, during which Megge damned Clarice to an eternity of monthly courses without benefit of monk's pepper, was not so terrible in its execution as in the contemplation of it. With Alice shouting encouragement from above and Henry from below, Megge clambered down the thick rope from knot to knot until, with Henry's guiding hand, she alit on a ledge and found herself in small cave dimly illumined by daylight from below.

"You're a brave one, my lady, you are," said Henry as he tied another rope around her waist. "Your father'd be proud of you, he would. Bravest man I ever knew. Now down you go. I'll just put a few of these stones back in place in case anyone happens by. Sir Olyver set some of his men to searching the cliffs even before they finished setting up the camp, and if they didn't find it then, like as not, they'd not find it now, but we don't want to be taking any chances. Good luck, my lady. Alice and I will be waiting for you, don't you worry."

Megge took a few minutes to review her plan and gather her courage before she crawled out from behind the enormous slab of fallen rock. She would make sure no one was about on the river bank, head straight for the thick stand of trees fifty or so yards upriver, make a wide circuit around the siege camp through the dense woods, slip into the village, and return by the same route.

She had purposely chosen to wear a cloak somewhat

too large, but not so long that she would be tripping over her own feet, with a hood that would keep her face in shadow. If she had been perhaps a bit too clean and neat, thanks to Missy's insistent ministrations, when she set out, the scramble through cavern and the descent through the nasty darkness of the flume had transformed her into an entirely credible, wretchedly poor peasant woman likely to cozen any passerby.

Seeing no one about and certain that one such as she would not merit so much as a second glance, Megge trotted along the riverbank and in less than a minute gained the safety of the trees. Once beneath the dripping boughs, she grinned at her own baseless fears, gave herself a mental pat on the back, and made her roundabout way toward the village of Little Rising.

Happily away, if only for an hour or two, from the pressures of command, Megge could feel the ever-present headache, which no amount of betony could relieve, lift; her teeth unclench; and the knotted muscles of neck and shoulders relax. Petty squabbling, a difficult birth in the early hours of the morning, the want of monk's pepper, even the prospect of facing down the Limb of Hell himself notwithstanding, Megge stepped lively.

She was whistling a jaunty little tune as she entered the village. With her hood close about her face and head bent, she passed unremarked along the main street to Mistress Annie's thatched hut behind the bake house. Everything had gone without a hitch. All she had to do now was collect the precious herb and take herself back the way she had come.

How hard could it be?

Chapter Nine

"Hey, Lady Megge, look at me!"

Startled witless, Megge froze in mid step. Her eyes slid to the left, to the right, seeking a physical body to which to attach the childish voice. She peered at the waist high grasses that stretched away along the riverbank from the spot where she stood in the deep shadow of an ancient oak. Nothing stirred. She peered back over her shoulder: no one, nothing.

"I'm a monkey. See? But I don't got a tail."

Megge tilted her head back. A young boy, naked as the day he sprang from his mother's womb, hung upside down by his knees from a branch almost directly above her head. He grinned down at her. "I scared you, didn't I?"

Megge's heart resumed beating. "You certainly did. How did you get up there?"

"Climbed."

"How will you get down?"

"Easy," the boy informed her, and executed a little flip to land neatly on his feet.

Now that he was upright Megge recognized the child as the foundling Lancelot who worked in the stables at Flete. "How come you to be here, little Lancelot?"

"Sir Olyver has need of me, my lady," he replied, quite as though the most formidable knight in Christendom could not lay siege to a castle full of women and children without his help. "I'm to be his eyes and hears."

"His hears?"

"Aye. I'm to creep about and listen and tell him if any of the men try to sneak into the castle. I already caught two," he boasted, impressed with his own importance. "Well, I didn't catch them exactly, but I told Sir Olyver and he put them in the pillory for a whole day and we got to throw rotten food at them. That was fun. But then Sir Olyver made everyone listen to a long boring sermon by Father Boniface about skins of the flesh and human sacrifice."

"Human sacrifice? Could it perhaps have been self-sacrifice?" Megge inquired with a smile.

Lancelot shrugged. "I guess. I stopped listening when Father Boniface got to the part about fortification."

"Probably just as well," Megge said. "Lancelot, where are your clothes? Why are you running about like this?"

"Sir Olyver wouldn't let me sleep in his tent until I took a bath. With soap. I never had a bath before. John—John's Sir Olyver's squire—helped me. It wasn't so bad, but I smell funny now."

"You smell just fine," Megge assured him as she scanned the riverbank for sign of this John. "I don't see him . . . oh, that must be him in the water, with the red hair."

"That's him," Lancelot shouted as he bounced away through the tall grass like a skinned rabbit, then whirled around and sprinted back. "Lady Megge, aren't you supposed to be up in the castle?"

What to do about this wholly unexpected encounter? What to tell the boy? Young as he was, Lancelot would understand by now the nature of fealty to one's liege lord. He would have to tell Sir Olyver that he had encountered Lady Megge outside the castle walls.

Megge wondered if she could buy his silence. Probably not for long, but perhaps long enough to slip past John and make her way to the rock fall.

"You are absolutely right, Lancelot, I should be up in the castle. I have much to do to get ready to meet with Sir Olyver on Sunday." She reached into the satchel and extracted the tidy little packet of sugared fruit fritters Mistress Annie had pressed on her after she had purchased the herbs. She had been looking forward to savoring them in the privacy of her chamber that evening, but present necessity required that she forego that anticipated pleasure.

"I must be on my way, Lancelot. Why don't you take these sweets and share them with your friend John?"

"I thank you, Lady Megge," said Lancelot with a courtly if awkward little bow. "I think you are a very nice lady. Lord Humphrey says you're a holy nuisance, and John says you're the enemy, even though you are just a silly woman, but I think you're a nice lady."

"Thank you, Lancelot. And Sir Olyver? What does he say?"

"Oh. Sir Olyver calls you the prize."

Having delivered himself of this cryptic remark, Lancelot bounded away. When he reached the bank above the spot where John floated lazily upon his back, he set the packet carefully on the grass, plunged into the water and pounced upon him, setting off a furious water fight.

Thanking the Good Lord for the impetuosity and innocent exuberance of youth, Megge hurried past the two laughing shrieking combatants. Well pleased that she had encountered nothing more sinister than young Lancelot, she headed for the safety of the rock fall.

Chapter Ten

Run, hide! Run where, hide where? The tall grass, the bottom of the river. Sprout wings, fly away. Vanish into thin air.

If she hadn't cast one last amused glance at the thrashing, splashing boys, Megge wouldn't have seen another head bobbing in the river thirty feet downstream. She wouldn't have frozen to the spot or abandoned all semblance of self-preservation. She would have realized that the owner of that head had not seen her.

But no, she simply stood like the village simpleton and stared slack-jawed, as the man shook streaming, long blond hair from his face and emerged slowly and majestically like the god Poseidon rising from the sea to confound mortal eyes.

Still facing the far shore, the man stretched, rolled first his long thick neck and then his powerful shoulders. With his hands pressed firmly to the sleek muscles at the base of his spine, he arched his back and began slowly to rotate his hips the way men did upon dismounting after a long ride or some strenuous training exercise.

Look. Away.

Megge stood as one ensorcered, her eyes following the sinuous motion of the river god's hips and a goodly portion of tight buttocks. A curious fluttering sensation began in that most secret place of her own body, and she only just caught herself before her own hips began a synchronous rhythm with his.

God's teeth, what in the name of all that was holy was she doing? The horror of Megge's situation came crashing through the shock of her own licentiousness like a boar through a thicket. Sir Olyver— for it could be no other—had not yet seen her. She gauged the distance to the cliff, then to the woods, decided the latter was the safer bet, and began backing away from the riverbank into the waist-high grass, only to stumble and land smack on her backside with a despairing little whimper. She scrunched down low, hoping the high grass would conceal her, and so it appeared to be for a few seconds as Sir Olyver made no move toward the shore. But where he had been rubbing his hands through his hair, he now stood stock still as though aware of being watched.

Don't turn around. Dear God, don't turn . . .

Oh.

Now there was a sight a girl didn't see every day. A brute of a man, a giant risen from the waters, standing stark naked in sassy little wavelets that lapped at the juncture of his thighs, with just the suggestion of that manly part bobbing just below the surface. From what little of it Megge could see—or imagine—it appeared to be a part most men would sell their immortal souls to possess.

Here was no pale masculine rump unsatisfactorily espied in the ancient ritual dance in some dark cupboard or corner at Winchester or Durham; no stripped-down, sweat-begrimed torso straining against another in a wrestling match; no dandified, posturing courtier in padded hose and codpiece. No, here before her very eyes was the male animal arrayed in all its ascendancy, potency, and dominion.

Male and female He created them. Never had Megge reflected upon the distinction so prophetically pronounced in the Book of Genesis. "Man and woman" was not at all the same thing as "male and female," not by any stretch of the imagination. For one irrational moment while the blood thundered in her ears and a wave of lust swept from the top of her head to the tips of her toes and back up to settle in her womanly center, Megge wondered if the priests might have it right: the male created by God to command, the female to yield. The male standing upright between heaven and earth, the female prostrate at his feet. The male the hunter, the female his rightful prey. The male to take his pleasure, the female to confer it. All ordained by the Creator on the sixth day of His creation and signed and sealed as Holy Writ. Who could be so blind as to gainsay the truth of the matter with such an example of God's transcendent artistry standing before her?

"Lady Margaret de Languetot, that's who," Megge muttered, somehow managing to snap out of her erotic thrall and recognize the bronzed god before her for what he was: the commander of a siege army bent upon dispossessing her of her rightful property and returning her to the sway of men who held their own interests in far higher regard than they did hers.

"You there, stand, or prepare to die where you cower like a craven dog." The voice of doom. What to do, what to do? Stand. Yes, stand and stand tall. Was she not the daughter of the blood of the conqueror, the mistress of Castle Rising, the commander of an army of staunch souls who had entrusted their hopes and dreams to her?

Well, perhaps standing tall at the moment would not be in her best interest. She was, after all, supposed to be a lowly peasant, and if little Lancelot did not come barreling out of the water to betray her true identity, Megge thought she might very likely fool the shrewd Sir Olyver. She could but try, as she had no other option and even now could hear him approaching. Bending her head and rounding her shoulders so as to appear properly humble and submissive, she stood.

"Come out from there."

"Yes, my lord. Please, my lord, I mean no harm. Please don't kill me, my lord," Megge stammered as she inched forward.

Please be wearing something, if only your tunic.

"What do you here, girl?"

Megge ventured a quick peek from the shadow of her hood. Her eye traveled up from huge bare feet along steel-muscled legs to. . . . Thank you, God, there was the edge of an ivory linen shirt at midthigh. She dared look no higher, lest that unsettling stare she recalled so vividly from their brief meeting at Westminster strike fear to her heart.

"My grandmother sent me to gather, er, cress and stile, my lord," Megge improvised.

"Cress? Stile? Your grandmother is bald?"

Damnation, why couldn't she have said yarrow or feverfew? Why the herbs healers used for treating baldness?

"Um, no, my lord. Her hair is stringy and gray, but there's sufficient yet to cover her head. No, it's for the soldiers in the camp, them that's bald, you see. She has to lay in a goodly supply of cress and stile now that there's so many men about anxious to cure the baldness."

He was staring at her, she knew he was.

"Look at me."

Megge had had quite enough of looking at the imperious Sir Olyver for one day, but raised huge frightened eyes only far enough to stare at the wicked scar that slashed a pale puckered line along the left side of his jaw, stopping just short of his upper lip.

Taking her chin in his huge hand, he lifted it until she was forced at last to look into the palest blue-gray eyes she had ever beheld, intelligent, piercing, and above all, suspicious.

It was all Megge could do to maintain her composure. She had to look appropriately terrified—no great difficulty there, actually—and pray that Sir Olyver would see in the trembling, grime-faced girl with greasy curls escaping from beneath her hood the dull-witted peasant she pretended to be.

Whether he would or not, Megge was never to know, for at that moment a shout of alarm arose from the water upstream. "My lord, my lord," the red-haired squire was shouting. "Come quickly. Lancelot!"

Sir Olyver's head snapped around, and with a fearful oath he took off running in the direction the squire was pointing. Far out in the river where the current ran swift, Lancelot was being swept away. Unaware of his danger, his delighted cries of, "Look at me, my lord, I can swim!" and "Wheeeee!" sent Megge's heart slamming against her ribs. Without breaking stride Sir Olyver made a running dive into the water. A few powerful strokes brought him to the boy. He flipped him over onto his back, secured an arm across his chest, and began towing him back to where John stood on the shore hopping from one foot to the other in alarm.

Megge stood rooted to the spot until she noticed Lancelot was grinning from ear to ear, and with a little wiggle of his fingers was signaling her to make good her escape. What a dear, dear boy, Megge thought as she sprinted toward an outcrop of the towering cliff and flattened herself on the far side. Peeking around the corner, she saw a stern Sir Olyver berating the boy, who was managing to look appropriately contrite, for venturing out so far.

Megge knew at some point he would confess to Sir Olyver, as his honor demanded, that the peasant girl had been Lady Margaret herself and he had pretended to be in distress so that she could escape. Sir Olyver would not be pleased to hear it.

Not just a dear little boy, but a shrewd little boy. Sugared fruit fritters were not nearly sufficient compensation for the good deed Lancelot had done her. In that moment, Megge resolved that the someday she would take the canny little orphan into her household and see that he was trained to be the knight in shining armor he had shown himself to be that day.

A few minutes later, as she took hold of the rope

Henry let down to haul her up, Megge wished that she had thought to gather some cress and stile for the good man, whose few hairs clung optimistically to his round head.

"All went well with you, my lady?" Henry asked when they at last gained the cavern floor.

"It did, Henry. And with you?"

Henry and Alice grinned at one another. Megge could only conclude that things had, indeed, gone well with them, too.

Chapter Eleven

"Please, ladies, I beseech you—" said Lady Orabella.

"Pink!"

"Green!"

"Bah. You have no eye for fashion."

"And you do?"

"Perhaps a nice dark blue, to match her eyes?" Missy, Megge's timid little maid, ventured.

Lady Sybille and Mistress Gilly turned as one and glared the girl into silence.

"Give me that." Lady Sybille made a grab for the length of pink velvet she'd selected for the gambeson Megge would wear for the first meeting with Sir Olyver upon the bridge come Sunday.

Mistress Gilly snatched it back.

Lady Sybille lunged, seized a corner, and like a terrier with its teeth at the throat of a hapless hare, held on tight as Mistress Gilly, who outweighed her by a good three stone, yanked.

Lady Orabella lumbered to her feet and barked out, "Enough, I say!" in a tone that carried sufficient authority to bring the combatants to a standstill, although neither had any intention of surrendering the fabric.

"Sybille, Gilly, you will cease this unbecoming behavior immediately. Have we not enough difficulties to face without the two of you joining battle over so trivial a matter as fashion?"

"A lady," Lady Agnes opined, "must always be seen at her best. A woman in cuisses and gambeson, whether they be pink or green, cannot by any stretch of the imagination be said to be seen at her best. The very idea. Wearing men's garb and riding astride like some barbarian!"

That had Gunny Two launching into her favorite subject, great warrior women of old. "What about Boudicea? She was a queen. She went up against the Roman legions, her daughter right along with her. And what about Aife and Maeve and Queen Scathach of Skye? Aye, and don't forget all them Amazon women, cutting off a breast so's they could hold the bow without their tits getting in the way, though that must've hurt like the devil and I don't reckon Lady Megge'd take to the idea. Don't think none of them was wearing silks and ribbons," she scoffed.

Megge lifted her hands, scrubbed them over her face, and rose as though the weight of the world was upon her shoulders, which at that moment she felt certain it was.

"For once Agnes is quite correct."

"There, you see!" Lady Agnes crowed. "Megge agrees with me."

"Not for the reasons you think, Agnes," Megge said. "I agree that a woman should always be seen at her best. In the present case, however, it is imperative that

Sir Olyver see me as a woman. Cuisses and gambeson are not the proper garb to begin the negotiations."

"But, my lady," Gunny Two objected, "Sir Olyver will think you some weakling woman, not the commander of the keep. He will think he has the upper hand."

"That, Gunny, is exactly what I would have him think."

Megge had given the matter of her attire for the first meeting with Sir Olyver a great deal of thought as she stood the watch with seven others upon the walls the night before. Her first impulse had been to get herself up as a soldier; meet like with like. Here was a man who had lived his life among men, a mercenary soldier who knew naught but a life of war and violence. His thought had ever been directed toward conquest and surrender on the battlefield, in the siege, and at the negotiating table. Well would he know the minds of men.

Ah, but what of women? So far as Megge knew, Sir Olyver had never married. Most likely not, as he was the youngest son without property or coin for the bride price. He would have had mistresses, of course. Willing wenches and fine ladies alike would throw themselves at so legendary a warrior simply to have the bragging rights of having lain with him.

But a man in the act of swiving was most likely not a man in the throes of serious philosophical introspection. A man whose contact with women centered on an organ located considerably lower than his brain was not probing her . . . well, strictly speaking he was, but not her mind. . . .

Here Megge's own train of thought veered off into some distinctly unladylike speculation of her own as to how a woman could survive an encounter with a man of his size and strength without being flattened or torn asunder. Having seen in the flesh, literally, Sir Olyver's impressive generative endowment, albeit in a quiescent state and bobbing gently upon the waters, Megge felt certain that a woman who would be so rash as to find her way into Sir Olyver's bed must quite properly regret it ever after.

"Serves them right," she muttered with a nod.

"I beg your pardon, my lady?" asked a sentry.

"I apologize, Mary. I was just thinking to myself."

"That's about all there is to do up here of a night, my lady," Mary replied. "Quiet as a tomb it is. Even the geese are sleeping, their heads tucked under their wings all quiet like."

Megge leaned over the parapet to look down at the large covered, openwork basket hanging from the wall. A lot of good this goose would be if Sir Olyver set his men to scaling the walls in the dark of night. During the day the damnable birds squawked and flapped and scolded at anything that moved, be it bee, butterfly, or herring gull. At the moment this snoozing sentinel probably wouldn't ruffle a feather in the face of a full-scale escalade.

"You've been muttering to yourself above half an hour, my lady. You look like you have something on your mind."

"That I do, Mary."

"Might help to get it out. Share it like."

"Perhaps you're right. I was thinking about what to wear on Sunday when I meet with Sir Olyver on the bridge."

I was thinking about lying beneath Sir Olyver. Not on the bridge, of course.

"I'm sure you have a nice gown, my lady. Missy packed two full chests for you. Bound to be something pretty enough to make a man sit up and take notice."

Having been scrutinized from head to toe by Sir Olyver's cool, cryptic gaze that very morning, Megge would rather spend a week in the pillory than go through the experience again.

"Actually, I was thinking of borrowing one of the guards' uniforms. I think one of them is about my height."

"Better have Gunny Two wash it twice, my lady. Those guards don't smell all that good."

Silence.

"And how would you know what the guards smell like, Mary?"

Mary opened her mouth, closed it, and blurted out, "It's like this you see, my lady. A girl's got these needs, don't you know, and a few of us thought as the guards were locked up there for days on end and probably feeling lonely—"

Megge held up a hand, sighed. "How many went up to the tower, Mary?"

"It was three of us the first night, then—"

"The first night? No. Wait. Don't tell me. I don't want to know."

Mary wrung her hands. "I'm terribly sorry, my lady, but like I said, I got these needs, as my Ralph's over yonder in the camp."

Megge willed away a horrifying vision of crazed, love-starved women dangling from the high walls on frayed ropes or clambering down the treacherous cliffs that surrounded the citadel on three sides. Or, please God no, creeping out one of the postern doors in the outer wall and charging into the enemy camp to ravish the first available males they came into contact with. The sentries would probably go down in the first wave of the onslaught, then. . . .

So much for the bargaining advantage.

"Mary," Megge said urgently, "has anyone tried to leave the castle through the postern doors?"

"Two or three, I think, but the doors are locked, and Gunny One's got the keys, and a person would be mad to try to steal them from Gunny One."

Megge breathed again. She had never once considered that the women within the walls of Castle Rising would be at the mercy of such needs as well as their men over the river. Tomorrow she would have to appoint someone—preferably without needs of her own if she could find such a person—to keep a lookout for the little traitors.

"It seems to me, my lady, that you might have a leg up on Sir Olyver, so to speak, if you went to the bridge dressed like usual. Maybe he'll think you're just a silly woman—of course you're not—and you could throw him off the scent, if you know what I mean."

Megge all but hugged the girl. "Mary, that is a brilliant idea."

Mary blushed. "My fellow Ralph's been on two campaigns with Sir Olyver. He's always talking about how Sir Olyver does this and Sir Olyver does that, and how he thinks and all, so that's how I came to think of it. He worships Sir Olyver. Sir Olyver is crafty, and it's the kind of thing he'd do if he was a woman, but he wouldn't be thinking a woman could be that clever. And Ralph was just saying as how Sir Olyver's been distracted these last few days. He swears he even saw Sir Olyver smiling this morning after he came back from the river."

Mary clapped her hands to her mouth.

"Yes? You were saying?" Megge prompted.

"I never . . . we never . . . we just talked, whispered like. I swear by the bones of St. Perpetua, my lady."

"Come, Mary, stop dithering. Tell me."

Mary took a deep breath. "I was over on the west wall when I first came on the watch tonight. I hear this noise and I lean over the wall with my lantern, and as God is my witness there's my Ralph clinging to a ledge halfway up the cliff. He says he can't eat and he can't sleep and he can't hardly walk for want of me. I told him he's a madman, climbing up like that, and he can just take care of the matter with his own hand. Besides, I took a vow to Lady Megge, so he could just go back the way he came. He says God only knows what was going to happen because Sir Olyver is acting strange.

"And that's all that happened, my lady," she finished up, glad to have gotten it off her chest. "I swear it on my pa's grave."

Sir Olyver distracted? Smiling? Megge couldn't picture it, couldn't imagine what could ruffle the composure, chisel away at the intensity, or beguile the unwavering focus of the man she had encountered on the shore.

"You do believe me, don't you, my lady?" Mary entreated.

"I believe you, Mary. You know," Megge said after a few moments' deep thought, "I think your Ralph may prove very useful to us. I want you to try to recall everything he told you about Sir Olyver, even the smallest thing such as which dishes he prefers and if he bathes more than once a month. I need someone like your Ralph to help me read his character. Come to my chamber first thing in the morning and we'll get you started."

Megge started for the staircase that spiraled down through the wall and turned back. "Mary, might I ask a personal question?"

"Of course, my lady."

"You say that this Ralph is your, er, close friend?"

Mary nodded. "We been talking of marrying."

"If you are affianced to Ralph, how comes it that you, er, visited the north tower? I mean—"

Seeing that Megge was at pains to say outright what was on her mind, Mary interrupted her. "He'd do the same, my lady. Not take his pleasure with men, of course, though there's them that do. A quick tumble when the need's on you doesn't signify much. He'd be doing the same if Sir Olyver allowed women in the camp."

Megge knew all about Sir Olyver's strict rule against prostitutes plying their trade in his camps. She had counted on that in devising her scheme. The men would be without recourse, since nearly all the women of the village of Little Rising were safely within the castle walls, save a few of the very old who were unlikely to incite even the most desperate man's lust. Even Bessie and Alice had been willing to forego their usual trade for however long it took them to negotiate higher fees for some of their more specialized services.

"You don't feel you are betraying your Ralph when you lie with other men?"

Mary's eyes went wide. "Of course not, my lady. I love Ralph. Coupling's got nothing to do with love."

"I see. Well, that must make life considerably easier for everyone."

Mary grinned. "It does that, my lady."

Until that morning Megge would have thought such a breezy dismissal of the Church's teachings on such matters a poor rationalization for licentious behavior. However, having become acutely aware of some needs of her own as she spied on Sir Olyver at his bath in the river, she could not deny that one could desire without loving. She had met Sir Olyver but once before, so she could not say that she knew him. And she certainly did not love him, nor imagine she ever could love such a cold, hard man. And yet, desire him she did.

"Thank you, Mary. I think I understand. I shall see you in my chamber in the morning."

"Oh, I see the way of it," Gunny Two nodded. "You're going to deceive him. That's very smart of you, my lady."

"Actually, it was Mary's idea."

"Mary? You mean Mary the blacksmith's girl? That one has no more sense than a turnip."

Megge laughed. "Then a turnip must be wiser than you think. I have asked her to be my squire. No, Missy, my dear," she added as she took in her little maid's hangdog expression, "you mustn't feel hurt. I can think of no one better able to serve as my personal maid than you do.

"That too is an important job," she continued as she saw the proud grin spread across the girl's face. "I don't know what I should do without you. You always know just how my hair should be arranged and what colors suit me."

"Pink is the obvious choice," Lady Sybille declared.

"I say green," Mistress Gilly retorted.

Encouraged by her mistress's high praise, Missy spoke up. "I thought, my lady, that you should wear the blue wool with the wide sleeves faced with yellow silk. It matches your eyes."

Megge nodded. "So it does."

"The bronze girdle and the amber cross," Missy continued. "And the scarlet mantle with the fox fur lining. It will keep you nice and warm if the day is cool. Scarlet cloth is ever so grand, it being so dear, and I vow you look like a queen when you wear it. Sir Olyver will give over on the spot when he sees you."

"An excellent choice, Missy, although I rather think it will take a good deal more than a well-fashioned habit to bring Sir Olyver to his knees."

Chapter Twelve

"And Joshua, the son of Nun, sent out of Shit'tim two men to spy secretly, saying, 'Go view the land, even Jericho.' And they went and came into a harlot's house—"

"Hurrah for harlots!" cheered the men of the siege army.

Father Boniface glared down at his flock from his makeshift pulpit atop a baggage wain. He had selected today's text with special care, thinking to distract the men from the incessant demand of their fleshly appetites and redirect their attention to the gravity of the business at hand.

"Now Jericho was straitly shut up because of the children of Israel: None went out, and none came in. And the Lord said unto Joshua, 'See, I have given into thine hand Jericho, and the king thereof, and the mighty men of valor. And ye shall compass the city, all ye men of war, and go round about the city once. Thus shalt thou do six days—' "

"God's teeth!" someone groaned.

"Six days? One more hour without a woman and I'm going to throw myself off the cliff," another wailed.

"And seven priests shall bear before the ark seven trumpets of rams' horns: And the seventh day ye shall compass the city seven times, and the priests shall blow with the trumpets. And it shall come to pass, that when they make a long blast with the ram's horn—"

"I'll show you a blast of a *horn*!" someone shouted from the furthermost rank. The crowd roared.

". . . and when ye hear the sound of the trumpet, all the people shall shout with a great shout; and the wall of the city shall fall down flat, and the people shall ascend up every man straight before him—"

" 'Every man straight before him?' You have that aright! Ha, ha, ha!"

Father Boniface soldiered on with grim determination.

"And it came to pass that when the priests blew with the trumpets, Joshua said unto the people, 'Shout: for the Lord hath given you the city.

And they utterly destroyed all that was in the city, both man and woman . . ."

"Nay, we'll spare the women!"

". . . young and old, and ox, and sheep, and ass, with the edge of the sword. But Joshua had said unto the two men that had spied out the country, Go into the harlot's house, and bring out thence the woman . . ."

"Yea! Bring out thence the woman!" chorused the men.

Father Boniface, whose patron saint had been dubbed 'The Tamer of the Tribes' for his missionary zeal amongst the heathen east of the Rhine, threw up his hands in resignation, snarled a hasty benediction, and stomped off to the cook cart to break his fast.

Father Jerome, too, had given much thought to the lesson he would preach when the damnable women of Castle Rising finally unlocked the door of the chapel and allowed him to see the blessed light of the sun for the first time in two long weeks.

He had not exactly endeared himself to them upon their arrival by declaring that in departing the divinely ordained guardianship and protection of His Most Gracious Majesty Edward, Lord Humphrey, their husbands, fathers, and brothers, they had already traveled far down the road toward certain damnation. It fell to him, he had announced during that first Mass, to show them the iniquity of their folly. He would take it upon himself to make manifest the peril in which they had placed their immortal souls and instruct them in the proper duty of women according to the Word of God, His holy saints, and blessed martyrs.

The women had not received Father Jerome's exhortations with appropriate humility, and except for one sortie to baptize a new babe—escorted like a prisoner between the two formidable Gunnys— Father Jerome had been confined to the chapel where he had had ample time to reflect that one soul in particular merited particular attention.

His.

For Father Jerome lusted. He lusted mightily. He lusted by night, he lusted by day. Years of earnest prayer brought no surcease to the incessant cry of his loins; nor the cleansing act of confession and the supposed solace of absolution; nor acts of contrition, nor good works, nor mortification of his rebellious flesh.

Why, oh why could he not have been born in an earlier time when a priest might marry? All of the Apostles, except for young John, were married men with families. Had not Paul posed the perfectly reasonable question, "How can any man who does not understand how to manage his own family have responsibility for the church of God?"

True, in those long off days a priest might not know his wife in the Biblical sense on the night before he celebrated the Mass, but what were fifty-two nights of self-denial compared to three hundred and thirteen of blissful abandon between succulent white thighs?

Alas, in Anno Domini 366, one Damasus had succeeded to the throne of Peter and decreed that priests could continue to marry, but that they were not allowed to express their love sexually with their wives. Fortunately, no one paid him any attention; that is, until the sainted Augustine—once he had partaken of the full measure of his carnal appetites, and set his sights on literary immortality—decided that a woman's embraces were "sordid, filthy, and horrible. Nothing," he had declared, "is so powerful in drawing the spirit of a man downwards as the caresses of a woman." After that, it was downhill all the way—in Father Jerome's opinion—to that dark day when Pope Gregory VII decreed that a man who aspired to a life in the Church must first take a vow of celibacy.

Oh, celibacy had seemed a grand and noble undertaking when Jerome entered the monastery at age fourteen; he had yet to experience that first joy of male adolescence and knew no better. By fifteen, he had his suspicions when a pig keeper's daughter offered him the freedom of her slatternly body and he only just escaped damnation by fainting dead away. At sixteen, with hormones raging and libido run amok, Jerome knew he had made a colossal mistake, but by then it was too late: he had taken his final vows. He had pronounced his own doom.

If Father Jerome was not cut out for the rigors and sacrifices of the life spiritual and corporeal, physical martyrdom held no appeal whatsoever. Thus no nightmare could have compared to the reality of spending the past weeks inflamed by lustful imaginings, surrounded on all sides by women as sexually frustrated as he. But for that locked chapel door, he was certain he would have been well on his way to the fiery pit by now.

So it was that on the morning of the great day the negotiations were to begin, Father Jerome succumbed to temptation of a different sort: petty vengeance. The sirens of Castle Rising were going to pay for those extra years he'd be spending in purgatory.

"Hear ye, ye sinful women, the Holy Word of God as revealed in the Book of Proverbs:

> 'A virtuous woman is a crown to her husband:
> but she that maketh him ashamed is as rotten-
> ness in his bones.'

"Not again," Megge groaned.

> 'It is better to dwell in a corner of the housetop,
> than with a brawling woman in a wide house. It
> is better to dwell in the wilderness, than with a
> contentious and an angry woman.'

> 'A continual dropping in a very rainy day and a
> contentious woman are alike.'

"Boo!"

"Hear now," Father Jerome persevered, determined to make the most of the opportunity to put these women in their proper place, "the words of Paul in his First Epistle to Timothy:

> 'I will that women adorn themselves in modest
> apparel, with shamefacedness and sobriety; not
> with braided hair, or gold, or pearls, or costly
> array.'

"Pearls are so common," sniffed Lady Agnes.

"They most certainly are not," countered Lady Sybille. "Queen Eleanor is extremely fond of them, and you cannot say that the queen is a commoner."

"I *said*," snapped Lady Agnes, "that the pearls are common, not the person who wears them."

"Oh. Well, I rather like them myself. Frederick says they suit my delicate coloring."

Father Jerome glared down at Lady Sybille.

" 'Let the woman learn in *silence*. I suffer not a woman to teach, nor to usurp authority over the man, but to be in silence. For Adam was first formed, then Eve. And Adam was not deceived, but the woman being deceived was in the transgression—' "

"Takes two to transgress," Gunny One called out.

Father Jerome affected not to have heard and forged ahead. "Likewise, we read in the First Epistle General of that most holy apostle Peter:

'Ye wives, be in subjection to your own husbands—'

"Nay!" chorused the women.

Megge could stand it no longer. If the man went on in this vein much longer she would have a riot on her hands. "I beg you to conclude your lesson, Father. I must prepare to meet with Sir Olyver immediately after the noonday meal. If you will pronounce your benediction, you may join us in the hall rather than have your meal delivered to the chapel."

"Nay!"

Father Jerome took in the indignant, hostile faces before him and wisely opted for the chapel.

Chapter Thirteen

"Where in the name of heaven has Sybille got to?" Megge demanded.

"She went to change her gown and fetch the flag," Mary reported.

"Change her gown? Again? That is the third time today. This is not a court revel we are preparing for. Negotiating a treaty is serious business."

"Oh, I do so agree with you, Megge," called Lady Sybille as she dashed down the steps, "which is why I have finally settled on the pink and green striped silk rather than the orange samite, which I am sure you will agree was far too merry for the occasion."

With her burgeoning belly, little Lady Sybille now resembled nothing so much as the lavishly ornate ladies' pavilion at the annual spring tournament at Windsor. The "far too merry" orange samite looked like mourning garb by comparison.

"Did you bring the flag, Sybille?" asked Megge as she wriggled back against the padded cantle of the sidesaddle and planted her feet on the wooden stirrup board. She far preferred riding astride in a comfortable split-skirt riding gown, but to lead the little procession across the drawbridge and down the steep winding road in such militant style would not be in keeping with the genteel, accommodating, non-threatening demeanor she wished to convey to Sir Olyver. Given his reputation for facing down even the most treacherous, antagonistic, unyielding foes, he would think it no matter at all to best a seemingly tractable woman in parley and bring the siege of Castle Rising to a speedy conclusion, to his own advantage, of course.

Megge had considered at length the wiles the great Sir Olyver would bring to the table this day. She had concluded that like every other man, his assurance that his ascendancy over woman was divinely ordained—she being the lesser in understanding and resolve—would be his point of greatest vulnerability; the underbelly of the wild boar, as it were. He could only intimidate her if she allowed him to do so, and since she had lately taken on both Lord Humphrey and the king of England himself, Megge felt quite certain she would not be quailing before the legendary warrior this day.

Of course, it was all very well to congratulate herself on the soundness of her plan with Sir Olyver safely out of sight. But if her reaction when they came face to face was anything like it had been during the heart-stopping moments by the riverbank when those cold eyes had paralyzed her like a hapless bunny in the shadow of a swooping hawk, she was going to be in for a bad time of it.

"Here it is," Sybille announced with pride, producing the triangular swallow-tailed pennant with a proud flourish. "I will have you know I worked far into the night to get it finished. It's come out splendidly, don't you think?"

Megge's jaw dropped. Upon the stark white cloth that from time immemorial had signified absolute neutrality there now flew a delicately embroidered blue dove bearing an olive leaf in its little yellow beak.

"It's supposed to be pure white," Megge managed.

"Oh pooh. White is so boring. I thought and thought what to put on it to make it pretty. At first I was just going to put some little pink rosebuds, and then it came to me. The dove is the symbol of peace."

The dove, Megge thought glumly, is the symbol of docility, appeasement, capitulation. Not exactly the image she wished to carry before her as she entered into negotiations intended to wrest control over her own life from the self-serving grasp of men. Still, it might prove useful in further deceiving her opponent into thinking her willing to settle for peace at any price.

"Don't you like it, Megge?" Lady Sybille inquired anxiously. "Should I have used the rosebuds?"

"This will do very well, Sybille. The dove may prove the perfect choice," Megge assured her.

Lady Sybille produced a tangle of blue and yellow ribbons. "I've brought along some pretty ribbons to tie it to the lance," she announced, and set about the task while the rest of the party assembled beneath the arched passageway of the outer gate. Up above in the guardhouse the well-pleasured soldiers of the Castle Rising garrison manned the pulleys that would raise the massive iron gate.

Megge gave the signal, and soon the little procession appeared on the dirt rampart outside the wall and began its descent. Mary led the way on foot, holding high the truce flag. Then came Megge upon her white palfrey, bearing the colors of the ancient house of de Languetot: the red and azure chevron, with two lions above *combatant gardant*, and below the golden fleur-de-lys. Walking abreast behind strode Gunny One and Gunny Two, the former bearing the satinwood chest containing Megge's papers, a small stoppered vial of ink, and two newly prepared swan-feather quills; the latter Megge's delicate chair, upholstered in red, blue and gold damask. Bringing up the rear trotted a wildly apprehensive Missy with her lady's scarlet cloak draped neatly over her arm.

High atop the walls, like a flock of exotic birds in full mating plumage, the ladies of Castle Rising fluttered and tittered and flounced. They waved brightly colored handkerchiefs, and threw kisses. A mighty roar of approval echoed back from the siege army gathered in the sheep meadow across the River Lis.

It needed only a few knights in gleaming mail astride brightly caparisoned destriers, a wandering minstrel or two, and stalls selling meat pies, fruit fritters, ale, and gewgaws to beguile a casual observer into believing the scene a pleasant afternoon's entertainment at some country fair.

Megge was in no danger of being so beguiled as she guided Lady Skye around a sharp bend in the path and came face to face with a glowering Lord Humphrey of Flete, whose eyes were fixed on a point above the barbican gate.

"Megge, you will pay dearly for this foolishness," he growled as his roan gelding crowded Lady Skye precariously close to the edge of the drop. He rode on to the great gate, which had now been lowered again.

"Orabella," he was roaring as Megge urged her horse down the last of the incline, "you will come down from there at once."

"Nay, husband," the good lady called down with commendable aplomb, given the enraged purple face below. "We must talk."

"Talk? Talk?" seethed Lord Humphrey. "What can a husband possibly have to discuss with his wife?"

And therein, reflected Megge as she trotted on toward the wide stone bridge that spanned the river, lay the crux of the matter. It appeared that nothing short of barricading themselves behind high walls—be it atop the Acropolis of Athens or the granite cliffs of Devon—and denying men the relief of that most primal urge that informed their every thought and action, could women command sensible discourse with their men. It was all too absurd. A man need only open his ears and so avoid being forced to his knees. But no, the intransigent son of Adam would have none of it, and so must be led like a recalcitrant donkey in pursuit of a proffered carrot toward the paddock, or a child lured by a sugared wafer toward his little cot.

Engrossed in such thoughts Megge found herself suddenly at the bridge and pulled up. Several paces ahead Mary had planted herself like the great Colossus of Rhodes, holding high the lance upon which fluttered Lady Sybille's daintily embroidered dove. At the far side of the bridge, a fire-haired squire, similarly posed and equally self-important, bore a gleaming lance to which was affixed a plain white triangular pennant.

And looming behind him atop an enormous, sinister, mottled gray destrier sat Olyver of Mannyngs,

Scourge of the Saracen, the Limb of Hell. Clad from head to toe in shades of brown and black, he might have been carved from the same granite as the walls of Castle Rising.

With barely a flicker of an eye, Sir Olyver took in every detail of the odd little party before him, from the regal tilt of Lady Margaret's chin to the ridiculous little bird embroidered upon the truce flag. Without a word he swung around and led the way toward a square white tent that had been erected beneath an enormous copper beech at the river's edge.

Drawing a deep breath for courage and launching a fervent Hail Mary toward the heavens, Megge rode forward to embrace her destiny.

Chapter Fourteen

Olyver dismounted with the nonchalant grace, economy of effort, and elegant strength of a man in consummate mastery of himself and his realm. He tossed the reins to an earnest Lancelot, quivering with pride at his new and exalted station in life, and turned to watch Lady Margaret and her curious little entourage advance across the meadow.

Another, less prudent, commander would dismiss an adversarial force consisting of a headstrong, presumptuous, spoiled young noblewoman, a quaking maidservant, a mulish standard bearer, and two scowling giantesses as beneath his notice and contempt. It had been Olyver's experience, however, that one must know one's enemy as well as one knows oneself, and that loyalty above all other considerations of character determines who will win and who will lose. That four obviously ignorant peasant women would march with their lady against a seasoned siege army was sufficient to alert Olyver that the battle to be joined would be like no other he had ever fought.

He would win, of course, he always did. The two prizes to be won—the great castle bathed in the golden light of a summer's afternoon and the intriguing woman trotting across the meadow on her dainty little palfrey—would be well worth the nuisance and tedium of sitting through negotiations she could not possibly conclude to her advantage.

Lady Margaret would have no understanding of the protocols, the myriad subtleties, the feint and thrust of proposal and counterproposal. Intelligent and bold she might be, but she was after all only a woman when it came down to it: predisposed toward seeing things as she thought they ought to be rather than what they were, wary of confrontation, anxious of resolution.

And if the unthinkable should transpire and Lady Margaret prove to be his equal in reasoning, cunning, and resolve, he could always seduce her.

Megge stared down at the proffered hand and chided herself for not bringing Henry along in the capacity of squire to assist her down from the damnable sidesaddle. It would be unseemly for Mary to set aside her banner, and besides, she was fully occupied in trying to stare down Sir Olyver's squire. Missy and the Gunnys had their hands full, and Megge was well aware of the perils a stirrup board held for a woman attempting to dismount without getting her feet tangled in her skirts and plunging to the ground. Such a ludicrous scene was not likely to do much in the way of bolstering her self-confidence. It might, however, reinforce, if any reinforcement was needed, that she was but a helpless woman who could not even dismount from a small docile palfrey without the assistance of a gallant male with a strong arm.

Heaven knew that the arm attached to that huge hand would be strong enough to assist an ox down from a tall tree, should the beast find itself in such a predicament, although whether a knight would undertake such an ignoble task. . . .

Megge brought herself up short. Good heavens! The fact that such an idiotic thought should cross her mind at this first critical moment in her association with her formidable adversary gave proof that she was not as calm and collected as she had believed herself to be, and needed to be, under these trying circumstances.

It was the size of that hand, the uncompromising strength of long thick fingers encased in the dark leather of a half gauntlet, that led to the apprehension that once she placed her own slim white hand into its grasp, she might never get it back.

It's a just a hand, you ninny, Megge scolded herself. It will get you out of this hellish contraption, set you firmly upon the ground, and return to its other duties.

"My lady?"

"My lord?"

"Allow me."

"But of course. I thank you."

A split second too late she realized that one hand, however capable, was not sufficient to lift a lady off a stirrup board with any degree of dignity, and sure enough a second hand appeared. Gently cradled about the waist, she had no choice but to steady herself by laying her own hand on a shoulder as hard as iron.

Rather than being crushed between Sir Olyver's massive paws, Megge found herself being lifted as though she were the most fragile butterfly and set gently upon the earth. For the briefest moment she knew what it must be like to fly, to float weightless upon the wind. For one breathless moment she understood the wildly erotic interplay that could explode between a man and a woman.

And in that moment she had obviously lost every wit she possessed and would likely find herself being led off to some place of confinement for the mad. How the simple act of dismounting from a horse could translate into the most intimate mating ritual she could ever have imagined was utterly beyond her.

She eased back from Sir Olyver the moment her half boots touched the ground. With a regal little nod she gave him a wide berth and swept toward the tent.

Sweet Jesus, what had just happened here? He'd barely touched the woman.

The prize Olyver had so coolly demanded for lifting the siege of Castle Rising had suddenly and inexplicably become the most desirable woman he had ever known. She had fired a sexual arousal so powerful and immediate that he feared to take a step in any direction lest he shame himself before two hundred equally frustrated men.

Sir Olyver was no stranger to the demands of powerful lust. He had always prided himself on his ability to school his carnal appetites. He would yield to them when the need was hard upon him and an alluring woman was willing; rein them in when they were inappropriate or interfered with his sworn obligation to his liege lord and the effectiveness of his command. As for romantic love, he was perfectly content to leave that to the gallants, the fops, and the rogues who lured gullible maidens to their beds with the lovesick sigh and the dewy rose.

Only once, when he was but three and ten and had yet to gain his growth or sprout a single whisker, Olyver had believed himself madly in love with the delectable Allyson, she of the large bosom and flirtatious ways. Alas, the tempting globes had found their way into the hands of each of his four older brothers in succession, his own father, two uncles, and the archbishop of York.

Olyver nurtured his chaste infatuation for Allyson for years, but at the age of seventeen when finally he was ready to gift her with his virginity, he discovered she had taken to harlotry in earnest. What had once been given freely to all and sundry now commanded a substantial sum. As the young Olyver had not a penny in the world, love had withered on the vine for lack of funds, and he had gifted his virginity elsewhere at no expense whatsoever.

Sir Olyver was seriously considering making for the nearest thicket when he became aware that Lady Margaret's so-called squire was watching him closely. A quick waggle of her thick brows and just a hint of a smirk around her mouth proved sufficient to douse the fire in his loins.

With a foul curse he stormed toward the tent. The sooner he proved to Lady Margaret that she stood no chance against him in this ridiculous negotiation, the sooner he would take the rebellious little troublemaker to his bed.

Chapter Fifteen

"The Lord bless thee and keep thee. The Lord make His face shine upon thee and be gracious unto thee. The Lord lift up His countenance upon thee, and give thee peace," intoned Father Boniface with all the solemnity of Jesus blessing the bread at the Last Supper. "In the name of the Father, the Son, and the Holy Ghost, Amen."

"Amen," murmured Megge.

"Amen," echoed Sir Olyver.

It might have been more timely had the good father pronounced his blessing ten minutes earlier when the atmosphere within the tent had been anything but peaceful.

"Surely you cannot expect my lady to sit in *that*," Gunny One had barked at the young soldier in charge of seeing to the preparations.

"What's wrong with it? She has an arse like everyone else, doesn't she?"

"It has no cushion."

"That is why God gave us arses," he snickered.

"Remove it at once."

"I don't take orders from women."

"You'll take them from me."

"Children, children, this is most unseemly," Father Boniface managed to interject before the first blow could be struck. "Edgar, take it away. I believe Lady Margaret has brought her own chair."

"And while you're at it," Gunny One snapped, "bring a whisk and brush out this carpet. Lady Megge is not some godless infidel slopping around in the mud in some godforsaken jungle."

"You're an ignorant old bat," retorted the soldier. "Infidels live in the desert where it's sandy not muddy, and I can tell you they smell a good sight better than you do. Ow!"

The ensuing brawl brought Sir Kay, Sir Olyver's second in command, on the run to oversee the last minute details with a firm hand. Woe unto the soldier newly admitted to Sir Olyver's elect company who misread Sir Kay's jocular manner and peculiar appearance—stubby torso, bowed legs, huge beaked nose, bright pink jug ears—as outward proof that a buffoonish temperament dwelt within. A clown did not fight by the side of Sir Olyver of Mannyngs from one end of Christendom to the other, stand for him in his absence, and enjoy his privileged friendship and absolute confidence.

In no time at all, the crimson tapestry carpet was duly swept, Megge's chair installed, and the contents of her satinwood chest arranged neatly on the table. Only then were the flaps of the tent secured back.

"After you, my lady," said Sir Olyver with a ceremonious bow.

Megge sank into a graceful curtsy. "My lord."

"You may leave us, Father," said Sir Olyver.

"But, my lord," the priest protested, "the Conventions of the Siege mandate the presence of a man of God to offer divine counsel."

"We shall be sure to summon you if the need should arise."

"But—"

"Leave us."

Father Boniface sailed off in a huff.

Sir Olyver motioned to Lady Margaret's little maid-servant, who was perched on a chest in a dark corner, that she too should leave. To his astonishment she actually shook her head at him, clutching Lady Margaret's cloak to her breast as though she held the winding cloth of Christ himself.

Sir Olyver fixed her with a stare that had sent seasoned warriors to their knees. "You defy me, girl?"

Missy quailed, but stood her ground.

"Please, my lord," Megge interjected, "allow me. I am, as ever, grateful for your concern, Missy, but as you see it is a fine day and I am quite comfortable as I am."

"It might snow, my lady."

"Missy, it is July."

"Or rain frogs, like it did in the Bible."

"That is highly unlikely to happen."

Missy sought for inspiration. "The sky could fall!"

Megge heaved a sigh. "If it should happen that the sky is falling I shall take shelter under a tree."

"An angel could fall on you," the girl hazarded. "They do that sometimes, you know."

"Enough." Sir Olyver pushed back his chair. With surprising gentleness, he pulled Missy to her feet and ushered her from the tent.

"What does she do with herself in the winter?" he

inquired as he settled his powerful body into his huge high-backed chair. "Has she a purpose in life?"

Megge smiled. "She certainly does. She follows me about with cool cloths lest I become over warm in my mantle. Missy means well, my lord. She takes her duties very seriously."

"So it would appear. Now, my lady, let us begin. It occurs to me that you may be unfamiliar with the protocols of formal negotiation. I would be happy to provide a brief explanation of them if you so desire."

"I should be glad of any instruction you care to give, sir," Megge said. She folded her hands upon the table and gazed at him like an avid student waiting for pearls of wisdom to fall from her master's lips.

Sir Olyver was not so easily deceived. From the look of the thick sheaf of papers covered closely with neat notes in a dainty hand he suspected the lady had come to the table well prepared. Nevertheless, there was a certain advantage to be gained by speaking first. It would allow him to direct the discussion and intimidate her with his expertise and experience. The drawback was that it afforded his adversary the opportunity to gauge his strengths and weaknesses without yet having to expose her own.

For her part, Megge was perfectly content to let Sir Olyver take control of the proceedings. She had expected nothing less of the man. He was accustomed to playing the leading role and assigning the roles he wished others to play. He would assume they would conform to his expectations. Megge was a woman. Women required the guidance of men and sought validation from them. Ergo, Megge would be grateful for his superior understanding and his condescension. He would have the upper hand from the outset, or so he believed.

Megge propped her chin on her hand and fixed her eyes on Sir Olyver, giving him her earnest attention. In truth she was paying little heed to his words, taking instead the opportunity to study at close range that remarkable face without seeming impertinent or unduly interested.

The cast of his countenance was austere and uncompromising, but his features when taken individually were really quite appealing. His hair was the color of winter wheat; had it not been drawn tightly back from his face and tied with a strip of dark brown leather, it would have swept well past his shoulders. Straight sandy brows defined a high brow, and thick lashes framed eyes of quicksilver blue. His face was all hard planes and sharp angles, with a slashing scar along the left jaw.

But it was the mouth that betrayed the man. Sir Olyver had certainly perfected the art of concealing his thoughts and masking his emotions, but something about shape of his lips and the tiny dimple at the right corner of his mouth hinted at a softer, sensual—possibly even mischievous—man behind the impenetrable façade.

All in all, it was a face that would haunt a woman's dreams. If she were foolish enough to allow herself to be so beguiled.

Just look at the little minx, gazing at him with her big eyes the color of ripe bilberries and a tiny vertical frown of earnest concentration between those gently arching mahogany brows. She wasn't listening to a word he was saying. No, she was taking his measure, weighing her options, plotting her strategy. He must remember that she had been raised amidst the vicious intrigues of the court. She would have mastered the art of concealing a clever mind behind a gossamer veil of social grace, faultless deportment, and charming naivete.

And she would know exactly how to flatter a man by hanging on his every word, as she was doing now.

"Have you any questions, my lady?"

"No, Sir Olyver. You have explained everything so clearly. I really had no idea how to go on."

"I hope you will not hesitate to ask for clarification on any point you do not understand as we proceed. I am your servant."

Megge almost laughed aloud. Her servant? Never in a thousand years would the warrior lounging in lordly self-assurance across from her be anyone's servant. If ever a man had been born to command it was Olyver of Mannyngs.

"Then perhaps we can proceed to examine the root cause of the issues that confront us. I should be glad to hear your views on the matter, my lady."

Megge sat a little straighter and cleared her throat. "Thank you. As you may know, my mother died when I was but four years and my father when I was eight. His Majesty assigned himself my guardian, and I lived happily in his household for many years. He took his responsibility to find me a suitable match most seriously. Through no fault of his, or mine, it was not to be. I am now four and twenty, and once again His Majesty would have me marry. I have informed him that the man he is considering, Lord Humphrey's brother, Sir Walter, is not acceptable to me and I would decline to consider the offer."

"That cannot please Edward," Sir Olyver observed.

"No, I expect it does not. But it is my right under John's Great Charter." Megge shuffled through her papers. "Here it is: 'Heirs may be given in marriage, but not to someone of lower social standing.' As I am a direct descendant of King William, I may rightly be considered of superior rank to Sir Walter. But as I am also thrice a widow the following provision is more pertinent to our deliberation: 'No widow shall be compelled to marry, so long as she wishes to remain without a husband. But she must give security that she will not marry without royal consent, if she holds her lands of the Crown, or without the consent of whatever other lord she may hold them of.'" She handed Sir Olyver the page that he might read for himself the relevant passage.

Sir Olyver scanned it. "I trust you will excuse my indelicacy, Lady Margaret, but though you are thrice widowed it is my understanding that those unions were unconsummated due to the unfortunate death of your husbands, and are therefore invalid in the eyes of the Church. Edward's judiciars could argue, with some credibility, that this passage does not apply to you."

Megge schooled her features. Did every soul in the kingdom know of her virgin state? It would not do to let Sir Olyver see her discomfiture. "That, sir, lies in the province of Canon Law, and if it comes to it I shall take the matter to the Holy Father in Rome. In civil law, however, having taken my vows in good faith, I am a widow."

"My apologies, my lady. I did not mean to offend. Let us move on. It is my understanding that King Edward assigned your guardianship to Lord Humphrey some time ago."

Megge stiffened. "You might be interested to know, sir, that a guardianship is not *assigned,* it is *sold.*"

Sir Olyver shrugged. "I stand corrected."

"Which is as much to say," Megge continued, "that the ward is herself sold to the highest bidder; in my case, that bidder was Lord Humphrey, who desired the use of my extensive forest preserves, which border upon his."

"Hmmm. I see."

"No, sir, I apprehend that you do not see at all," Megge retorted. "I, a noblewoman of the highest rank, am treated no better than a slave upon the block, to be sold to the highest bidder." Realizing that her anger was threatening to cloud her judgment, Megge once again took a page in hand and read aloud:

" 'For so long as a guardian has guardianship of such land, he shall maintain the houses, parks, fish preserves, ponds, mills, and everything else pertaining to it, from the revenues of the land itself. When the heir comes of age, he shall restore the whole land to him. . . . '

"And that, Sir Olyver," declared Megge, tapping an emphatic finger upon the paper, "is the crux of the matter that brings us here today. Lord Humphrey's administration of my holdings has been irreproachable, but he has made no effort to restore them to me now that I am of age. He gives as his reason that I will have to marry again, and in that event my property will be transferred to the jurisdiction of my husband. He does not see the need to go through the business of restoring it to me when it will only have to be transferred again."

"But you do not intend to marry?"

"I do not say that. But I vow that I shall have a say in the choice of a husband this time, and should he gainsay me the right to retain control of my own lands and fortune, I shall not have him.

"In short, Sir Olyver," Megge concluded, "I will never again suffer myself to be treated as some bit of chattel to be sold now to this man, now to that. I am not a brood mare to be secured for the sake of my noble ancestry. I am not a prize to be awarded to some upstart who is trying to better himself in the world."

Sir Olyver regarded the angry young woman—for she was very angry, though she masked it well enough—with some little admiration. She had analyzed her situation well, understood her rights under law, and organized her arguments in a clear and logical fashion. He forbore to point out, however, that Edward's advisors and judiciars would make short work of finding a way around the law, and failing that fall back upon the dictates of common practice and received wisdom. In the end the king would do whatever he damned well pleased anyhow. Surely she knew that.

"In taking possession of your principal holding you think to force the issue?"

"I do. Would you not do the same in my position?"

Ah, thought Sir Olyver, she had unwittingly opened the door for him to employ an important negotiating tactic: connection and commonality.

"As to that I cannot say, my lady. It is true that I am

free to marry where I will. At the same time, since I am possessed of no property of my own, being the youngest son, I can have no expectation of an advantageous marriage. It is possible that my efforts on behalf of my liege lords will earn their gratitude in the form of a small fiefdom, but I do not count on it. It would appear that although our situations are very different we are dependent upon the good will of others for our good fortune and our happiness."

Megge responded exactly as he had intended. "I am so very sorry, my lord. I spoke without thinking. I too know what it is like to have no home; to be constantly on the move from here to there, wanting only to be assured of my place in the world. It had never occurred to me that a man might feel similarly dispossesed."

Sir Olyver shrugged. "It is the way of things, my lady."

Megge could not put her finger on it, but some instinct warned her she had just been finessed. The man looked entirely too pleased with himself. She was sure of it a moment later when he suggested with an unexpectedly charming smile that they adjourn for refreshments. He had drawn her out, then elicited her sympathy and so had the advantage of her. For the moment.

"Allow me to summarize what we have covered here today," said Sir Olyver. "We have concluded that your disagreement with King Edward cannot be properly addressed through these negotiations. Am I correct?"

Megge nodded.

"You demand that Lord Humphrey forthwith transfer full authority for the conduct of all your business affairs and the administration of your properties into your hands now and in perpetuity. You demand that he order the siege of Castle Rising be abandoned and foreign troops depart from your lands immediately. Finally, you demand that he petition the king on your behalf to desist from any consideration of Sir Walter's suit for your hand in marriage."

"That is correct, my lord," Megge said, feeling suddenly overwhelmed by the enormity of the task she had set herself. She very much doubted there were ten men in the kingdom who would be fool enough to defy the monarch, issue demands to a powerful earl of the realm, and match wits with a master strategist who also happened to be a legendary warrior knight. They would need an army at their backs and a ready ship to bear them away to the farthest corners of the world should they fail. For a woman alone in the world to attempt it was madness, pure and simple.

Sir Olyver felt an unaccustomed surge of pity for Lady Margaret as he watched a storm of emotions chase over her expressive features. It could not be easy for her, alone in the world save for a gaggle of silly women who could have no understanding of the principles for which she was fighting.

This business must be concluded as quickly as possible for everyone's sake, especially his, since he was going mad looking at that perfect little cherry bow of a mouth and could hardly keep from yanking her across the table and plundering its sweet warmth.

"Ahem. My lady?"

"Oh, I beg your pardon, sir. I'm afraid my mind was wandering. Yes, let us proceed."

"As Lord Humphrey's representative in this matter, I must advise you that he has every right to expect some just compensation should he accede to your demand."

Megge bristled. "I seek only what is mine by right, sir. I would not have been forced to this had he acted in accordance with John's Charter."

"Perhaps Lord Humphrey has only your best interests at heart."

"I would never deny it. I am willing to offer him access to my forest preserves and a half share in the revenues derived therefrom while he lives, and thereafter an eighth share to his heirs. As he is particularly fond of the hunt I believe it a fair compensation for all that he has done for me and for the upright manner in which he has seen to my affairs these past four years."

Sir Olyver nodded noncommittally. "I will put the matter to him this evening."

"You do not think it fair?" inquired Megge.

"It is not for me to make such a judgment, my lady. I am merely Lord Humphrey's emissary in this matter."

"Yes, of course," Megge said as she began to gather her papers and writing instruments to return them to the satinwood box. "It is interesting, is it not, my lord, that though your role here is crucial to the successful resolution of our dispute, in the end you have no real stake in the outcome. It must be a most curious position to find oneself in."

"Most curious."

Something in his tone caused Megge to glance up. He was idly swirling the wine in his cup, and she was startled to find him in an unguarded moment. A small smile played over his lips, bringing out that adorable little dimple—yes, it really was very adorable, she had to admit—but it was the smile of someone with a secret, and for some reason that worried her.

Megge closed the cover of the box, then opened it again and searched through her papers. "I almost forgot. I have here a list of the women who wish to negotiate with their husbands and, er, friends. You will see also that I have set up a schedule beginning tomorrow shortly after morning prayers. I thought it advisable, and I am sure you will agree, to limit each meeting to one hour, else we shall never be done with it. No man will be admitted to the castle precinct; they must converse through the outer gate. I will of course ensure each couple complete privacy. However, they cannot be reunited until all negotiations are successfully concluded."

"Are you so sure of a successful outcome in every case, my lady?" inquired Sir Olyver as he held back the tent flap to escort her out.

Megge blushed. "One can only hope, my lord, that the, um, stress occasioned by their long separation will prove a potent stimulus for a speedy resolution."

"I have no doubt that will prove the case," he said wryly as he fastened the half gauntlet onto his left hand.

Mary appeared leading Lady Skye, followed by an anxious Missy, ready to fling the scarlet mantle about Lady Megge's shoulders should the sun take it into its head to pass behind a fluffy cloud, thereby causing her lady to take a chill and go to an early grave.

Megge eyed the awful sidesaddle in dismay. Frankly, she'd prefer to make the long trek up the castle mount on foot despite the heat. Besides, Sir Olyver would most likely insist on helping her into the saddle, and she would once again feel those powerful hands about her waist and she would go all breathless and soft and weak at the knees again. If she could just get away without touching him again.

"I will walk, Mary. Come, Missy. Oh, there you are, Gunny. Yes, we'll just leave the chair here. Well, we must be off," she said briskly, turning to Sir Olyver.

"I suspect you find that saddle not to your liking, my lady. You are welcome to ride with me to the gate." Sir Olyver instantly regretted his offer. It was the chivalrous thing to do, of course, but to have Lady Margaret snuggled between his thighs and her sweetly curved little bottom rocking against his shaft would likely kill him. To his relief she politely declined. Now if he could just get away without touching her again.

"My lord," Megge murmured as she curtsied.

"My lady," said he as he automatically held out his hand to raise her to her feet.

Feeling all breathless and soft and weak at the knees, Megge led Lady Skye toward the bridge.

His shaft throbbing unbearably, Sir Olyver headed toward the river for a long cold swim.

Chapter Sixteen

It had taken Father Boniface, whose mission insofar as he understood it was the salvation of souls, only a day and a night with the siege army to conclude that matters of personal hygiene in his flock also fell under the obligations of his office. How Noah had endured one hundred and ninety days in the close confines of his ark—forty days of flood and the following one hundred and fifty before the waters receded—he simply could not imagine.

The siege camp itself was kept in good order. Sir Olyver would allow no less. Cook tents were scrupulously maintained, vermin kept under control by a multitude of cats, and ditches far removed from the camp for the men's personal needs treated with lime daily. But the stink of unwashed bodies, unrestrained flatulence, and foul odors from two hundred mouths wafted like the breath of hell over the camp.

Accordingly, Father Boniface had searched out Biblical texts, of which there was no lack, to exhort the virtues of personal hygiene and the favor a man would find in God's eyes—not to mention his own—by washing more than once a year. He was therefore pleasantly surprised, nay astonished, to see men tramping down to the river, some as many as four or five times a day, to plunge about in the frigid water. The most popular time seemed to be immediately upon rising, but even in the dead of night splashing could be heard. A good deal of cursing accompanied this constant traffic, but all things considered, Father Boniface could congratulate himself on a job well done.

This day he trotted after Sir Olyver, who usually bathed in the early evening after the sun had imparted some degree of warmth to the water. He was anxious to find out what progress had been made with Lady Margaret. Sir Olyver seemed especially eager to bathe—well, the day *was* warm—as he was already tearing at the laces of his braies by the time he reached the riverbank. With a foul curse he flung off the last of his clothes and made a running dive into the river before Father Boniface could catch up. He struck out toward the far bank with powerful strokes, the water streaming over his massive shoulders.

"My lord," called Father Boniface, trying to catch Sir Olyver's attention as he plowed back and forth like a man with the demons of hell close behind.

"Later," Sir Olyver growled, flipped about, and headed away.

"Leave the man alone," Lord Humphrey snarled. He too appeared to be intent on bathing, having just returned from the castle, although Father Boniface had seen him in the river only that morning. The earl waded in and paddled about muttering darkly to himself.

"I say, my lord, how is it with your lady?" the priest

called out. "I trust you found her in good health?"

"My *wife* is going to be a widow if we don't get this damnable business settled soon," the earl snapped.

"Surely not, my lord," gasped Father Boniface. "You are in your prime yet. You are blessed with the best of health. Is not your lady even now increasing? The Psalmist assures us that the righteous man shall bring forth fruit in his old age . . . er, that is, you are vigorous still, my lord," Father Boniface stammered, backing away. Lord Humphrey had gained his feet on the river bottom and was wading toward shore with murder in his eye.

"If you have half a brain left in your head, priest," advised Sir Olyver, who had ceased his exertions and was now treading water closer to shore, "you will take it and yourself away at once."

"The man is a simpleton," growled Sir Humphrey as Father Boniface hurried off. He turned on to his back with his ample belly floating like a hairy little island above the water line, and glowered at the sky. "She wants to *talk*," he snorted. "*Negotiate.* Why, I hardly know the woman anymore. I blame Megge. She has put this foolish notion into Orabella's head."

"Perhaps," allowed Sir Olyver who floated a few feet away. "But like any good politician Lady Margaret has only exploited an existing discontent, not created it. Each of these women confronts a dilemma or harbors a complaint, real or imagined, that she cannot resolve on her own. Her husband will not hear her; her priest exhorts her to put her hand beneath her husband's foot and subject her will to his; the law accords little recourse. Lady Margaret offers a solution: By acting in concert one small voice becomes the roar of a multitude."

"Bah. I always knew Megge was too clever for her own good," grumbled Lord Humphrey. "I imagine Edward is seriously annoyed by all this bother, and if I know my brother, Walter will show up any day to make good his claim, whatever it takes."

"Is Lady Margaret in danger of him? Would he try to take her by force?"

"I wouldn't put it past him. Walter may be my brother, but I do not like the man. Nor does Edward, which is why I was surprised to hear that he had taken Walter's suit under consideration. I tell you, Olyver, there is more to this than meets the eye. There always is with Edward. For some reason he has his eye on Walter and is dangling Megge in front of him like a bone before a hungry wolf. I wish I knew the truth of the matter. I won't have Megge in danger. Perhaps it is just as well she is safely behind the walls of Castle Rising."

Sir Olyver had by now had gained the bank. Down river, closer to the camp, a steady stream of soldiers clambered in and out of the frigid water. "She has informed the king she will not consent to a union with your brother. She demands that you petition the king on her behalf."

"You did not inform her that I have already done so?"

"I thought it best to withhold that information for the present. Nor did I think it prudent to inform her of our arrangement."

"Wise man."

Sir Olyver then provided Lord Humphrey with a detailed account of that day's negotiation and the plans for the following day. "According to Lady Margaret's schedule—she is a very organized young woman—

you and Lady Orabella will be the first. In deference to your station and her warm feelings for you both, you are to be allowed two hours instead of one."

"Dear Christ," groaned Lord Humphrey. "Two hours! Whatever can I have to say to a woman for two full hours?"

"I believe the point of the exercise is that you should listen."

"Listen?"

"Listen."

"God help me."

While Lord Humphrey huffed and humphed his way into his garments, Sir Olyver lounged on the bank and gnawed at a stalk of dry grass and thought about Sir Walter. He had seen more than one rapist off to hell at the end of his sword and watched without pity as others gasped their last breath at the end of a rope for the same crime. A sound whipping awaited the man under his command who so much as laid a finger on a woman without her consent. He took seriously his knightly vow to protect the weak, and ten years earlier had nearly died from a knife thrust to the ribs after coming to the defense of well-used tavern whore who refused the attention of a drunken lout.

But it would be no knightly vow that would send Sir Walter into the eternal fire if he dared laid hands on his Lady Margaret. *His.* It would be personal vengeance, pure and simple. But a month ago she had been little more to him than a trophy, a means to an end. Then came the indignant fairy being upon a high wall; the ragamuffin in the tall grass who could not conceal behind a carefully applied layer of grime her noble pedigree; and the gamester at the table willing to play for the highest stakes of all, her freedom.

And though she knew it not and might never forgive him for it when she did, the woman beneath him, the mother of his children, the mistress of his hall.

Chapter Seventeen

"The man thinks he is so very clever," declared Megge, "but I see exactly what he is about, and I will not allow him to play his games with me."

"Who is that, dear?" inquired Lady Orabella. She reclined among soft cushions on a small bed that had been set up by the west hearth in the great hall.

"Sir Olyver, of course."

Lady Orabella shifted to a more comfortable position. She had only just escaped a nasty fall earlier in the evening when she was taken with dizziness. A maidservant had spotted her tottering on the top step of the treacherous spiral stairway in the Rose Tower, thrown her arms around her, and borne her back to the floor just in time. Try as she might to make light of the matter, the ladies of Castle Rising had decreed she should climb no more stairs until her time came.

Lady Orabella smiled. "I did not think you referred to my Humphrey. He is a most capable man, but I cannot in all honesty call him particularly clever. I should never say so aloud, of course, but at some level he knows it is so, which is why he places so much reliance upon Sir Olyver.

"No, dear," she said, waving Lady Clarice away. "I appreciate your concern, but if I drink one more drop of your potion I shall be to and from the garderobe half the night."

"You will do no such thing," announced Lady Agnes. "The servants will set up a little place right here in the hall where you can use a chamber pot in privacy; they are fetching the screens now. We have sent for Mistress Annie in the village to tend to you. You are only eight months along; this excessive fatigue and dizziness is not normal."

"Really, Agnes, you are making far too much of this. I am only a little tired."

"Oh? You have been with child five times. Can you say this has happened before?"

"Well, no—"

"There you have it," Lady Agnes said with finality.

"Agnes, Clarice, you will tire her ladyship even further with your fussing, however well intended," Megge said. "Missy, Lady Orabella has no need of another fur coverlet. She will go up in flames if you go on like this. Please, ladies, if you will excuse us, I must speak with Orabella in private."

"Thank you, Megge," Lady Orabella said when the hall had been cleared. "My father used to say that great damage could be done with much kindness."

Megge perched on the edge of Lady Orabella's bed and took her hand. "Agnes is right, isn't she? There is something amiss."

Lady Orabella sighed. "I fear so."

"Shall I send for Lord Humphrey?"

"Heavens no! He will go distracted. The one time he was at home when I was in childbed—it was dear little Arthur, I think—he drank himself into insensibility and fell into the moat."

Megge plopped back into her own chair. "Perhaps you should bring that up when you meet with him tomorrow."

"He will not appreciate being reminded of it, and I foresee enough difficulty as it is without embarrassing him into the bargain." Lady Orabella smiled at the fond memory. "But you were speaking of Sir Olyver? What is it you think he is about?"

"He intends me for Sir Walter."

"What foolishness is this, Megge? How can it possibly profit him?"

"Sir Olyver seeks an advantageous marriage; he told me as much today. He cannot hope for one unless he possesses property. He has served the king and Lord Humphrey some fifteen years with honor and commendation, yet he has not been enfeoffed."

"I am sure Humphrey will—"

"No, Orabella, I do not believe Sir Olyver is as patient as he would like the world to think. He is not content to wait upon that day."

Megge bounced up from her chair and paced back and forth. "It took me a while to work it out, but this is what I think he has in mind. He will advise Lord Humphrey that the best way to deal with me is to allow me to remain in Castle Rising. Your husband will be appropriately grateful for my offer to share my forest preserves with him, and will begin the process of restoring my property to my care."

Orabella had gained her feet and lowered herself

into the chair Megge had vacated. "Is that not what you hoped for, dear?"

"It is. But Lord Humphrey cannot give his consent that I should retain that control in the event of my marriage; only Edward can do that. Whether he will or no, Lord Humphrey will continue to do everything he can to protect my interests when I marry."

"Of course he will," Orabella said indignantly. "He is so very fond of you. But Megge, I thought you said you would not marry unless it be the man of your choice."

Megge sighed. "I am not such a fool as to think Edward will not have his way eventually. He will bring the power of the Church to bear, and if that fails will see me to a convent and absorb my property into the Crown. I cannot allow that. My inheritance is a sacred trust."

Lady Orabella shook her head in bewilderment. "But what has Sir Olyver to do with all this? What is this scheme of his?"

Megge stopped in front of the hearth and stared at the flames as though seeing there the events that would unfold if Sir Olyver had his way.

"Sir Olyver will advise Lord Humphrey to support Sir Walter's suit—"

"No, Megge," Lady Orabella cried. "I cannot believe Humphrey would ever—"

"Oh but he will! Walter is his brother. He may dislike him, but what better way to keep an eye on my interests than have his own brother installed as my lord?"

"But Sir Olyver?"

"Before he sets the matter before Lord Humphrey, he will forge an alliance with Sir Walter. In return for wielding his influence with Lord Humphrey he will

demand as payment one of my estates once Sir Walter and I are married. Likely in France, as he does not
appear to care to live in England. Then he can make
his advantageous marriage," she concluded with a
nod, confident with her own reasoning.

"Oh dear," said Lady Orabella. "It all seems rather
complicated. But I tell you again, Megge, Humphrey
will never countenance a marriage between you and
Walter. I know him."

"And," Megge continued, hands on hips, "while all
this is going forward, Sir Olyver will man the garrison
here at Castle Rising, ostensibly to see to my protection until Sir Walter is installed. Actually, he will be
keeping an eye on me by ensuring that I do not again
raise the gates and force another siege."

For long moments neither spoke.

"It saddens me, Megge," said Lady Orabella at last,
"that you have so little faith in my Humphrey. He is a
good man. He could not be persuaded, even by Sir
Olyver himself, to see you wed to a man who would
treat you ill."

Megge dropped to her knees beside Orabella and
seized her hand. "Please, do not misunderstand me. I
know Lord Humphrey to be the kindest of men. But
it is the lot of men that they must deal with the reality
of the world as it is, even the most exalted of them. I
am one of the greatest heiresses in England; Edward
must see me wed. It is his duty. As my guardian, Lord
Humphrey must find the best way to safeguard my interests. It is his duty. Sir Olyver owes it to his noble
line to make an advantageous match. It is his duty.
Each will do what he must to achieve his goal."

Megge pushed to her feet. "As Sir Olyver says, it is
the way of things."

"Perhaps," Lady Orabella ventured, "Edward will choose someone else, even if Humphrey does petition him on behalf of his brother. There is no lack of applicants, I am sure, and there is always the hope that this man would permit you to retain control of your interests in exchange for the privilege of marrying into William's line."

"Hah!"

"Yes, I suppose you are right," Orabella conceded. "Perhaps some joint arrangement?"

Megge had to laugh. "Orabella, you are a dreamer. There is not a man on the face of the earth who would agree to such a thing."

"But if he loved you . . ." Orabella's voice trailed off at the look of incredulity on Megge's face.

"Love? What has love to do with this? We are discussing marriage!" Megge cried.

Orabella did not reply for a moment, then said softly, "I love Humphrey."

"I apologize, my lady—"

"And he loves me, in his way."

Megge realized she had offended. "I am sure he does," she said contritely.

"You are clever, my dear, but sometimes I think you lived too many years at court. You are far too cynical for one so young. I pray that one day you will open yourself to the possibility of love in your life, however unlikely the prospect may appear to you. Now I should like to sleep. Would you give me your hand?" she added wearily.

"Of course." Megge helped Lady Orabella to her bed and saw her safely tucked in. "I have sent Gunny One to the village to fetch Mistress Annie. She should be here any minute. She will sit with you tonight."

Lady Orabella took Megge's hands between her own. "What ever will become of you, Megge? If what you say is true, you are in a pretty fix indeed. What can you do?"

"It is quite simple, Orabella. I too will do what I must."

"Oh dear," sighed Lady Orabella as her eyes fluttered shut, "I don't like the sound of that at all."

Chapter Eighteen

Yes, Megge would do what she must. She would honor the sacred trust that had come to her down through so many generations. She would dedicate herself to the stewardship of the lands and holdings given into her care; see to the welfare of her people; adjudicate their disputes with wisdom and compassion, and see to the impartial and fair administration of the law. She would serve and esteem her liege lord Edward—even when he did not deserve it—and play her proper role in the administration of his realm.

It was an awesome trust indeed, one rarely confronted by a young woman alone in the world, and insofar as Megge knew, never before in the distinguished line of the conqueror himself.

And, Megge reminded herself as she lay staring up at the gold fleurs-de-lys sprinkled like stars over the blue canopy of her bed, a sacred trust that she must pass on to future generations.

Edward would see her married a dozen times if necessary, bedded, and successfully impregnated—if he himself had to stand over the marriage bed to see it accomplished.

Edward had exhibited a fatherly concern for her welfare during the years she had lived in his household, and Megge knew in her heart that he wished her happy. Which made it all the more puzzling that he would think of marrying her off to Sir Walter. It worried her that she had not received a reply from him with regard to her letter.

Knowing she would find no sleep this night, Megge reached for the loose wool tunic and soft leather slippers Missy laid across the bottom of the coverlet on even the warmest night. She picked up the ivory beeswax candle that burned low on a carved chest beside the bed, and pushed aside the thick curtains that protected against draughts. Ever so quietly so as not to wake the girl, who lay curled up like a little kitten on a soft pallet in the corner, she stepped down from the high dais and tiptoed out of her chamber.

The blessed nighttime quiet of the great castle embraced her—such a relief after a day of wailing babes, shrieking children, and chattering women—as she made her way through the great hall. A small fire still burned in the west hearth, illuminating a dozing Mistress Annie in a chair close by Lady Orabella's bed. Megge tiptoed past, rounded the carved wooden screen that shielded the hall from draughts when the buttery door was open during meal times, and left the keep through a small side door. She climbed the steep wooden steps to the walkway of the east wall and gazed up at the stars.

The night was far cooler than she had expected. She thought about going back for one of the many cloaks Missy had ever ready to hand, but the brisk sea breeze was more invigorating than uncomfortable. It helped clear her mind to focus on the present state of her scheme and the difficult choices that might lie before her. And to cool the delicious little quivers and wanton ripples of pleasure that heated her womanly center each time she recalled the touch of Sir Olyver's strong callused fingers.

Never in her life had Megge experienced such an undignified and scandalous reaction to the simple execution of an act of formal etiquette. Perhaps, as Lady Orabella had pointed out, she could not, or would not, allow herself to experience such a personal and intimate response to a man. Megge suspected the right man had not made an appearance in her life before. That he might very well be Sir Olyver was not at all a comfortable thought under the circumstances, especially since he could have no interest in Margaret de Languetot beyond seeing her wed to Sir Walter, thereby securing his own future.

Megge gazed down at the sprawling siege camp. Moonlight washed over it, laying down long shadows across a field of sleeping bodies and cold fire pits. It cast into sharp-edged silhouette tents and wagons, and silvered the flanks of drowsing horses. Dogs skulked in the shadows, cats stalked reckless prey, and bored guards traced a tedious itinerary around the camp perimeter. Rarely if ever in history, thought Megge with a smile, had so destructive a force been assembled to challenge such a patently innocuous foe, who nevertheless wielded the most potent weapon of all: the means to relieve men's elemental and insatiable sexual desire.

"Male and female He made them," proclaimed the Book of Genesis. So He had, Megge thought smugly as she moved along the rampart toward the light of a sentry's lantern, but how blind men had ever been to the paradox of God's plan: that a *man* might hold mastery of a *woman*, but the male would ever be ensorcelled by the female.

"Look, my lady!" Megge followed Mary's pointed finger and was amazed to see a rider just topping the steep road that led to the castle gate. He angled right and moved into the deep shadow of the outer curtain wall. He appeared to be alone, but Megge immediately sent Mary to warn the other sentries and make ready the vats of rancid pig grease should an attack be under way.

"Don't let them make it too hot," she reminded Mary. "We don't want anyone to get burned. If it comes to it and we must pour it down over the flanking wall and the cliff, we must shout out warnings so the men won't slip and fall."

She sprinted down to ground level, checked that the massive gate was lowered, then hastened toward the postern door.

"Someone's out there," Gunny One said as Megge rushed up.

"I know. I think it must be Sir Olyver, judging by the size of both horse and rider."

Gunny peered through the door's small iron grating. "Aye, 'tis the man himself," she reported. "He's dismounting."

Megge crowded close. "Whatever can he be thinking?" she whispered.

"I reckon he's come on some urgent business he has with you."

Megge stepped back, unconsciously smoothing her skirts only to remember she was clad only in the wool tunic and slippers. "I cannot imagine what could be so important that it cannot wait until morning. He cannot think to continue our negotiations in the middle of the night."

"You are dim as a donkey, if you don't mind my saying so. A man doesn't call upon a lady at one in the morning to discuss business. Like as not he has more *urgent* matters on his mind, if you take my meaning."

A firm knock sounded upon the door. "I wish to speak with your lady on an urgent matter."

Gunny One grinned at Megge. Megge glared back.

"We won't answer," Megge told her. "Maybe he'll go away."

"He knows we're here."

"Not necessarily. Perhaps he can't hear us through the door."

"I know there's someone there," said Sir Olyver. "I hear you whispering. You will summon Lady Margaret at once."

The cook bristled. "Says who?"

"Sir Olyver of Mannyngs. Whom do I have the honor of addressing?" Sir Olyver was nothing if not a clever tactician.

Gunny One squared her shoulders and preened. "You have the honor of addressing Mistress Gunnilda, chief cook to her ladyship and guardian of this here door."

"Well, Mistress Gunnilda, might I ask you to fetch Lady Margaret?"

"I'll not rouse her ladyship from her bed at this ungodly hour of the night. She needs her rest, what with all the mischief you bring to her door."

"I am sure she does," soothed Sir Olyver. "But trust me, my good woman, she will not thank you when she learns you have turned me away. Might I suggest that for your own sake, you do as I say at once or suffer the consequences?"

"As you're on that side of this door, Sir Knight," Gunny One replied, "and I'm on this side, I don't have to do anything, and that includes rousing my lady at this ungodly hour."

"Gunny—" Megge began.

"And don't think I don't know what urgent business you have on your mind," Gunny continued. "A man wants only one thing this time of night."

"Really, Gunny, perhaps—"

Sir Olyver's patience was clearly slipping. "Mistress Gunnilda, if you were under my command—"

"A good thing for you I'm not," Gunny retorted. "I'll not be ordered about by the likes of you. Lady Megge is the mistress of this castle. I answer only to her."

"Most commendable," replied Sir Olyver, "and if you value her safety, you will fetch her here at once."

"That will not be necessary, my lord," Megge interjected before Gunny could open her mouth again. "I am already here. What is this urgent business you have with me?"

"Ah, I thought I saw you upon the wall, my lady. I must have private conversation with you concerning a message I have received from His Majesty."

"Well, you aren't coming in here, that's for sure," Gunny snapped despite Megge's restraining hand upon her arm. "Whatever you have to say to Lady Megge, you'll say through this here door."

"Lady Margaret, if you will kindly muzzle your guard dog—"

"Dog!" Gunny lunged at the door. "I'll show you who's the dog—"

Megge jerked her back, an impressive feat since she was half Gunny's size. "Stop it at once," she hissed.

Gunny fumed. "He insulted me."

Sir Olyver, who could hear every word, sought to defuse the situation. "Please accept my apologies, Mistress Gunnilda. I expressed myself poorly." He hadn't, but it seemed a good idea to mollify her or he might never be able to have a word with Lady Margaret. "I only meant that although you are admirably zealous in the performance of your duty, you may not fully understand the importance of the news I bring, else I would not think of disturbing Lady Margaret in this way."

Gunny One could not be expected to appreciate the clever tact that a master negotiator might employ to take control of a choleric subordinate, but she was not immune to a bit of flattery delivered in so courtly a manner. "Well, that's better then," she muttered.

"Lady Margaret," Sir Olyver continued, "since I cannot come in, perhaps you would join me for a brief stroll."

"She will do no such thing," Gunny informed him. "She's not even dressed!"

"Gunny! Sir Olyver doesn't need to know—"

"Just look at you, my lady, you can't go walking out with a man in your nightclothes in the middle of the night. It's not seemly."

"I assure you, Mistress Gunnilda, Lady Margaret will be safe in my hands," said Sir Olyver.

"That's what I'm worried about," Gunny muttered.

"This is absurd," said Megge. "Give me your cloak, Gunny. Sir Olyver is a knight of the realm and has agreed to honor the Conventions of the Siege. It is quite in order to for us to speak together."

"Speak, yes," said Gunny darkly, "but who knows what else he—"

"Your cloak, Gunny," Megge repeated sternly. "If the king has sent a message I must know of it. Lock the door immediately after me and wait here for my return. Now don't fret; I shall be quite safe. We have Sir Olyver's word of honor on it."

Tsking and tutting all the while, Gunny secured her voluminous rough cloak about Megge's slender frame, twisted the huge iron key in the lock, and opened the postern door only wide enough to allow Megge to slip out. "You just remember, Sir Knight, you'll be answering to me if any harm comes to her ladyship."

"It will be uppermost in my mind, Mistress Gunnilda."

"Harrumph," said she, and slammed shut the door.

Heart pounding, Megge curtsied, but not so low as to require Sir Olyver's assistance in rising. "Shall we, my lord?"

"After you, my lady."

Gunny One pressed her ear to the door, tracking the murmur of their voices as they moved along the wall toward the seaward side of the castle. Then she tucked up her skirts and marched purposefully toward the keep to call out reinforcements. For all she knew, Olyver of Mannyngs might be the finest specimen of chivalry since Sir Galahad graced the Round Table at Camelot with his golden presence. But he was a man for all that.

Chapter Nineteen

"I apologize for rousing you from your bed, Lady Margaret, and thank you for your willingness to speak with me. Perhaps I should have waited until morning, but I could not rest easy until you knew about a new and unsettling development in the conduct of this siege and our negotiations."

I could not rest at all for thinking of you.

"Your dedication to seeing this situation resolved to the satisfaction of all parties is most commendable, my lord. Nor should you concern yourself about disturbing me, as I was not yet asleep."

I could not possibly sleep for thinking of you.

"Mistress Gunnilda's cloak is over large for you. Take care lest you tread upon the hem. You are warm enough? Perhaps you would prefer to return and dress more, er, appropriately? I will be happy to wait outside."

You look absolutely charming, and the thought of you clad only in your nightclothes beneath that ugly cloak is going to drive me to distraction.

"I am quite comfortable, I thank you."

I am not remotely comfortable. You don't even have to touch me and I go all breathless and weak at the knees.

"This will not take long. I will have you back in your bed in no time."

Sweet Jesus, what did I just say?

"I can ask for nothing more."

Mary, Mother of God, what can I be thinking by saying such a thing?

Sir Olyver cleared his throat.

Megge coughed a delicate little cough.

Sir Olyver wondered how a lifetime of iron self-discipline and exemplary presence of mind in the face of the most dire of circumstances could so readily desert him. Without further preamble he explained the reason for his untimely visit.

"Edward comes."

Megge's eyes went wide. "Here? To Castle Rising?"

"Aye. He is already upon the road. We may expect him in four or five days' time."

Megge shivered. "I see." It could mean only one thing: The king had reached a decision regarding her next husband and intended to see the matter concluded himself. Edward Longshanks was not a patient man. He did not countenance disruption in his realm, be it the armed insurrection of Simon de Montfort or an assertion of independence by a defiant young noblewoman.

Sir Olyver looked down at the motionless figure beside him, wishing he could see her face in the deep shadow of her hood. This must be devastating news for her. She had to realize that her daring scheme had come to naught. No one bargained with Edward.

"Is that the sum and substance of the king's message, that he travels to Castle Rising?"

Sir Olyver wondered at her composure. Surely she understood the implications? "Not quite, my lady. I fear the rest may not be to your liking."

Megge pushed back the hood, and straightened her shoulders. "Have no fear, Sir Olyver. Let me spare you any distress you may feel in delivering your news.

"The king has dismissed my request to consult with him as to the choice of my next husband," she said calmly. "He has settled on Sir Walter and will see us married here at Rising within the week."

When Sir Olyver did not contradict her, she continued, "I had hoped that Lord Humphrey might prevail upon him to deny Sir Walter's suit, but I do understand why he failed to do so. I don't doubt that you can be most persuasive when the stakes are so high."

"Lady Margaret, I believe you misunderstand the situ—"

"And how relieved you must be, sir," Megge continued with a thin smile, "to know that the part you have played in this matter has turned out so well for you."

Sir Olyver frowned. "My part?"

Megge gave a dismissive little wave of her hand. "You have no need to explain yourself, my lord. I fully understand."

"Well, I'm damned if I do," he snapped.

"A fine property—Château de la Madeleine at Chevreuse would suit you very well, I think. And a suitable marriage sanctioned by the king. I hear that the Lady St. Aubert would be most grateful for your attentions. His Majesty is as eager to see her wed as is myself, so you should encounter no difficulty there.

All in all, you must think you have done very well for yourself."

"What are you babbling on about, woman?" demanded Sir Olyver.

"I do not babble, my good sir," Megge retorted. "You know very well what I am talking about: your arrangement with Sir Walter. Well, it grieves me to inform you," she announced, quailing only a little before the fierce scowl that etched his normally impassive countenance, "that there will be no Château de la Madeleine for you at Chevreuse, and no buxom Lady St. Aubert in your bed. I have no intention of marrying Sir Walter, whether His Majesty wills it or no, so you must come up with some other scheme. As it is late, might I suggest that you retire to your bed and find what sleep you can in the few hours of the night that remain, and begin afresh in the morning? If you will excuse me, I will leave you now. I have no wish to discuss this further."

Megge sketched an ironic little curtsy, and marched away toward the postern door, only to be spun around and backed against the castle's massive foundation wall.

"I do not," said Sir Olyver, emphasizing each word, "have any idea where you came by the mad notion that I have some 'arrangement' with Sir Walter."

Megge glared up at him. "It is the only logical explanation to account for your willingness to command the siege of a castle held only by women and children," she declared. She could not be certain whether she was frightened or wantonly excited by the looming presence above her, perhaps a bit of both. "An endeavor, you will agree, my lord, that is so far beneath your rank and dignity as to be laughable. There must be some advantage in it beyond your usual fee for your services, a prize that is worth the expenditure of your time on such a trivial matter."

There is indeed, my lady. You.

Sir Olyver had to admire her logic. Lady Margaret's only error, of course, lay in assuming that it was Sir Walter who would be taking her as the delectable prize. He did not think that this would be a particularly propitious moment to apprise her of her mistake.

"You will believe me, my lady, when I tell you that I do not consider it a waste of my time to fulfill my obligation to my liege lord, Sir Humphrey, when he so commands. As he does not consider the matter trivial, neither do I."

He could smell the flowery fragrance of her unbound hair, feel the delicate line of her shoulders beneath the coarse wool of her mantle. "In fact," he said softly, "I am finding it most—"

"Entertaining, I suppose," Megge grumbled. She tried to slip around him, only to find an arm as strong as an iron pike blocking her way.

"I wouldn't say entertaining, no."

"Tedious?" she supplied testily as she feinted to his left, then made an unsuccessful dive to wriggle beneath his outstretched right arm. Sir Olyver was a superbly trained soldier; he could intuit an opponent's intent by the slightest twitch of a muscle. He had only to bend his elbows a few inches to keep her safely confined within the cage of his arms.

"Definitely not tedious, my lady. Quite the opposite."

"Um, intriguing?"

"Close." He snaked a thickly muscled arm around her waist to draw her softness against him; cradled the back of her head in his huge hand.

"I really must be going, my lord," she managed. Truth be told, at this point Megge could barely recall that there *was* anywhere else, much less that she should have a reason to go there.

He bent his head toward her. "I don't think so."

In some dim corner of her mind, Megge felt she owed it to the dictates of propriety to make one last desperate stand before she melted like tallow in his arms. "That, sir, must be my decision, not yours."

Sir Olyver looked up at the stars as though seeking guidance on an important point of etiquette. "Hmmm. You are quite right, my lady." He stepped away, and tucked his hands behind his back.

"Oh." She adjusted her cloak.

"Well then." She backed up a step.

"I'll just . . ." She faltered.

And launched herself straight into his arms.

She bridled at the deep growl of male satisfaction as he caught her up and anchored her against his big hard body.

Megge glared up at him. "You don't have to look so smug, my lord."

"Why should I not, my lady? It appears I have negotiated the point to my advantage."

She could not let that pass. "I conceded the point, sir, you did not win it."

"Ah. In that case, I must offer you a concession of equal value. Nay, of greater value, as you were so gracious as to open this negotiation with your own. A moment, my lady, while I think on the matter. What have I to offer that you cannot live without?" He made a great show of pondering the possibilities. "Hmmm. Yes, I think I know just the thing," he said at last.

Megge did not care for this exhibition of condescension. "Really, my lord, you of all people should know that under the rules of fair negotiation there is no need—"

"Oh, but there is need, my lady," he murmured, backing her toward the wall, "a most pressing need."

"I believe I must protest, my lord." Protest? She hadn't a complete thought left in her head, and if only the man would stop swirling the tip of his tongue in her ear, she might be able to make sense of the few pitiful shards rattling about in there. If only she cared enough even to try.

"You must?" he said on a puff of breath that inexplicably hardened her nipples and tickled the soles of her feet.

"I suppose it could wait," she mumbled as the vexatious tongue traced a path of ice and fire down the arched column of her neck to the pulsing hollow of her throat, then back up to tease along the line of her lips.

"Open, my lady."

"Open? Oh."

The sweet assault of lips, tongue, and teeth that followed would have sent Megge to her knees had she not been supported at her back by the unyielding stone wall of Castle Rising and in front by the unyielding muscled torso of a huge superbly trained warrior. A momentary rush of panic at finding herself imprisoned so, unable to wriggle an inch in any direction, gave way almost immediately to a curious sense of freedom, of relief. The power of choice was taken from her, and with it went the burden of responsibility and the whole pesky business of sin and expiation and eternal damnation. All she had to do was . . .

Let go.

"Give over, my lady," said a deep voice.

Surrender.

"Know at the outset, my lord, that you should harbor no hope or expectation that I will surrender myself into your care or jurisdiction."

Apparently Sir Olyver had not given Lady Margaret's enjoinder the serious consideration it deserved, if the pace and fervor of the present seduction was anything to go by. Nor had Lady Margaret herself taken into account the persuasive power a man's fierce desire had to compel a woman to offer herself up so that he might find his release, and if she was so fortunate, find her own.

Male and female He created them, and apparently He knew exactly what He was about when He did it, for in the deep concealing shadow of her citadel Megge's composure crumbled into chaos. A lifetime of propriety fled before the onslaught of his passion, and hers, and self-control gave way to wild abandon.

"I want . . ."

"What, my lady? How may I serve you?" Olyver whispered, and Megge heard in his voice the contented rumble of the predator that knows his prey.

"This perhaps?" He held her to the wall with the strength of his hips, and yanked a handful of the woolen cloak and linen gown up to her waist.

"And this?" He bent his knees slightly, and slid up so that the hard heavy bulge of his arousal settled firmly between her legs, practically lifting her from the ground.

"Please," she thought she heard herself say as he began to move against her naked flesh, "stop."

"You don't want me to stop, my lady," he murmured.

"I don't want you to stop," Megge echoed into the crook of his neck. And when the coiling tension and the liquid heat became almost more than she could bear, she opened her eyes, seeking escape, and was bewildered to see him there above her, watching her, waiting for something, waiting for her.

"Please," she said.

Please what? Stop? Don't stop? Help me?

"Help me."

She almost screamed when he eased back, so devastating was the sudden absence of his heat and the rough friction of leather against her quivering flesh. "No, don't leave me, come back!" she gasped.

And when a moment later his big callused hand cupped her, and his long thick fingers parted the folds of her sex and teased the spot that throbbed unbearably, and stroked deep, she thought she would surely die of the pleasure. "Oh, dear God, please . . ."

A split second before she spiraled out of control, she buried her face against his chest, and the thick velvet of his tunic muffled her wild cry of release.

How he managed to draw back from the brink of his own release as Megge fell to pieces in his arms Olyver would never understand. Two things he did know for sure: Another chilly session in the River Lis awaited him, and he wouldn't be sitting his saddle with any degree of comfort until she lay beneath him in his bed and he could find his release deep inside her.

All the more reason, he thought, as she righted her

garment and settled the ugly cloak about her shoulders, to conclude this business the moment Edward arrived. If he could manage to wait that long.

Megge cleared her throat. "My clasp. It seems to have—"

"Here it is, my lady."

She plucked it from his hand before he could move to secure it to the cloak. "Thank you, Sir Olyver," she said crisply. "I can see to the matter myself." She slipped around him and set about securing the mantle in the fussy way a woman who is embarrassed might employ to distance herself from the cause of her confusion.

Sir Olyver spoke from the inky shadow of the wall, his deep voice unusually gentle. "You have nothing to be ashamed of, Lady Margaret."

Megge's head snapped up. "I think, sir, that this unfortunate episode is best forgotten by us both. I cannot imagine what possessed us. We will never speak of it again."

Lust, my lady, is what possessed us.

"As you wish," was all he said.

"Well, if that is the only business you had with me," Megge began. That didn't sound right. She tried again. "What I mean, of course, is the message from His Majesty that he is upon the road. I bid you good night, Sir Olyver."

Anxious as she was to put a safe distance between them, she resisted the urge to dash pell-mell toward the safety of the postern door. She set off along the rocky path with head held high and a calm measured gait.

"Not quite all, Lady Margaret," Sir Olyver called after her.

Megge swung around. "Sir? What more can we possibly have to discuss?"

"You are correct in your belief that His Majesty has made his choice for you," he replied as he strolled toward her. "That choice, however, is not Sir Walter."

She went very still. "Not Sir Walter? Are you quite sure?"

"Quite sure, my lady."

Megge swallowed hard and steeled herself. "Who?"

In all of his adult life, Sir Olyver had rarely had recourse to tell an outright lie. Honesty and dignity were as one to him. The man who must speak the truth, however unpalatable, in holding his own honor high enabled the one who must hear it to do likewise.

"Lady Margaret," he began carefully, "I think perhaps His Majesty will wish to inform you of his decision himself. It is not my place—"

"Don't you dare patronize me," Megge snapped. "You know. I demand that you tell me."

"No."

"No? Is that all you have to say to me? No? Oh, I see. Your clever scheme to see Sir Walter installed here failed, and you are taking out your frustration on me by withholding the name of the successful candidate. No doubt you hope to make some arrangement with this mysterious lord before Edward arrives; perhaps occupy Castle Rising to ensure my compliance and secure your property withal. Your payment for a few weeks' work," she added with a sneer.

Sir Olyver said nothing.

"Well, let me tell you, Sir Olyver of Mannyngs, I will defy Edward himself if I must. If Castle Rising cannot stand against him, against you, I will cede it to the

Crown, and gladly. I have other properties, well out of his reach and that of any other man who seeks to claim me against my will. I have done with being auctioned off to the highest bidder, sold like some brood mare at Smithfield. And now, if you will excuse me, I have much to do to prepare for the morrow. The women under my command will at least have their day, even if I will not. I owe them that much."

Olyver watched her march proudly away. He could not mistake the tears that threatened to intrude on her righteous anger, and wondered how she managed to hold herself together as she rapped smartly upon the postern door and waited until the key grated in the lock and the door opened to admit her. He did not doubt that the moment it slammed shut behind her she would give over to the fear and shame she didn't want him to see.

What her reaction would be when she learned that the man to whom Edward had awarded Lady Margaret was none other than Olyver himself he really did not want to think about.

Chapter Twenty

"Is she safely within?" Mary called down from the wall above the postern door.

"Aye," Gunny One replied. "And in a state, I can tell you. Where's that rogue got to now?"

Mary's head disappeared; in a moment she was back. "He's just standing against the wall, real still, like he's watching something. Now he's moving along the wall, keeping back in the shadow. Yes, he sees someone. Wait! So do I. There's a man; two men, three; no, four—"

"God's teeth, girl," Gunny One scolded, "can't you count? I'm coming up there myself."

By the time Gunny One reached the parapet, Mary and three other sentries had been joined by Gunny Two and three strapping serving girls. They had extinguished the lanterns, and were peering over the wall at some drama unfolding below.

Gunny One shouldered her way to the fore. "Stand back," she whispered, taking command. "Let us see what we have here."

What they had was the sight of four shadows just hauling themselves by means of stout ropes over the lip of the rock face that fell some sixty feet to the landward side of the castle. The men paused for a few moments to catch their breath, coiled their ropes, then crept along the base of the wall straight past the spot where Sir Olyver stood concealed in deep shadow.

"Quiet, you fool," Sir Walter snarled when someone's boot dislodged a small rock.

"Sorry, my lord. Can't see a blessed thing, what with the moon setting the other side of the wall. This here is the best-defended castle I ever did see."

"No talking," ordered Sir Walter. "There were sentries on the wall a while ago. I don't see their lanterns now, but they may still be about."

"Women." Someone snorted. "What we got to fear from a few weakling women?"

The men had by now reached the guard tower that surmounted the outer gate. "Not so weak if they can crank that gate up and down," someone observed. "I like a strong woman. Get her legs up over your shoulders real tight, gives you a good angle to work from, if you know what I mean."

"If you don't curb your tongue," growled Sir Walter, "I will see it removed from your mouth myself. Now be quiet and let me think."

High on the wall the women tiptoed along, tracking the men below. "Where are those vats, Mary?" Gunny One whispered.

"Down the far end of the wall, near the cliff. I sent Emmy, Clara, and Long Ida for them. They stink something awful."

"Can't stink enough for these fellows, you ask me,"

declared Gunny Two. "Look, isn't that Sir Olyver over there to the left?"

The big knight was moving stealthily toward the group gathered before the gate.

"Damnation," muttered Gunny One. "Lady Megge won't be thanking us for emptying a vat of rancid pig grease on the man, no matter what he said that upset her so. Where are those girls, anyhow? Mary, go hurry them along."

"Good evening, gentlemen."

"What the . . . ?" Sir Walter whirled around, his hand already grasping the hilt of the long dagger at his waist.

Sir Olyver stood with arms crossed, to all appearances at his ease. "You are abroad rather late, Walter. What do you here?"

"I might ask you the same question, sir."

Sir Olyver smiled. "You might. And I might answer if I thought it was any business of yours."

Sir Walter swaggered forward. His men took up positions around Sir Olyver. "You always were an arrogant bastard, Olyver."

"The youngest of five, but no bastard I assure you."

"True," replied Sir Walter. "But a runt, if I recall."

"No more. As you see."

"True also. I will admit that you have done well for yourself, Olyver, but you will never rise higher in the world than where you are now. Humphrey is so much the buffoon that he dare not water a bush without you at his side. You can have no expectation he will release you from his service and reward your loyalty with a holding of your own. You will live, and die, a paid soldier at the beck and call of others."

Sir Olyver shrugged. "Perhaps. Tell me, Walter, what lies in store for you? Do you think to become lord of this place? I understand you have petitioned Edward for Lady Margaret's hand in marriage, and he has denied you and shown his favor to another. Is it that which accounts for your presence here tonight? Perhaps you seek to force the issue by compromising Lady Margaret?"

"Edward would pimp his own grandmother to fill his coffers for his war with the Welsh," Sir Walter said. "Someone made him a better offer for Lady Margaret. When I discover his identity I will kill him with my bare hands."

Sir Olyver nodded. "I see. You thought to purchase the lady. Tell me, what did you, as a second son, have to offer the King of England that he could not obtain elsewhere? Evidently it was not enough, as another will be taking Lady Margaret to his bed and enjoying the enormous income her holdings will bring him."

"My lord," one of Sir Walter's men whispered, "there is someone on the walkway directly above us."

"Back against the wall," Sir Walter ordered.

"Here, dearie, shine that lantern right there," came a voice from above. "I swear I saw some big strapping fellows down there."

"Oooh, let me see. I could use one of those right about now. A woman shouldn't have to go weeks without a man between her legs."

"I vow, I'm like to go mad if I don't get a man under me soon," someone groaned.

"You down there," a woman entreated, "show yourselves. If we like the looks of you, maybe we'll invite you in for a bit of sport."

Two of Sir Walter's men swaggered into the pool of

light before he could so much as open his mouth to order them to stay put.

"I got all a woman could want," bragged one.

"Which of you fine ladies likes to ride astride? I'm your man," offered the other.

"Hell," muttered the third as he shook off Sir Walter's restraining hand and joined his comrades, "I'm not being left out if there's good swiving to be had."

Sir Walter strode forward. Shielding his eyes against the blinding light of lanterns and rush lights, he tried to pick out the leader of the group atop the wall. "I am Sir Walter. There will be no sport and no swiving."

"You have that aright, my lord," agreed a large woman, who appeared to be balancing an iron pot on the edge of the wall. "Ready, ladies?"

"Ready, Gunny One," the women chorused.

"Pour!"

A moment of horrified silence followed the sound of warm pig fat splashing down upon the heads of Sir Walter and his men. An unholy stench filled the air.

"Aaagh!"

"God's balls!" one of the men yelled as he lost his footing and landed flat on his face in a puddle of fetid pig fat and greasy mud.

"Greek fire!"

"It isn't Greek fire, you horse's ass," snarled Sir Walter as he tried to wipe the foul muck from his face with the hem of his tunic.

"I'm going to be sick," groaned one of the men, and was. A woman laughed. "I don't know, Emmy, I'm not sure I like the looks of these fellows after all."

"What in heaven's name is going on up here?" Megge joined the group at the wall, having been alerted by Lady Agnes that the Saracen army was storming the gates of Castle Rising and they were all about to be raped and murdered in their beds. "What is that horrible stench?"

"The pig grease, my lady," Gunny One informed her. "We have some visitors."

Megge peered over the wall. "Good lord! Is that Sir Walter down there?"

"Aye, my lady. So he says."

"Who are those men with him?"

Gunny One sniffed. "The devil's spawn most likely. Sir Olyver was standing there a moment ago."

Megge gasped. "You poured *pig grease* on *Sir Olyver*?"

Gunny One shrugged. "If he didn't have the good sense God gave him to get out of the way, I suppose we did."

"I don't think he was still standing there when we tipped the vats, my lady," said Mary.

"Thank the Lord for small mercies. Hold the lantern out so I can see better, will you, Mary? Thank you. Sir Walter," she called down, "what do you think you are about, my lord, sneaking around my castle in this manner in the middle of the night?"

"I came to see you on urgent business, my lady."

"Here we go again," muttered Gunny One.

"There can be no business so urgent that it cannot wait until morning, sir. In fact, I can think of no business we need to discuss at all. I understand that Edward has denied your petition for my hand. Although I am sorry for your sake, I am entirely content with his decision for my own. That is the end of the matter. Now take yourself off at once."

"On the contrary, my lady. I leave now, but we have

not seen the end of this discussion yet," replied Sir Walter, and strode off after his cursing men with as much dignity as a man slathered in pig fat might be expected to assume.

Sir Olyver was still chuckling as he arrived at the bridge and looked back at the massive walls of Castle Rising. Throughout his exchange with Walter he had been aware of the furtive activity on the walkway high above them. When the women began to call out to the men below, luring them into the open just as Homer's sirens lured sailors to their doom upon the rocks, Olyver had slipped away to observe from a safe distance what they planned for their hapless victims. Almost as shocked as the men themselves, he watched in fascinated horror the greasy, rancid stream wash over them; held his breath against the stench that filled the air and carried on the sea wind; and heard the guffaws and jeers from above and the retching and blasphemy below.

Now as he gazed up at the great citadel against a sky poised between deepest night and the first thin wash of dawn, he could not help but admire its staunch defenders and the woman who commanded them. A woman's nature might not lend itself to violence, murder, and mayhem—mercifully, God had not ordained it so—but she had at her disposal a veritable arsenal of trickery and ingenuity when it came to the matter of defending herself or gaining her point. In her way, Lady Margaret was every bit as able a warrior as he. She knew to entice the enemy then strike; feign weakness that he might become arrogant; set one man against another for her favors. Olyver had dedicated the days and years of his life to perfecting his skills on the training ground, at the tournament, and on the battlefield. Lady Margaret had done it in the women's solar and the court.

Lady Margaret might very well be his equal when it came to the art of war, thought Sir Olyver as he strolled through the camp toward his tent, but strength of will would decide the matter in the end: his or hers. And no one possessed a stronger will than Olyver of Mannyngs.

Chapter Twenty-One

"Has the man lost his mind?" Megge whispered.

Lady Orabella shifted in her chair, trying to ease the strain on her lower back. "It would appear so, my dear. Whatever did you say to Father Jerome after his last sermon?"

"I cautioned him against choosing a text that did not reflect kindly upon our sex."

"Behold, thou art fair, my love; behold, thou art fair; thou hast doves' eyes within thy locks; thy hair is as a flock of goats, that appear from Mount Gilead. Thy teeth are like a flock of sheep that are even shorn, which came up from the washing."

"Well, he has certainly taken your words to heart," observed Lady Orabella.

Lady Sybille scrunched her perfect little nose. "Who would want hair like a goat? It is so very coarse. And teeth do not look at all like sheep, nor for that matter, do sheep look like teeth."

Lady Orabella leaned over and patted her hand. "Hush, dear. The Song of Solomon is an allegory of love between Christ and His Church."

"I sleep but my heart waketh; it is the voice of my beloved that knocketh, saying, Open to me, my sister, my love, my dove, my undefiled . . ."

Lady Sybille gasped. "His *sister*?"
"I'll explain later, child."

"My beloved put in his hand by the hole of the door, and my bowels were moved for him . . ."

"Oh dear," sighed Lady Orabella as giggles erupted across the great hall, "this is most unfortunate."

Megge rolled her eyes. "Whatever has gotten into the man?"

"You'd do better to ask what the man's been getting into," Mistress Gilly suggested. "Clara would be my guess."

Breathing hard, his face flushed, Father Jerome launched into Chapter Seven.

"The joints of thy thighs are like jewels. Thy navel is like a round goblet. Thy belly is like an heap of wheat set about with lilies."

Megge shook her head. "Definitely not Clara."

"Thy nose is as the tower of Lebanon."

"Edith?" suggested Lady Agnes.

"The hair of thine head like purple . . ."

"Do we know anyone with purple hair?" inquired Lady Orabella.

"This thy stature is like to a palm tree, and thy breasts to clusters of grapes."

"A palm tree: Long Ida!" cried Megge.

Lady Orabella nodded. "I believe you are right, my dear."

"Clusters of grapes, indeed," said Lady Agnes. "More like old prunes, if you ask me."

A frown creased Lady Sybille's alabaster brow. "I didn't know grapes grew on palm trees."

"If you will only try to understand my reasoning, my lord," urged Father Boniface as he scrambled up the steep road in Sir Olyver's wake.

"Reason had nothing to do with it, priest," the big knight growled. "You nearly caused a riot."

"I will confess the text I chose was not in the ordinary way, but there is much wisdom in the Apocrypha, particularly in the first book of Esdras."

Sir Olyver glared down at the panting, red-faced priest. "And where, pray tell, lies the wisdom in telling a man that the Lord has ordained that his woman is stronger than he? That she holds dominion over him? That he is beholden to her for his very life? That he is helpless in the face of her flattery, her displeasure, her charms?"

"Ah, but you see, my lord," cried Father Boniface, "I thought to play upon their manly pride and inspire them to assert themselves when they meet with their women today. This unfortunate period of abstinence has so sapped their will that they would likely agree to burn the Holy Father at the stake to relieve their discomfort."

"Let me understand," said Sir Olyver. "You quote some prophet so obscure as to be relegated to the marginalia of Holy Scripture, whose teachings appear to contradict the received wisdom of both the Old and New Testaments as to God's purpose in creating man and woman. You do this so that my men will in turn reverse the message in their own minds and act according to God's plan."

Father Boniface's face lit up. "Exactly so."

"Does it not occur to you," inquired Sir Olyver, "that you had only to preach the standard text to achieve the same end?"

"Well, put like that—"

"And save me the trouble of fishing you out of the well?"

"Yes, but—"

"The standard text from now on," ordered Sir Olyver and strode on up the road.

"Yes, my lord."

This morning's experiment had not quite achieved the results Father Boniface had hoped for, but he could not dismiss the idea out of hand.

The usual way of things was to warn a man not to do what he ought not. Often as not, the man did not heed the warning and went out and did what he ought not to do.

But if one told a man to do what he ought not, and a man did not heed the warning, he would end up doing what he ought!

He could not wait to hear Father Jerome's opinion

of the matter. If anyone could see the wisdom of con-
vincing a man to sin in order to prevent him from doing so, it would be Father Jerome.

"Sir Olyver has arrived, my lady."

"Thank you, Mary. Is everything ready?"

"Yes, my lady."

"You sent the message to Lord Humphrey that
Lady Orabella is indisposed and cannot meet with
him today?"

"I did, my lady. As to the preparations: Gunny Two
had the maids out at dawn scraping away the muck
from the pig grease and spreading scented rushes
about. We've set a stool outside the gate for the men
and a small table for the flagon and ale. Within the
gate there's a nice padded bench and watered wine
for the women. I saw the castle banner raised myself."

"What of Lady Sybille's truce flag?"

"I fashioned a holder for it above the gate."

"Excellent. Well done, Mary. Did Clara make
enough nosegays? I think we have seven couples
scheduled for today. If several of them can reach accord quickly, we may be able to squeeze in one or two
more."

"I'll check on the flowers, my lady. We can always
send someone down to the lower garden for more if
it's needed."

"Please inform Sir Olyver I'll be down to greet him
in just a few minutes."

"Very good, my lady."

"You look lovely in the purple, my lady; it suits your
coloring and deepens the blue of your eyes," Missy
declared as she secured the net of silver threads that
bound Megge's hair with a braided silver circlet. "I've

set out your pale blue silk shawl and the scarlet mantle and the velvet—"

"Thank you, Missy. The shawl will do nicely." Megge sighed. "Well, I suppose we must get started."

Missy brushed a minuscule speck of dust from Megge's fitted sleeve. "If you don't mind my saying so, my lady, you seem low in your spirits this morning."

Megge bustled about her chamber. "I'm perfectly well, I assure you. Perhaps a bit tired after all the commotion last night."

"I slept right through everything. It must have been ever so exciting. Did you think so, my lady?"

"I certainly did," Megge agreed. *And more, much more.*

"Long Ida said Sir Olyver looked ever so handsome out there in the moonlight, like a Viking warrior from the old days. Do you think he's handsome, my lady?"

"I haven't really thought about it." *Oh yes, you have.*

Missy draped the silk shawl around Megge's shoulders. "She says as he's such a big man he must be, well, *big*, if you know what I mean. Do you think he is, my lady?"

"Really, Missy, I am not sure it is quite proper to speculate on such things." After last night's encounter, Megge certainly had no reason to speculate. She knew.

Missy gathered up Megge's mantles and draped them carefully over her arm. "Long Ida knows these things," she affirmed with a little nod, clearly impressed with the older woman's powers of observation. "She predicted Father Jerome would be a virgin, and so he was."

"Missy—"

"She says he's a slow learner," the girl prattled on,

oblivious, "but she doesn't hold it against him, him being a priest and all."

Megge tapped a toe. "Missy."

"Yes, my lady?"

"Father Jerome took a vow of celibacy upon his ordination: He is *supposed* to be a virgin."

Missy shrugged an airy little shrug.

"You do not find it troubling that Long Ida should be intimate with a man ordained in the service of God?"

Missy pursed her lips as she considered the matter. "No," she concluded with a firm shake of her head. She brightened. "It's a family thing is what it is, my lady. You see, Long Ida's father is a priest, so—"

"Please." Megge closed her eyes and held up a hand. "No more. I see you and I need to have a little talk."

"Did I say something wrong, my lady?" Missy bit a trembling lip. Tears threatened.

Megge sighed. "No, dear. It is just that I think you may rely overmuch on Long Ida's view of what is acceptable behavior and what is not."

"Yes, my lady."

Missy managed to hold her tongue as they made their way down the tower stairs, out through the keep's enormous oak doors, and across the inner bailey.

"My lady," she ventured as she trotted along beside a clearly distracted Megge, "I wish Long Ida hadn't told me about Sir Olyver. Now all I'm going to be thinking about is his lance, and I just know I won't be able to help looking and maybe he'll know I'm looking and then what should I do?"

"Close your eyes," Megge replied through clenched teeth.

"Are you going to close your eyes, my lady?"

"No." *It wouldn't help anyway.*

Missy stumbled to a halt. "There he is, my lady," she whispered.

"You needn't whisper, Missy. He is too far away to hear us."

"Yes, but I *see* him. What should I do?"

Megge was done being patient with the girl. "What you should do," she said firmly, turning Missy around and aiming her in the direction of the keep, "is return to the hall and attend Lady Orabella. As her maid is occupied elsewhere, Mistress Annie will be glad of your assistance in seeing to her comfort."

"But what if you should take a chill, my lady?" Missy protested.

"Go."

Missy went.

Megge squared her shoulders. Whatever her personal feelings might be this day, she would see the promise she had made to the women of Castle Rising fulfilled. It mattered not that she herself would likely not prevail. It had been her mission to prove to these women that not only did they deserve a greater say in the matters that most closely concerned them, they possessed the means to do so. Not just their sexual favors—although that was proving particularly successful—but the will and the strength to be found in numbers.

Sir Olyver awaited.

Lady Margaret de Languetot, descendant of the conqueror, chatelaine and defender of Castle Rising, a woman with a mission, advanced to meet the warrior at her gate.

Chapter Twenty-Two

"Gray peas, pullet mash, hung cabbage; pottage of whelk and lamprey."

"Aw, Gunny, that be food for babes and them that's old and sick and like to die," Magnus groaned. "What of roasts and stews, fritters, caudles, and chowets? Sweet marrow, salted lard, spicy entrails?"

"Fear not, husband," replied Gunny, who was not moved one jot at the sight of the piteous figure clutching at the bars of the castle gate. "You shall have them again come the day you can see your lance down there beyond the bulge of your belly and guide it to the mark."

"I shall sicken, I shall die!" Magnus keened.

"You will certainly sicken and die if you do not leave off your gluttonous ways, both in this life and the next," Gunny remarked.

Magnus paled. "What do you mean, wife?"

"Lady Megge!" Gunny shouted.

Megge's head popped around the corner of the bailey end of the tunnel that ran some twenty feet beneath the guardhouse. "Did you call, Gunny?" she asked in a cheery voice.

"I did, my lady."

Megge hurried forward and joined Gunny at the gate. "Good day, Magnus," she said. "I trust you and Gunny are making good progress."

"We are not making any progress at all, my lady." Gunny folded her hands across her ample bosom and glared at her husband.

"Oh dear," said Megge. "I am so sorry to hear it. How may I be of help?"

"He's a glutton, my lady, and if you'll pardon my language, he's too fat to swyve. A woman shouldn't be forced to put up with such a man."

"Oh my, how very unfortunate, Magnus," said Megge, her voice filled with compassion. "You are in a pretty fix, I'm afraid. I believe it is a sin for a man to abstain from his conjugal obligation because some unwholesome behavior on his part renders him unfit to do so. On the other hand, the sin of Gluttony is of the very worst kind. The Apostle says that those "whose god is their belly" will be in for a very bad time of it when called to account. Each deadly sin carries a specific punishment in hell.

"Let me see if I can recall them all," she continued with a little frown. "Oh, I have it. He who commits the sin of Pride will be broken on the wheel; Envy, immersed in freezing water; Anger, dismembered alive; Sloth, thrown into a pit of vipers; Greed, bathed in boiling oil; Lust, smothered in fire and brimstone."

"G-g-gluttony?" Magnus managed, his tiny porcine eyes bulging alarmingly from their sockets.

Megge cocked her head, then smiled brightly. "Ah,

yes, I remember now. The Glutton is force-fed rats, toads, and snakes for all eternity."

Magnus crashed to the ground.

If Sir Olyver wondered at the little posy tied with yellow ribbon Magnus clutched in his hand as he plodded across the bridge, he did not think it wise to bring it up. From the slump of the man's shoulders and the vacant look in his eye, it was an easy surmise that first blood had been drawn by the ladies of Castle Rising.

"Rats, toads, snakes, Mother of God, rats, toads, snakes," Magnas was muttering as he went on his way.

Sir Olyver did not inquire.

It took but fifteen minutes for Gunny One and her husband to arrive at a cordial understanding: one bath every month, taken together. It was an unexpected dividend of cleanliness he had not before considered. His ribbon was pink.

Mistress Gilly's husband returned without a posy, which was not particularly surprising since his mother had insisted on accompanying him. He was rescheduled to return, alone, at three on Thursday.

A mutinous Sir Siward had just started up the path to meet with Lady Agnes and, as he vowed, "put the woman in her place," when Lancelot came bounding across the meadow. "Sir Olyver, Lord Humphrey has called for another flagon," he reported. "It's his third this morning. He is not at all happy that Lady Orabella refuses to meet with him."

"Lady Orabella is indisposed, I understand," said Sir Olyver.

"That's what Lady Megge's message said, but Lord Humphrey claims it's a ruse to drive him mad. He's threatening to have himself catapulted over the wall."

Sir Olyver pinched the bridge of his nose. He felt a headache coming on. He never suffered from headaches. "Tell John to fetch as many flagons as may be necessary to render Lord Humphrey insensible. And inform Lord Humphrey that I will question Lady Margaret myself as to the truth of Lady Orabella's indisposition."

"Aye, my lord." Lancelot scampered happily away. Suddenly he was back. "My lord?"

"Yes, what is it, Lancelot?"

"I like Lady Megge. She's nice to me. She gives me sweets, and treats me like I'm somebody."

"You are somebody."

"I don't like Sir Walter. Nobody does. I don't want Lady Megge to have to marry him."

"Don't worry, Lancelot. Lady Margaret is not going to marry Sir Walter."

"Sir Olyver?"

"Yes, Lancelot?"

"You should marry Lady Megge. I bet she'd like that."

"Go."

Lancelot went.

Megge reached through the bars and pressed the cold compress to Sir Siward's left eye. "Mistress Annie is preparing a poultice to help with the swelling, my lord. I will have it sent down to you. I am afraid it is going to take some time for the bruising to disappear."

"I never saw it coming," Sir Siward complained. "One moment I standing here instructing Agnes as to her duties as my wife, the next thing I know her fist is in my eye and I am flat on my arse."

Sir Olyver eyed the square openings of the gate. "You have to admire her accuracy."

Sir Siward stepped back and brushed the broken rushes from the seat of his breeches. "Much as it pains me to do so, Lady Margaret, I must tell you that I lay the blame for this debacle squarely upon your shoulders. Agnes was the most reasonable of women before you urged her into this foolishness. Or as reasonable as one might expect of your sex."

Megge cocked her head. "Was she indeed, sir?"

"She most certainly was. The last time I saw her she expressed herself most sensibly on a number of topics. I cannot recall at the moment what they were, but I do recall thinking I had secured a most acceptable spouse."

"Acceptable. I see. And when was that, my lord?"

"When was what?"

"When she expressed herself most sensibly on a number of topics."

Sir Siward frowned. "Let me see. I believe it was two years ago. September I think it must have been. I know I had stopped in at Flete for two days en route from the harvest games at Leeds to the joust at—"

"Siward," interjected Sir Olyver, "the afternoon grows late. I suggest you give over the evening to examining what might have incited Lady Agnes to plant her fist in your face. I am sure, given time, it will come to you."

Having recovered something of his dignity, save the alarming discoloration that now graced the left side of his face, Sir Siward maintained he need waste no time analyzing his wife's assault upon his person. "Either she has lost her wits or she is with child," he declared. "Likely both. It is a well known fact that women act most peculiarly when breeding."

"I think I should point out, my lord," said Megge, "that you have not visited with your lady wife for almost two years."

"What has that to do with it?" Sir Siward huffed. "Do you imply, Lady Margaret, that I am incapable of paying the marriage debt? Let me assure you—"

"Siward," Sir Olyver interrupted, "pray don't make more an idiot of yourself than you already have. Lady Margaret is merely pointing out that a lady does not breed for two years."

"She doesn't?"

"She does not."

"Well, how was I to know that?" Sir Siward demanded.

"I don't think I can stand another minute of this," Megge groaned. "I shall go mad."

Sir Olyver steered Sir Siward toward the path. "Lord Humphrey is presently enjoying some excellent Beaujolais. He would be glad of your company."

Sir Siward balked. "But what about Agnes? I am sorely in need of—"

"The river."

"Hell."

Chapter Twenty-Three

"My lady."

"My lord."

She looked, Sir Olyver thought, as though she bore the weight of the world on her shoulders. Last night's intelligence must have been a severe blow, and her surrender to her own desire in the arms of her enemy would not, in the light of day, have sat well with a woman of her stubborn pride. Nevertheless, she maintained her regal bearing as she regarded him through the iron barrier with a cool eye.

"Lady Margaret?"

"Sir Olyver?"

"What, may I ask, has occasioned Magnus's sudden interest in rats, toads, and snakes?"

The tiniest trace of a smile softened the firm line of her lips for a fleeting moment. "I believe Magnus is reconsidering his options."

"Ah."

A cool breeze eddied through the tunnel at Megge's back. She drew her shawl closer about her shoulders, and sank down on the bench Lady Agnes had quitted when her negotiation with Sir Siward had taken such an unfortunate turn. "It has been a most trying day."

Sir Olyver rested a booted foot on the stool. "Agreed, but not entirely unsuccessful. The ladies Gunnilda and Gunredo seem to have achieved their aims. Three of my men may expect an enthusiastic reconciliation in a few days' time, though I fear it cost them dear."

"Whatever could Mistress Gilly's husband have been thinking to allow his mother to accompany him?"

"I must apologize for that, my lady," Sir Olyver said. "I was at the midday meal at the time, else I would not have let her slip past me. I haven't the slightest idea how the woman came to be here; I have placed her under guard, where she will stay until Mistress Gilly and Alfred reconvene on Thursday."

"Let me see," said Megge, ticking off on her fingers the couples scheduled to face off on the morrow. "We still have Lady Clarice, Lady Sybille, Lady Belinda, Lady Joan, Cook's assistant, Mary and her Ralph, Emmy . . . Oh, and I understand Father Boniface has begged an interview with Father Jerome; apparently it is of the utmost urgency. Have you any idea what that is about?"

Sir Olyver winced. "I daren't speculate. But what of Lady Orabella? Humphrey is near to distraction. If she continues to refuse to meet with him, you may very possibly expect to see him sailing over your wall and dropping at her feet like a downed wigeon."

Megge moved to the gate. "I must make a confession, Sir Olyver. At Orabella's insistence, I worded the message to Lord Humphrey in such a way as to lead him to believe she declined to see him. The truth is far more serious."

Olyver joined her, speaking low. "Is her ladyship unwell?"

"I'm afraid so. She is only in her eighth month, but we have seen fit to confine her to her bed. She suffers from dizzy spells and unnatural fatigue. I felt it prudent to bring Mistress Annie from the village two days ago. She is a most excellent midwife, and concurs in my opinion that something is amiss with the babe." Megge gazed out over the sea. "I fear for her, my lord."

Sir Olyver laid his huge hand over hers, where it gripped the iron crossbar. "Lady Margaret—Megge—Humphrey needs to know of this."

Megge nodded. "I know, but she will not hear of it. She won't have him worrying about her."

"He will not thank her—or you—for keeping it from him."

"She loves him," Megge added unnecessarily.

"And he loves her. Does that surprise you?"

She shrugged, and withdrew her hand from beneath his.

Sir Olyver stepped back, observing her closely. "You do not believe in love?"

Megge did not reply.

"Or perhaps you believe love is for others, but not for one such as you?"

Her lips tightened.

"Who was it, my lady, who taught you that an heiress can have no expectation of love in her life," Sir Olyver persisted, "but she must sacrifice her tender heart for the greater good?"

Megge glared out at him. "You know very well who, sir."

"Tell me."

"It is as plain as the nose on your face: men! The priests, the king, the lords of the realm, the lowliest swineherd, you yourself!

"Do you dare condemn me?" she went on. "Do I betray my woman's nature? I have learned through bitter experience that I am nothing more than a commodity and cannot expect to be appreciated for the *tender heart* you claim still beats in my breast. You will believe me, sir, when I tell you that I let go my dreams long ago, and can think of no reason to regret their loss."

If Sir Olyver thought to begin his courtship of this woman by seizing on the subject of love it was clear he had made a poor start of it. Lying in his bed at the dawn hour as the camp stirred to life around him, he had sketched out the strategy by which he might win Lady Margaret's favor even before Edward's arrival. He had considered only those means that would lessen, if possible, the shock of the king's announcement of their betrothal, and her probable reaction to his own complicity by not informing her in advance.

The subject of love had not figured in his calculations, and he had been caught unawares when she herself unexpectedly introduced the subject into the conversation. Instead of hearing her out and assessing her vulnerability, as any tactician worth his salt would have done, he had alienated her.

Knowing the strategic value of retreat when one has miscalculated, Sir Olyver sought to remedy the situation. "Forgive me, my lady, I spoke out of turn. I can know nothing of the circumstances of your life that inform your feelings on the subject. You have spent many years treading the perilous waters of life at court, a world I eschew in favor of the soldier's life. You cannot have had an easy time of it."

Megge swallowed. "I have not."

"I have lived my entire life among men. What do I know of a woman's heart? Of what destroys her dreams? How she survives their loss? Perhaps in time I . . ." His voice trailed off.

She had abandoned her defensive stance and moved closer to the barrier that separated them. "Yes, my lord? You were saying?"

Captivated by those blue, blue eyes, Olyver hadn't the faintest notion what he had been saying. Instead, he found himself reaching through the bars to cup her face in his rough hands and draw her to him. His mouth settled on hers in a kiss soft as a whisper. "My lady."

"Megge, my lord."

"Olyver, my lady."

It was all they needed to say.

Chapter Twenty-Four

A cry so desolate, so piteous, so utterly devoid of hope and succor it could only have issued from the fiery pit of Hell itself pierced the night. It echoed from the massive walls of Castle Rising, eddied through its dark twisting corridors, spiraled up to its loftiest chambers and down into its deepest dungeons; soared high above the majestic towers and the River Lis and out over the sea.

"Or-a-bell-a!"

Megge shot from her bed. "Dear God!"

"Ora-bellllaaaaa!"

Sir Olyver staggered from his tent. "Christ Jesus!"

"Orrrr-a-belllllllaaaaaa!"

A fearful threnody arose. "Aga-nes-aga-nes-aga-aga-aga-nes."

Banshees were upon the land. "Gilleee-gillillilleeeee."

"Ora-aga-aga-lillee-aga-be-be-be-nessssa-lee-lee-lalala!"

195

Father Jerome erupted from the chapel. "Repent!" he shrieked. "The Day of Judgment is come!"

A mind-numbing crack of thunder rent the air—in after years many would swear it emanated from the great cavern beneath the castle—and a post-apocalyptic silence settled over the world.

"Pickled sheep's eyes."

"No, Clarice. That's a silly old wives' tale. Rabbit droppings boiled in vinegar is much more effective."

"Raw eels," Mary offered. "My ma always swore by raw eels."

"Hemlock," Gunny One grunted. "That should do it."

"But hemlock's a deadly poison," someone reminded her.

"Exactly."

Megge, who was now enduring her second night in a row without sleep, was not feeling in charity with the three men sprawled in drunken stupor on the ground outside her gate. "I think the best thing we can do is nothing at all. Suffering may be the best cure."

"I heartily agree, Lady Margaret," said Sir Olyver as he and eight soldiers appeared at the top of the road. "Good evening, ladies."

"Good evening, Sir Olyver," chorused the women gathered on the walkway above the guardhouse.

"Oh dear, is that my Humphrey down there?"

"Orabella," Megge cried. "What are you doing out of bed?"

"One does not sleep through the end of the world, my dear. You there, sir," Orabella called down to a soldier who was wrestling her husband onto a canvas litter, "do take care. Lord Humphrey is prone to bruising."

"Yes, my lady."

"He has such beautiful white skin, like a baby," she confided to Megge. "Except for the hairy patches, of course."

"We need to get you back to bed," Megge told her.

"Not just yet, dear. It's a lovely night, so soft. I feel like a sluggard, lying about all day. Oh look, Agnes, Sir Siward has tumbled off his litter. That had to be painful."

"Nothing more than he deserves," Lady Agnes muttered. "Frightening decent Christian women from their beds at all hours of the night. I'll wager not even the Saracens would countenance such behavior. They would have his head from his body before he could so much as belch."

"He may wish they had when he wakes up," Megge said.

Lady Orabella watched the torch-lit procession with its oblivious cargo wind down the road to the river. "I think it was sweet. Rather like a nosegay or a love token. Noisier, of course. But then, men have their own special little ways of expressing their feelings."

"Like vomiting in the roses?" Lady Clarice asked.

"Well, I was thinking more along the lines of—" Lady Orabella began.

"Pounding one another into a bloody pulp?"

"Passing wind at table?"

"Spitting at flies."

"Cracking their knuckles."

"Fondling their ballocks."

"Staring at your breasts."

"Falling asleep on top of you."

Raucous laughter swept the heights. Far below in the siege camp men glanced uneasily at one another. A woman's laughter was a troubling thing.

Chapter Twenty-Five

"Sweet Jesus, let me die."

Sir Walter leaned back in Lord Humphrey's capacious chair and crossed his ankles atop the camp chest at the foot of the bed. "Good morning, brother. You're looking well."

"Oh, God."

"No? A bit worse for wear?"

"Kill me."

"The ladies of the castle have kindly sent down these little pots to see you through your distress. Let's see what we have here. I cannot say what these little brown blobs are; they smell like vinegar. Raw eels in this one."

"Help."

"Eyeballs? It can't be. Yes, I believe it is."

"Have pity."

"Let the man be."

Sir Walter swiveled around to see Sir Olyver looming in the doorway of his brother's huge tent. The big warrior stood at his ease, but always there was about the man a disarming stillness that made the wise man wary and the fool reckless.

"I'm leaving. He'll not be fit company for two days at least."

"I was just going to exercise my horse. Perhaps you would care to join me?"

"You surprise me, Olyver. I did not think you particularly cared for my company."

Sir Olyver shrugged. "I don't recall ever having said so outright, Walter. Be that as it may, I should like to speak with you about Lady Margaret."

"Then I'll join you. Humphrey is certainly in no condition to talk. The man never could hold his drink."

They strolled through the nearly deserted camp toward the paddocks that had been erected along a branch of the Lis that always ran fresh, despite the salty backwash when the tide came up the main river. Out on the broad sheep meadow, men trained with sword, lance, and falchion. A group of mounted knights trotted by, returning from the morning hunt. Their squires trooped along behind bearing bloody haunches of deer, the carcass of a huge boar, rabbits, and wood ducks.

"Your brother is under stress," Sir Olyver remarked. "He is anxious about Lady Orabella. She is with child, and he would see this situation resolved."

"I know what kind of *stress* he's under," replied Sir Walter. "I have never understood why you will not allow women in your camp, Olyver. Your men have their needs. They must have relief almost daily; some more often. Why deny them?"

A page rushed up to hand Sir Olyver his riding gloves. "Will you ride Aries today, my lord?"

"Yes, Jason. It is not," Sir Olyver replied turning to Sir Walter, "a matter of relief but of discipline. The presence of willing women is bound to sow discord. It is our nature to wish to mate with the most comely; when we are challenged we may kill even our closest comrade."

Sir Walter swung up onto his dappled gelding and took up his whip. "Where's the harm in a good brawl now and then? It flatters a woman to have a man fighting for her favors."

Sir Olyver steadied the destrier as Jason adjusted his stirrups. "Lady Margaret is evidently not such a woman," he observed.

"Bah," said Sir Walter as they set off. "For all her airs, the lady is not out of the common way. All this nonsense is but a ploy to force the king to marry her into a royal house. Mark my words, she has her eye on Castile."

"I see. You think it possible Edward has capitulated. Perhaps he travels to Rising to see what she will offer him to achieve her goal. She is a great heiress, and Edward is ever in need of funds."

Sir Walter slapped his whip against his high boot. "I would have her if that fool in Milan hadn't gotten the pox."

Sir Olyver brought Aries to a stop, rested his hands on the tall saddle horn, and looked back over the Lis Valley toward the great castle on the cliff. Megge would take the veil before she would give up Castle Rising for a royal title.

"I had the Alfieri family willing to loan Edward a huge sum at a fairly reasonable rate," Sir Walter said. "Those Lombardy bankers are a wily lot; he has never been able to get such good terms with them before.

Then that wastrel Alfonso got the pox from some whore and gave it to Marco's wife who gave it to him. Both brothers were dead in a matter of months and that was that."

"A sad tale."

"When Edward heard the news," Sir Walter continued, "he gave Lady Margaret to someone else. The bastard must have paid a fortune for her."

Sir Olyver shrugged. "Not necessarily."

"Bah. Edward is no fool. He is not about to waste such a valuable asset on some nobody." Sir Walter gave an impatient pull on the reins and started back down the hill. "Damn Humphrey to hell. He knows who the bastard is, and I can't get a coherent word out of him. Well, I can't wait. Edward is already at Exeter."

Sir Olyver stared straight ahead. "You have a plan?"

"I have a plan. I realize we have had our differences since we first trained together at Chester, but if you will hear me out, Olyver, you may come away from this silly siege a man of property and greater consequence than you ever dreamed possible."

"The man might as well tie the noose around his own neck and save Edward the trouble," Sir Kay observed.

Lord Humphrey grunted his agreement. His tongue might be too numb to speak more than a few sentences at a time, but at least he could sit up without toppling over. He took up his cup, held his breath, and forced down another swallow of the tonic Lady Orabella had sent down from the castle. "God Almighty! What foul stuff!"

"Consider the alternatives and be grateful," Sir Olyver suggested.

Lord Humphrey opened one eye and glared at the

three pots. The brown matter had turned out to be pieces of coarse bread soaked in vinegar; the sheeps' eyes, little onions coated with lard; and the raw eels—well, they were raw eels. "I will have the cook's hide. Two is the cook, I think. No, it's One. One, Two, they are both ugly as sin."

"What I find extraordinary," Olyver remarked after his squire had refilled his flagon and left the tent, "is that Walter's proposal was almost exactly the same as Lady Margaret suspected. In return for my assistance I should have one of her properties in France once they were wed."

"Clever girl, Megge," said Lord Humphrey.

"The difference being," Sir Olyver continued, "that rather than wielding my influence on Edward and you, Humphrey, I should organize an assault upon the castle so that he could, as he so delicately put it, make it impossible for the king to refuse to legitimize the union."

Lord Humphrey slammed down his cup, winced. "Edward will hear of this, by God."

"I told Walter I would have to consider how best it could be done, as Humphrey had forbidden a direct assault in favor of negotiation, and that I would again survey the area for some way into the cavern beneath the keep."

"But we already know where it is," Sir Kay pointed out.

"True, but Walter doesn't know we do. And I intend to keep it that way."

Sir Kay threw back the last of his ale and got to his feet. "I'll have a watch set on him."

"Hold off, Kay. I have a better idea. John!"

The squire appeared promptly. "Yes, my lord?"

"Have Lancelot attend us immediately."

"I'm here, my lord!" Lancelot popped into the tent.

"You seem ever to be 'here'," Sir Olyver remarked.

Lancelot threw back his scrawny shoulders. "I am here to serve at your pleasure, my lord."

"Thank you," Sir Olyver replied gravely. "Lancelot, I have a mission for you that will require the utmost discretion." At the boy's look of evident confusion, he explained, "Discretion means that you must watch your tongue and think carefully before you act. You must carry out your orders to the letter, and if you find yourself in a difficult or dangerous situation you must withdraw if possible and summon assistance."

Lancelot positively quivered with pride that the great warrior should be placing his trust in his lowly self. "I understand, my lord."

"This is a serious matter, son. You are devoted to Lady Margaret, are you not?"

"Oh yes, sir!"

"We have reason to believe that Sir Walter may wish her harm. You will keep him in your sight night and day. He has appropriated a manor house just outside the village for his own use rather than stay here in the camp. I want you to act the beggar boy. Hang around the place, offer to fetch and carry in exchange for food. Make yourself indispensable—necessary—so that he ceases to take notice of you at all."

"I won't let him hurt her, I swear on the Bible, my lord," Lancelot declared.

"I know you won't, son, but you must not put yourself in danger, else she will have no one to assist her. That is why you must come to me or Lord Humphrey or Sir Kay if Sir Walter tries to enter the castle. No one else, absolutely no one, must know what you are about, is that understood?"

"Shouldn't you warn Lady Megge, my lord?"

"No, we are not warning Lady Margaret, nor must you. Do you understand?"

Lancelot didn't, but so far as he was concerned, Sir Olyver of Mannyngs spoke with the same authority as God himself. "Yes, my lord."

"Off you go then."

Lancelot turned smartly and marched away, head high.

"This is the damnedest business," Lord Humphrey growled. "Women rampaging through the countryside; manning the ramparts; making this demand, making that demand; denying their husbands their God-given privileges."

Apparently his lady's tonic was doing its work, as a rosy tinge was creeping back into his cheeks. It was not all that much of an improvement; the general cast of his face remained a sickly pease-porridge green, and the two colors did not sit well together. "A man deserves better, I tell you. The next thing you know our wives will be telling us where to put our lances and how to wield them."

Chapter Twenty-Six

"Supreme joy? What the hell is supreme joy?"

Lady Sybille lifted her sweetly rounded little chin. "It is a moment, if you must know."

"A moment?"

She nodded vigorously. "And I want one."

Sir Frederick had been delighted to acquire a young wife who was possessed of beauty in abundance and no real intelligence at all. Now he was beginning to wonder what he was going to do with one who hadn't one coherent thought left in her pretty little head.

"Everyone else has them," she reported. "It's not fair. Father Boniface never mentioned it, which is strange, don't you think, since it's in the Bible? Let me see if I remember what Father Jerome's text said. Oh yes. You are to put your hand by the hole of a door—he didn't say which door—and then I move my bowels for you. Or perhaps you move yours for me. I don't think I have it quite right, but it goes something like that."

Sir Frederick dropped onto the bench and buried his head in his hands. "God help me."

"Really, Frederick, I don't believe it can be all that difficult. I expect it takes practice, but as you come so often to my bed we'll soon get the hang of it. And then I can have my moment of supreme joy, too."

His head snapped up, understanding dawned. "Who put such an idea into your head?" he demanded.

Lady Sybille thought back. "Well, Megge asked me what I desired most in the world. I said rose-colored silk shifts, of course, and she said no, that was not what I desired most in the world, I desired a moment of supreme joy." She frowned. "Of course, it occurred to me at once that Baron Broward couldn't have enjoyed his moment of supreme joy very much, since he died in the middle of it. I suspect he may have been using the wrong door and—"

"Sybille, I beg you be silent," Sir Frederick groaned, tearing at his hair. "You are driving me mad."

A tiny snuffle sounded from behind the gate.

Sir Frederick leaped to his feet. "Don't cry, my little pigeon. You know how I hate it when you cry."

"I w-was, I was only trying to explain—"

"I know, lambkin—"

"Th-that—"

"I understand, my sweet pomegranate, my pumpkin, my peach, I understand."

Lady Sybille managed to choke back another sob. "You d-do?"

Sir Frederick reached through the gate to gently wipe away a tear as delicate as a drop of liquid crystal from his wife's long silky lashes. "I do, I do."

"I will have a moment of supreme joy?"

"You will, you will."
"You can help me?"
"I can, I can."
"Oh, Frederick."
"Oh, Sybille."

Chapter Twenty-Seven

Oh bliss, Megge thought, as the second day of negotiations drew to a close and she could finally retire to her bed. All in all it had gone rather well. Six couples seemed to have resolved matters on a positive note; two were at an impasse; and one couple had fought and screamed at one another to the point of exhaustion and had to be carried away.

She had only caught a distant glimpse of Sir Olyver in the camp below, but had received a message from him suggesting that the private negotiations be suspended on the morrow in favor of another meeting in the tent on the meadow, at which they should discuss progress to date and the king's imminent arrival at Castle Rising.

He had not, Megge noted, made reference to the incidents of the past two nights: the 'Greasing of the Pigs,' as it was now referred to by the women of the castle, and the impromptu cacophonous serenade by Lord Humphrey, Sir Siward, and Alfred the steward. Nor, to Megge's profound relief, had he made mention of their impulsive intimate encounter at the gate, which had left her with such conflicted feelings that she resolved to put the matter out of her mind, not altogether successfully as it turned out.

Amid alternating waves of desire, disquiet, and doubt, there lurked a suspicion that Sir Olyver might be about some mischief: a clever ploy perhaps to distract her from her purpose or entice her to submit to his authority. A man of his renowned strategic skill would not be above seducing a woman for his own ends.

Still, she could not mistake the tension of his hard body as she came apart in his arms and the heat of him as they shared that exquisitely gentle, stupefyingly erotic kiss. He desired her, just as she desired him.

And therein lay the problem, and the danger.

Lady Margaret de Languetot, a noblewoman of the realm and coveted object of the attentions of greedy, ambitious suitors from her earliest years, had long ago schooled herself to step back and weigh the consequences of giving in to her emotions. A man might go to any lengths to attract her notice or gain her favor. Words of love fell as easily and sweetly from the lips of a man intent on winning her fortune as on winning her heart. In the end, it did not matter, of course, as Edward would make the choice for her, so Megge had learned to shield her emotions lest she come to love someone she could never have.

She must be on her guard. She would never have Sir Olyver. She could not and would not allow herself to come to care for him.

Megge tossed and turned in her great bed, willing her body to sink into the deep sleep it so badly needed. The night was blessedly free of commotion;

she could hear the plaintive urgings of frogs in the castle's fishpond, the frantic chirp of crickets, the eerie call of the owl and the nightjar. Wrapping herself in the fur coverlet, she padded out of her chamber and descended to the great hall.

A fire still burned in the west hearth, stoked throughout the night to ensure Lady Orabella did not catch a chill. Megge smiled down at the sleeping woman, as much a mother to her as she had ever known. She lay on her side with soft cushions tucked between her knees to ease the strain on her back. At the age of thirty she had already borne Lord Humphrey five sons; this pregnancy must be her last, else she might die in childbirth as so many women did delivering year after year. She was a good wife to her lord, loved him, and Megge was certain, was loved in return.

Megge swallowed hard. She wanted to cry. She would probably never know the certainty of her place in the world like Lady Orabella, the blessing of love and belonging. She must face the fact that she would not find such a life in the union Edward had planned for her. Either she must accept the inevitability and go forward as her duty dictated, or depart England and face a life alone forever.

"My lady?" Mistress Annie jerked from her doze. "Is there something I can do for you?"

"No, Annie, I am merely restless tonight. Why don't you find a pallet and take your rest. I will sit with Lady Orabella."

Megge settled into Annie's chair and drew the coverlet close around her. In time, lulled by the warmth of the fire and the sweet stillness of her castle around her, she slept.

* * *

"She bids you come, my lady."

Megge struggled from her slumber, blinked, and blinked again. A small child, exquisitely formed and delicate as a butterfly's wing, gazed up at her with luminous eyes as green as new moss.

She shook her head, thinking she must be dreaming.

"It is not a dream, my lady," the child informed her, as though she could hear the thought. "She bids you come."

"Who, child?"

"The queen."

Megge frowned. "Queen Eleanor is here? Is the king with her?"

The child's laugh was the tinkle of a silver bell. "The moon is not full, my lady," she said as if that explained the matter. She held out her hand. "Come. We must hurry."

Compelled by the child's earnest entreaty, Megge let fall the coverlet, took the little hand, and allowed herself to be led, clad only in her thin linen gown, from the hall, across the inner ward, and down the staircase that descended from the guardhouse into the great cavern below the castle. It was the same route she and Henry had taken, except now the slimy stone steps and weeping walls were dry and smooth to the touch, suffused with an otherworldly glow, and the air smelled not of damp and decaying matter but sun-kissed earth, cool-running waters, and freshening spring breezes.

A woman's voice, rich as sweet cream, deep as velvet, spoke in the half-light. "Welcome, Megge, we have waited long for your return."

Megge curtsied low. "Your Majesty."

"Rise, child. You may approach."

Tytania, queen of the Fay, sat at her ease upon a moss-cushioned throne hewn from fragrant cedar, her elegant bare feet resting upon silk cushions redolent of sweet herbs and wild rose. Round about her dais were strewn golden and purple flowers of the field, and in her long delicate fingers she held a crystal goblet of golden nectar.

A memory, as elusive as mist, teased at the edge of Megge's mind. Had she once stood in this very spot, gazing up at this fearsome fairy being with her slanted eyes of deepest jade and cascading waves of silver-spun hair?

"Yes."

"I don't remember," Megge confessed.

"But you have always known, in your heart. The child in you has not forgotten."

Megge gazed about her. "I passed through this place but a few days ago, my lady, and saw only dank stone and ancient bones and fetid pools. How could I not see you and your people, the splendor of your court?"

"We did not wish it. Surely you know we reveal our presence to few mortals. Few truly believe, few are deserving."

"I cannot think I am one of them," Megge replied. "I am not sure I do believe, and frankly I think this can only be a dream. Likely I shall wake soon."

Tytania shrugged. "Make of it what you will, I care not. But as I have summoned you, you will hear me out. As a child you believed in us. Your lady mother and her lord brought you to us, and you danced among us, twirled and skipped and shouted with childish glee. We loved you, and grieved when they passed and you were taken from us."

"My mother, my father? They knew of you?"

Tytania sipped at her nectar. "Of course. We embrace those mortals who love truly, and the children of their love. Your parents knew the meaning of true love, a rare blessing among your kind."

Megge found she could not speak for the loss and longing that welled up within her.

"You have assumed your rightful place as mistress of Castle Rising, Megge, yet because you have abandoned all hope of love in your life and refuse to open your heart to it, you would sneak away like a thief in the night, ceding it to the unworthy. And as you must go, so then must we, for we will not dwell in a place bereft of love."

"What would you have me do, lady?" Megge cried. "Others hold my feelings of no account, so why should I? What good does it do me? I only seek to safeguard my heart. Is that so wrong?"

"What is wrong, Megge, is that you have lost faith in your own knowing. Long ago a man came to you; you felt the first stirring of love, but you were young and the time was not right for you or him. Fate has granted you a rare grace—as rare as the great love your parents found in one another—yet you will close your eyes to it. Take care, child. It will not be vouchsafed to you again.

"Go now," Tytania said. "Lady Orabella has need of you."

Chapter Twenty-Eight

Megge would never remember waking from the dream—if it was a dream—or summoning Mistress Annie to Orabella's side, or rushing about rapping out orders. The birthing chair must be brought down to the hall immediately. Water must be heated. Only women who had birthing experience could remain in the great hall. Someone must fetch Father Jerome to hear Orabella's confession lest she not survive the ordeal, and baptize the babe as soon as it should enter the world, whether the Lord ordained it should live or die.

Mistress Annie, Megge, Lady Agnes, and the Gunnys One and Two had consulted close together out of Orabella's hearing and agreed that she was having a difficult time of it. In the past week her belly had become so distended that she likely carried more than one babe, in which case a breech birth might be expected.

As she herself had never attended at a birthing and would likely only get in everyone's way, Megge took it upon herself to ride down to the siege camp to inform Lord Humphrey that his wife was in labor. She paid no attention to Orabella's protests that it would do neither him, nor her, any great service to rouse him in the middle of the night and perhaps send him into a fit of apoplexy.

"You will let me pass," she barked at the sentry who tried to stop her as she guided her palfrey through the sleeping camp toward the tent she knew to be Lord Humphrey's. She had only just dismounted when Sir Olyver appeared at her side, having been awakened by the ruckus.

"Is it Lady Orabella?"

"Yes. We are concerned for her. I believe Lord Humphrey may want to see her before she is too far along."

Lord Humphrey most certainly did, and raced toward Castle Rising wearing his tunic inside out, with his hose awry and the laces of his breeches tangled in knots.

Howling her displeasure, the girl child slipped from her mother's womb just as the first rays of the sun washed the towers of Castle Rising with a peachy glow. Ooohs and ahhhs greeted her entrance into the world; praise and words of comfort were heaped upon her exhausted mother.

Megge went in search of Lord Humphrey and eventually found him in the stable, where he had been confined by Sir Olyver and allowed judicious amounts of double-fermented mead during the long hours of Orabella's travail.

"Orabella is delivered of a girl child!" Megge called out.

"A girl!" Lord Humphrey leaped up from the bale of hay upon which he had finally succumbed to a fitful doze, clasped Megge to his breast, and thumped Sir Olyver heartily upon the back. "A girl, by God!"

"How fares her ladyship?" Olyver inquired softly of Megge while the new father stomped about in delight.

Megge just shook her head, and waited for Lord Humphrey to get over his first excitement and calm down enough to hear the rest of it. She had no idea how he would take it, and was grateful for Sir Olyver's calming presence.

"Humphrey," he said, "I believe Lady Margaret has more to tell you."

"Your lady is comfortable for the moment, my lord," Megge said.

The earl frowned. "For the moment?"

"I am afraid there is a complication," she said gently. "There is another babe still to be born and—"

"Another? What are you saying? Is my Orabella in danger?" Lord Humphrey cried.

Sir Olyver laid a hand on Lord Humphrey's shoulder. "Stay calm, Humphrey. Let Lady Margaret explain."

"Mistress Annie tells me the babe is not in the correct position. She will have to, um, make an adjustment, and—"

Lord Humphrey sank to his knees. "God, God, God, Sweet Jesus, Mother Mary, Orabella, my Orabella," he moaned.

"Father Jerome is offering prayers in the chapel, my lord," Megge said. "Why don't you wait there?"

Lord Humphrey leaped to his feet. "The hell with that. Out of my way!"

* * *

Mistress Annie, midwife, glared at Humphrey, baron of the realm, as he marched across the great hall. "A man has no business in a birthing chamber. You will take yourself away immediately, sir, or I will toss you out upon your ear."

"I should like to see you try," he growled. "Move aside, madam, or feel the full measure of my wrath."

Annie stood her ground. "Your lady wife is in no condition to receive you. You are in no condition to assist her in her task. Begone."

"Annie, I will see him," Lady Orabella called out in a weak voice from behind the screens that had been set up around the birthing area.

"It is not seemly," the midwife protested.

"Nevertheless, I will speak with my husband."

The midwife sent Lord Humphrey a dark look that said, "Upset her and you will answer to me."

Lord Humphrey replied with a glare of his own that clearly implied, "Get in my way again and you will be answering to your God, and soon."

His bravado and bombast vanished in an instant when he rounded the screen and beheld his Orabella, ashen-faced and drained, propped up in her bed with bolsters and cushions. Her maid hovered at her side, dipping cloths into cool water and wiping perspiration from her brow and neck.

Lord Humphrey sank to his knees beside her. "Oh, my love, my Orabella, forgive me, forgive me."

"Why, Humphrey," said she, "what have you done that I should forgive you?"

"I don't know, wife, but whatever it was, you must forgive me."

"Really, Humphrey, you are making no sense at all."

The earl leaped to his feet and aimed a shaking finger at her. "No more! There will be no more babes, Orabella."

"But Humphrey, that's what I wanted to—"

"I will not allow you to go through this again, do you hear?"

"Of course, my dear, but—"

"I have spoken," the earl declared. "You may bear this last one, but that is an end to it."

Lady Orabella raised a brow. "I may?"

He gave a regal nod. "You may. Henceforth we will find some other means to, er, conduct our . . . some other means."

"Humphrey—"

The earl scowled down at her, and folded his arms across his chest to show that he meant what he said. "Not another word, wife. I have spoken."

Orabella smiled up at her glowering lord. "Yes, husband," she said meekly.

"Good. It pleases me greatly that you see the sense of the matter. Now that we have that settled—"

Orabella gasped. "Go away now, my dear."

"Go away?"

"Now, Humphrey."

"Now? Oh God. Midwife!" he shouted. "Where is that blasted woman?"

Mistress Annie rounded the edge of the screen and elbowed the panicked earl aside. "Out."

Lord Humphrey staggered away. Megge sent for Father Jerome to take him in hand, and the terrified lord was led off to the chapel to offer up prayers to the Blessed Virgin for the safe delivery of his beloved wife and his last child.

* * *

Megge floated along that gentle current that bears the sleeper from the silent world of dreams toward the beckoning echoes of waking life. A kaleidoscope of shifting images flashed behind her closed eyelids: Orabella in sweet repose after her painful exertions, Lord Humphrey a snoring sentinel in a chair at her side; Father Jerome at the chapel font as he sprinkled holy water upon the heads of two tiny, squalling babes and pronounced the ancient words that welcomed them into the safekeeping of the Church; Sir Olyver beside her. . . .

Megge bolted upright, and felt about in the dimness of her curtained bed, relieved—and possibly just a bit disappointed, though she never would have admitted it to herself—to discover no one there but herself.

"Missy?"

The little maid drew back the velvet hangings. "Good morning, my lady," she said cheerfully.

Megge frowned. "Morning? You mean afternoon. We did not get everyone settled until at least three, I am sure, and as it is still light it must be afternoon."

Missy shook her head. "No, my lady. That was yesterday. Now it's today."

Megge glanced down and was surprised to see she still wore her riding gown. "You are saying I have slept through an afternoon, an entire evening and night? Why did you not wake me?"

"He told me I mustn't, my lady."

"He? He who?"

"Why, Sir Olyver, my lady."

"Sir Olyver was here?"

Missy giggled.

Megge remembered now, only vaguely, looking up

at the great staircase that led to her chamber and thinking she could not possibly face the long climb. She had stumbled to a stone bench in a recess off the great hall and collapsed into exhausted sleep. Then had come the sensation of being lifted in strong arms and the sound of heavy boots on stone and the soft whoosh of a feather mattress beneath her as she was laid gently upon it. And strong arms again, drawing her against a warm hard body, and a deep voice whispering, "Sleep now, my lady, sleep."

Chapter Twenty-Nine

Lancelot darted into the deep shadow of an enormous buttress. He crouched low and watched Sir Walter make his way toward the postern door.

Sir Walter bowed. "I must speak with you, my lady."

Megge peered out through the grate. "Sir Walter, I cannot think we have anything to discuss."

"Megge," he said, using the familiar form of address, "you must know I mean you no harm. You have lived in my brother's hall these four years. We are, in a sense, family. I have felt on occasion that you do not hold me in the highest regard, but believe me when I say that I truly have your best interests at heart."

Megge did not reply.

"Please. Walk a way with me and hear me out. I fear you have placed too much trust in Sir Olyver and he has misinformed you on certain matters."

"I find it difficult to believe that a man of Sir Olyver's character would lie."

"I do not say he has lied exactly, but only offered you his interpretation of the facts."

Megge hesitated. She must not allow her growing feelings for Sir Olyver to cloud her judgment. He had denied entering into an arrangement with the man, yet she had been informed that he was seen riding out with him two days past. He seemed intent on continuing negotiations until the king should arrive, which confirmed that Castle Rising remained under formal siege. He valued loyalty above all things, and although he might desire her, he would never set his honor above his duty.

Nor, she thought, could she. She had come too far, worked too hard. She must see this mission through to whatever its end must be, and to do so she must have a clear understanding of the forces that would bear on her choices, and ultimately her success or failure.

"Very well, Sir Walter. I will fetch my cloak."

On hearing that Lady Megge was going to leave the safety of the castle in the company of Sir Walter, Lancelot immediately set off to find Sir Olyver. He was halfway down the road when it occurred to him that he would not know where they had gone, and his intelligence would be of little value if Sir Olyver did not know where to find them. He skidded to a stop, slid down an incline on his bottom, and crouched behind a tangled yew until they came into view. Treading softly he followed the murmur of their voices. Rather than walking on toward the bridge and the meadow beyond, Sir Walter steered Lady Megge to the right and along a narrow trail at the base of the cliff that led down to a rock-strewn stretch of beach.

Lancelot watched them for a moment, then turned and ran like the wind, his heart pounding in his scrawny chest, back along the path, over the bridge and across the meadow. He zigzagged through the camp at full tilt, leaping over fire pits and sleeping bodies. Ignoring a sentry's order to halt, he crashed through the canvas flap of Sir Olyver's tent and collapsed at his feet.

"He, she," he wheezed. "They."

Sir Olyver was already on his feet buckling on his sword belt before Lancelot could summon the breath to deliver his message. "Kay, get Humphrey," he ordered his second in command. "We have trouble." He reached down to haul Lancelot to his feet. "Tell me, son."

"Sir Walter went to the castle and told Lady Megge he must speak with her, and she agreed and went with him, I don't understand why, and then I don't think she wanted to go with him anymore, but he had his hand on her arm, and it's dark and I couldn't see, and—"

Sir Olyver slammed his sword into its sheath. "Breathe, boy. Where did they go?"

"To the beach, my lord, on the seaward side of the cliffs."

"You will lead us. Ah, Humphrey, good. Your brother has lured Lady Margaret from the castle."

The earl swore a foul oath. "What is that girl thinking?"

"More to the point," Sir Olyver snapped, "is what your brother is thinking."

Megge was not so much alarmed as annoyed by Sir Walter's insistent hold on her arm. Not wishing to appear impolite lest he was merely lending support as they descended the steep trail, she looked for a way to

224

draw away from him, and found it in the rising wind.

"Allow me to fasten my hood," she said as they paused at a sharp bend. "I fear a storm is upon us. Perhaps we should return."

Sir Walter looked to the west. "We have time yet, my lady. This will not take long."

They arrived at the beach. With the tide at its lowest ebb, it was twice its normal width, but darkness was falling fast and Megge had no wish to venture further.

"Well, Sir Walter, I am ready to hear what you have to tell me. I assume it concerns your suit, which the king has denied."

"It does, my lady. I was sorely grieved when I learned of his decision. I offered for you with the most honorable of intentions, believing you would suffer no disparagement and that we would suit well in temperament and understanding."

Megge could believe no such thing, and wondered that he could. "His Majesty keeps his own counsel, Sir Walter, and often decides matters in the light of what may best serve his interests and those of the realm. I expect he seeks some advantage to the match that you could not provide."

"Now that is what I so admire about you, Megge," he said with a winning smile. "You are no naïve maid who will not let go her foolish romantic dreams. You understand the way of things."

All too true, she thought sadly.

"But what I cannot understand, my dear," Sir Walter continued with daring intimacy, "is how you think to defy Edward by installing yourself here at Castle Rising. You must know you cannot escape your destiny. You must marry."

Muffled thunder sounded far to the west. Megge was glad of her warm cloak with its deep, concealing hood. She would not have Sir Walter see how the truth of his words affected her. She shrugged. "Perhaps. I seek only the right to be consulted as to who his choice might be. It is not too much to ask."

Sir Walter could not have imagined a better opening to achieve his purpose. "Indeed it is not!" he cried. "Perhaps," he continued humbly, "I would not have been your first choice, Megge, but it is as they say, better to do business with the devil you know than the devil you do not. It seems Edward will announce his choice for you when he arrives from Exeter. Fortunately, he does not care to travel in inclement weather, so you may have a few days more to save yourself."

Megge stared up at him. "I don't understand, Sir Walter. Save myself?"

The first heavy drops of rain spattered onto the sand and rocks around them. "Come, my lady, we must take refuge. I believe there may be a small cavern a short way up the beach." He knew very well there was, as he had scouted it out that very morning. He hurried her along, and they had only just ducked under a slab of overhanging rock when the storm broke.

Megge cursed herself for a fool as she began to suspect that Sir Walter might have serious mischief in mind. She felt beneath her cloak to make sure her little eating knife was safely in its sheath at her waist. She could not believe he would try to take her against her will, thereby irrevocably compromising her and forcing a marriage whether Edward willed it or no, but the jeweled hilt designed specially for her small hand gave assurance that she was not altogether without the means to defend herself.

"I believe you came to me with information about Sir Olyver?" Somehow just the sound of his name settled her nerves.

"I have," Sir Walter replied gravely. "I do not trust the man, Megge. What has he told you of the king's message to Humphrey?"

Megge counseled herself to caution. "Nothing really. I had not realized your brother had shared that information with him. He said only that he knew your suit had been denied and that Edward had settled upon another."

"And you believe him."

Megge did not like Sir Walter's sarcastic tone, but replied simply, "I have no reason not to. Why, do you think he knows?"

"I believe he does, and I suspect you will be most unhappy when you learn who it is."

Megge could barely discern Sir Walter's expression in the thick gloom, whether it reflected real concern for her or a certain smugness that he possessed knowledge that she did not. "You know?" she asked in surprise.

"Not for sure, my dear, but I suspect, I suspect. And it grieves me for your sake."

Megge could honestly not imagine a less appealing suitor than Sir Walter himself. But then, Edward had a realm full of willing noblemen of or near her own station in life from which to choose: some too young to grow hair upon their faces, others too old to eat naught but pap and gruel. Domineering, timid; conniving, credulous; coarse, foppish; brutal, passive; lecherous, impotent. Many were given to excess, dissipation, drunkenness, and unnatural vices.

Even as she considered the alternatives, Megge could not mistake Sir Walter's purpose, and so it proved when he suddenly hauled her against him. "Megge, let me help you. Accept my suit; marry me now before Edward arrives. He will of course seek to have it annulled by Rome, but it will not avail him if we have consummated our union. Why wait? You know it is the only way."

Megge broke free and backed away until she came up against the rough stone of the cavern wall. "I know no such thing, sir," she declared out of the darkness. "Do you seek to force the issue? If what you say is true, then the man Edward has chosen for my husband must be the very worst of men. Whom do you suspect? I demand you tell me."

"You will not like it, my lady." Sir Walter's voice now held a nasty note of triumph. "But as you will not see reason, I shall tell you."

"Walter."

Sir Olyver's voice was flat, but the warning in that single word was unmistakable.

"Olyver!" Megge blinked against the sudden bright light of lanterns at the entrance of the cavern.

"You are unharmed, my lady?" Sir Olyver did not take his eyes from Sir Walter.

Despite the fact that her heart was pounding and her knees were shaking, Megge determined to put up a brave front. "Of course I am unharmed. Sir Walter was just—"

Sir Olyver stood like an avenging angel with his hand upon the hilt of his long sword. "I know what

Sir Walter is doing here. What I do not know, my lady, is what you think *you* are."

Lord Humphrey appeared behind Sir Olyver, his face purple with exertion and anger. "By God, you go too far," he shouted, advancing on Sir Walter. "If you were not my brother, I would cut you down where you stand."

"Please, Lord Humphrey," Megge said, "you misunderstand the situation—"

"No, Lady Margaret, it is you who misunderstand," Sir Olyver broke in, his voice cold and dispassionate. "Either you are unbelievably naïve or have lost your wits to leave the castle in the company of a man who will say anything to achieve his purpose."

Stung by his callous words, Megge retaliated with, "And I suppose you wouldn't?"

"Oh, but he would." Sir Walter stepped to her side. "Sir Olyver knows better than anyone the power of the words he wields so well and the value of silence when it suits him. Has he told you of our arrangement, my lady? Of the reward he can expect from our union?"

"Enough," Lord Humphrey barked. "I have no patience with your insolence, Walter. Sir Kay, escort my brother to his lodging and see that he stays there. Come, Megge."

"A moment, Humphrey. I want a word with her ladyship," Sir Olyver said. "I will myself escort her back to the castle. Lancelot, go with them."

"Edward cannot arrive too soon," Lord Humphrey growled. "I shall go mad if this damnable business is not soon resolved. As if I have not enough to contend with, what with Orabella and two new daughters I have barely come to know, now I must think what to do about my fool of a brother. And," he added as though the matter carried equal weight with him, "I am soaked through to the bone and have yet to have my supper."

With that, Lord Humphrey stomped off into the storm, leaving behind a silence so fraught with tension that the ominous onslaught of rain against the cliff face sounded like the happy laughter of little children by comparison.

Sir Olyver, as was his habit, waited out his adversary that he might have the advantage of assessing his—in the present instance, her—state of mind and consider his response accordingly. Lady Margaret, however, seemed in no hurry to fill the silence as women were wont to do, and so they stood for some time as the rain fell and the lantern light flickered across the rough walls.

Megge finally spoke. "You lied. You said you had no arrangement with Sir Walter."

"I don't have an arrangement with Sir Walter."

"He says you do."

"He thinks we do, as I intended he should."

"You said you did not know the name of the man Edward has chosen for me.".

"No, my lady, I said I thought Edward should be the one to tell you. I did not say I did not know."

Megge shrugged. "It is the same thing. You merely lied by omission."

Sir Olyver leaned back against the wall, crossed one ankle over the other, and folded his arms across his chest.

"What could you have been thinking, allowing Sir Walter to lure you to this place?"

Megge liked neither his lordly stance nor his overbearing tone of voice. "I assure you I was not lured. I accompanied him of my own free will. He and I had business to discuss."

"What business?"

"That, sir, is no concern of yours."

"From what I observed when I arrived, the 'business' he had on his mind did not accord with your own."

Megge felt the first flush of real anger. "I don't know what you *think* you observed, Sir Olyver, but I assure you I was in no danger. Sir Walter is not the first man to let his amorous instincts toward me get the better of him, and likely he will not be the last. I can take care of myself very well, thank you. And I will not be lectured to by you as though I were a child. I am a woman full grown, and know what I am about."

Sir Olyver abandoned his casual stance, wanting nothing more than to shake some sense into her, or perhaps kiss her: He wasn't sure which. "Believe me, my lady, what Sir Walter intended for you had nothing whatsoever to do with *amour*. If you believe that, you do not recognize true passion when it is before you."

Oh, but she did, she did, Megge thought as he pushed away from the wall and stalked toward her, never taking his eyes from her, daring her to back away, knowing she wouldn't. Somehow she managed to stand her ground, though her heart was racing like a mad thing and anticipation danced along every nerve.

She heard her own voice, shaky but determined. "You will stop where you are, sir. I am no more inclined to welcome your attentions than Sir Walter's."

It was a lie, but she was determined that he should not know it.

Olyver stopped, hooked his thumbs in his sword belt, and shrugged. "Actually, my lady, my intent in approaching you was not to force my attentions on you, but to shake you until your teeth rattled in your mouth and some dim spark of common sense sprang to life in your obstinate little head." That too was a lie, and he was equally determined she should not know it.

For a moment Megge did not know whether to be disappointed or insulted. Wounded pride won out. "At least I possess sufficient acumen in my obstinate little head to see you for what you are, Olyver of Mannyngs."

He cocked his head. "I await your judgment of my character, madam."

"You, sir," Megge declared, "are the most dangerous sort of man. You claim to serve others, yet in all ways that matter you are the master. You wield words with as much skill as you wield your sword, yet you allow your adversary to think he is winning so that he grows careless.

"You take great care not to tell the lie, yet you will not always reveal the truth. You encourage confidences, yet offer none of your own, nothing of your true self. You incite passion in others," she continued, waving her arms in the air as she paced a small circle around the cavern, "yet hold your own so firmly in check that one is left wondering why it is you don't go mad like any normal man. I vow I do not know who you really are behind it all, so artful is your disguise, or what to make of you."

A smile tugged at the corner of his mouth. "You appear to be making excellent progress in reasoning it out, my lady."

"I am in no mood to be made sport of," Megge huffed. "Now, if you wish to escort me back to the castle, sir, let us be off. If not, I can find my own way very well."

"I wouldn't dream of it, my lady," Sir Olyver murmured. He took up the lantern, and followed her erect little figure out into the night.

At the high, wide iron-studded doors that led into the stable yard, Megge sounded the clapper that brought a young lad racing from his snug sleeping spot in the hayloft. "Who goes there?" he shouted above the wind.

"It is Lady Megge, Robert," she shouted back, recognizing his froggy little voice. "Please open the door."

"Aye, my lady," he called, and using both hands, slid back the long heavy iron bolt and tugged one of the massive doors open wide enough to admit her. He froze when he spotted Sir Olyver.

"It's all right, Robert," Megge said. "Sir Olyver has been kind enough to accompany me back. Run along, now. You will catch a chill."

"But you left with that other man," he informed her.

"Yes, well, but now I have returned with Sir Olyver."

"But he's the enemy," Robert protested, backing away. "Hildegard says he does the devil's work and has horns and a forked tail. He eats little children and spits out their bones."

Sir Olyver threw off his hood and bent his head so the boy might see for himself that no horns sprouted from beneath his thick mane of golden hair.

"You could still have a tail," Robert pointed out.

"Don't you dare," Megge warned when Sir Olyver made to lift the back of his cloak. "Robert, you must trust me when I tell you Sir Olyver has no tail."

Robert looked unconvinced. "Are you sure?"

"Yes, I am quite sure."

"How do you know? Have you looked at his bottom?"

Megge blushed a deep crimson. "No! I have not looked at his bottom!"

Sir Olyver cleared his throat. "You know, my lady, as I have not yet had my supper and am feeling rather hungry, perhaps you would not mind if I had a quick bite to eat right now."

Robert stumbled back, croaked out "Gnoodight-mgldy," and ran for his life.

Megge could not help but laugh. "Really, sir, that was quite unnecessary. You've frightened the child out of a year's growth."

"You would have preferred that I dropped my breeches and allowed him to inspect my bottom so that he might be sure?" he inquired.

"Of course not. The weather is far too inclement for that sort of display," she replied gravely.

"So it is. Perhaps another day."

Rain dripped from the eaves of the stable. A horse whickered.

"Well then, I bid you good night, Sir Olyver."

"And I you, Lady Margaret."

The wind assailed the cliff face, scoured the massive walls; snatched at their hoods, whipped their cloaks about their legs.

"You are mistaken."

"In what way am I mistaken, my lord?"

"My passion. I cannot always hold it so firmly in check."

"Oh."

Lightning flashed far out over the sea.

"Still, it is good to know that I incite passion in others."

"Well, yes, I am sure it is most satisfying. To know," she thought to add.

He bent to her. "Do I incite your passion, lady?"

"It would depend, of course, on—"

"Desire?"

"Well, sir, as to that—"

"Heat?"

"Um—"

"Lust?"

"You—"

"Come to my bed, lady."

"I—"

"Lie with me, Megge. Please."

Chapter Thirty

She would, Megge thought as she shivered in the gloom, probably have followed him to the gates of hell itself as he led her down from the castle mount and across the raging waters of the River Lis to the tent beneath the great copper beech. Now she watched as he knelt before an iron brazier and struck tiny blue sparks off a flint that blossomed into a fire that washed the white canvas walls in an amber glow and the promise of safe haven and needful warmth.

Megge could not take her eyes off him as he rose and threw off his wet garments and stood revealed before her in all his raw power and uncompromising strength and animal grace.

Perhaps someday her heart would start beating again.

Male and female He made them. Indeed He had.

She really ought to take a breath. Else she might swoon and he would think her some goosey little virgin, which of course she was. She could, at the very least, pretend she still had her wits about her.

"No, let me." Now he stood before her, smiling down at her as though he could hear her very thoughts. He worked at the tangled knots of her hood, undid the clasp, and let the cloak fall to a puddle at her feet. He knelt before her, removed her half boots and hose, and drew her forward onto the tapestry carpet.

Megge stared down at her bare toes. "I don't know what I'm supposed to do," she mumbled.

"Let me see you, my lady."

Slowly, awkwardly Megge undid the braided bronze belt at her waist and the matching side laces, and slipped her gown over her head. Blushing, she fingered the pale blue silk of her shift, wondering if he expected her to remove it, too.

"Megge." Olyver reached out his hand to draw her down to him, gathering her softness against his hard body, breathing in the warm feminine fragrance, hearing her soft gasp as she learned the feel of him.

"Sweet Jesus," he groaned as he brought his hands up to cradle her head and trace the line of her lips with his tongue, then held her mouth hard against his as the kiss deepened and became a fiery plundering, leaving them both shaking and breathless.

Utterly consumed with a need she could barely comprehend, Megge began to move against him, slowly, then with greater urgency as his hands massaged her back through the whispering silk and explored up along the smooth, soft flesh of her thighs to the wet warmth between her legs. When he reached between them to feel her heat and mold her against his hardness, she could stand it no longer. "Please, Olyver, I want, I don't know, I want, I'm so empty . . ."

Cushioning her in his arms, he rolled her over. "Open to me, Megge."

There would be pain, she knew, but so compelling was the urgency that gripped her that when he seemed to hesitate she reached down to take hold of him and guide him into her.

And froze.

Her eyes flew open. "Oh. No. I don't think . . . It can't possibly . . . No."

Olyver winced as her grip tightened along with her growing consternation. "Gently, my lady, please, I beg you."

"Oh, I'm sorry. I just hadn't expected . . ."

"I know. Here, sit up." He knelt before her, took her hands in his, guided them up and down, then let her explore on her own the velvet softness of the skin over the hot, hard, pulsing shaft. He groaned as she reached lower and cupped him, and then to his utter amazement, bent her head to taste him and take him into her mouth.

"Sweet Jesus, Megge, no, stop."

"But—"

Gently he pushed her down onto her back. "You will kill me, lady."

"I will?"

He silenced her with deep drugging kisses; sucked her sweet taut breasts; teased and stroked with his long fingers until she was mindless with wanting. Only then did he brace himself above her, and with a single hard thrust make her his forever.

Olyver held her close, whispering words of comfort and reassurance as she wept against his neck, shuddered, and slowly relaxed to accommodate him. His own need was such that he wanted only to pound himself into her and find his release, but somehow he managed to hold back, even when she wrapped her legs around him and moved her hips against him in slow insistent circles.

"God, God, look at me Megge."

She opened her eyes. The single flame that was already burning fiercely where their bodies joined leaped up to consume her utterly, and she was lost as she swept out over the edge and found her release.

Olyver had given pleasure to many women, but this was beyond anything he could ever have imagined. She had given him a gift, not only of her virginity, but also of her trust. She had let go, knowing that as she fell he would be there to catch her.

Something almost savage took hold of him, the need to possess, and when she started to arch up against him again, he brought her firmly under control by pressing her down into the carpet with his full weight and imprisoning her arms above her head.

She was watching him, open to him as no woman had ever been.

"Megge," he groaned, burying himself in her heat, rocking against her softness, surrendering at last to his own release. "Megge. Mine."

Mine? What had Olyver meant, *mine?*

Megge lay curled against him, grateful for the warmth of his big body and the furs he had pulled from one of the chests pushed back against the tent walls. The storm had spent its full fury, and the world was silent save for the splatter of drops from the overspreading branches onto the canvas ceiling and an occasional gentle snore from the man beside her.

The thought of donning her wet clothes and making the long climb up to the castle was not a pleasant one, but she would have to, and soon, while it was still dark. How she would explain being out and about in the middle of a storm in the middle of the night she really could not say.

As she had last been seen in Sir Olyver's company by the sentries and little Robert, speculation would run wild that she might have given herself to him, which would certainly do her credibility no good in the eyes of the women she had convinced to withhold their own sexual favors from the men in their lives. It was not quite the same thing, of course, as she had not had a man in her life at the outset, but at the very least it would be terribly embarrassing that they might suspect that their leader had succumbed to her own unbridled desire. And so she had.

Just because she had lain with Sir Olyver, it did not necessarily follow that he *was* a man in her life. In point of fact, nothing had really changed between them. He still commanded the siege of her castle; she still awaited Edward's arrival before she determined her future course of action. Whatever happened, Sir Olyver of Mannyngs and Lady Margaret de Languetot would soon go their separate ways.

But she would always have this night with him, and although she knew the magnitude of the sin she had committed, she felt neither guilt nor regret. She had, as Tytania might say, been granted a rare grace that would not be vouchsafed her again.

"A moment of supreme joy," she murmured.

"Mmmm?"

"Sleep, my lord."

When he turned onto his side, dragging the furs with him, she decided she might as well get up and dress. Only the faintest glow emanated from the brazier as she pulled on her damp clothes, stuffed her wet hose into a deep pocket of her mantle, and stuck her feet into her stiff, wet boots.

For a moment she stood looking down at him, then turned and slipped out into the night. Dark clouds still scudded across the full moon, but there was light enough to see by as she made her way over the bridge and up the castle mount to her home.

She told herself she would not cry, but she did.

Chapter Thirty-One

"It is always so much better when a man believes it is his own idea," Lady Orabella remarked as she examined with a mother's uncritical eye the scrunched but serene little face of the newly arrived Lady Mary Eleanor. "It saves so much time and wear and tear on one's nerves."

Lord Humphrey had just departed his lady wife's chamber, having spent his allotted hour expounding on issues of childbirth—of which he knew absolutely nothing—and cooing over his identical twin daughters. Both would be christened Mary in honor of the Blessed Virgin, whose mercy had spared Orabella and the babes, but would be distinguished by their secondary names. The elder by some six hours would bear the name of Mary Eleanor, in honor of Edward's beloved queen. The younger would be Annabel, in honor of an irascible old midwife whose knowledge and skill had enabled her to turn the second babe in the womb. Tiny Lady Mary Annabel might not have arrived headfirst in the usual way of things, but her undignified entry into the world, bottom-first, had avoided the mortal danger posed by a feet-first birth, and likely saved Orabella's life.

It had been Humphrey himself who decreed the child would bear the name Annabel. The midwife had nodded curtly when so informed, then wept in private as no one had ever thought to name a child after her, though she had brought hundreds into the world. Humphrey continued to regard her as he would a snarling beast standing between him and a succulent joint of venison. For her part, Annie bristled at his bossy bluster and ordered him about like the lowliest servant, but in truth they were well pleased with one another.

"Men are so very complicated," Lady Clarice declared as she settled her awkward bulk on a cushioned chest. She had just carried up from the kitchen a cup of steaming broth that Annie decreed Orabella must drink several times a day, and the climb had not done her swollen ankles any favor.

Two days after the birth, Lady Orabella remained so pale and weak from loss of blood that Annie had sent to a renowned herbalist at Salisbury for a recipe to restore her strength. A concoction of herbs and dark green leafy vegetables had been prescribed, and Annie saw to it herself that Lady Orabella swallowed every bitter drop.

Lady Orabella smiled. "On the contrary, my dear, men are easily encompassed. Their physical wants are simple really and easily supplied. They must believe themselves in control even when the roof is crashing down upon their heads. They crave a well-regulated life and are ill equipped when confronted by the unexpected. They are baffled by their own emotions and terrified when called upon to deal with ours. They rely overmuch on the efficacy of logic, and disdain subtlety and the value of intuition, usually to their own detriment. Their pride is a sadly fragile thing and is to be handled with the utmost care, else they come undone. They really are the most extraordinary creatures: at once trying, imperfect, and endlessly fascinating.

"I don't know what I should have done with anyone but Humphrey for my husband," she concluded. "I account myself most fortunate."

"And I with my Frederick," chimed in Lady Sybille. She beamed round at the little group. "He is going to give me my moment of supreme joy. He says he knows how."

"Why does that not surprise me?" asked Lady Agnes of no one in particular. "Practice makes perfect, and Lord knows the man has had enough practice."

"I asked him how he's going to do it, but he wouldn't say," Lady Sybille informed them. "It's to be a surprise."

Mistress Gilly positively cackled. "I expect it will be."

Megge sneezed, prompting the inevitable query as to what she had been doing out in the storm the previous night. Pausing occasionally to stifle a sniffle, she gave a carefully edited account of her meeting with Sir Walter, "on business." Lord Humphrey and Sir Olyver had apparently been alerted unnecessarily that she might be in some danger from the storm and had come to fetch her back to the castle. Everyone seemed to accept the story at face value. If Lady Orabella suspected that there was more to it, she wisely kept her thoughts to herself.

Megge would be eternally grateful to Lord Humphrey that he had not even mentioned the episode. He couldn't know about her encounter with Olyver, of course, and she hoped he never would. Whatever her concerns might be that Sir Olyver had seduced her for some ulterior purpose of his own, she could at least be assured of his discretion, for the time being at any rate.

And who knew but that her fall might in the end work to her own advantage? Virginity in a woman of her high station was not merely desirable; it was mandatory. A village lass or merchant's daughter might enjoy an occasional dalliance here and there before she married, but a noblewoman must go to her husband's bed with her maidenhead intact. There must be no doubt that the child she bore him grew from his seed and his seed only, and thereby could be accounted his legitimate heir. He might strew bastards across the known world, but his wife must be above reproach. Would she dare, Megge wondered, to use her own disgrace as a last resort to convince this man Edward had chosen for her to turn from her in disgust, as he surely would?

"Bah," Mistress Gilly was saying. "There never was a perfect husband, and never will be."

A spirited discussion ensued as to what might constitute the perfect husband. They all agreed that he would sport a comely appearance, although when it came to particulars there were as many differences of opinion as there were women in the room: Eyes might be blue, green, brown, hazel. Hair might be golden, black, even red or gray, but as Lady Orabella commented, "A good head of hair is of course an asset in a man, especially to begin with, so that one barely notices over the years that it has been disappearing bit by bit."

Facial hair was defended and disparaged. Ears might lie close to the head or jut out adorably. Stature might be tall or average, but not squat; bodies hard or cuddly, but never bony or fat. Some favored the depressed navel, others a nicely rounded bump.

Eventually, after some initial embarrassment, a spirited discussion about cocks arose, and there was such disagreement about size and proportion—even color—that Mistress Annie finally put an end to the bickering by declaring, "Just as long as he's got one," which pretty much summed it up.

"No nose hair," Mistress Gilly declared.

"All his teeth, or most of them anyway."

"Warm feet."

"A long tongue," said Lady Clarice with a sigh.

"I don't see what the length of his tongue has to do with anything," Lady Sybille observed.

"You would be surprised," said Lady Agnes.

"Oh. I don't think I have ever seen Frederick's tongue. I must ask him to show it to me. I hope it is not too short."

Mistress Gilly sniggered. "For your sake, so do I."

Megge, who had been trying to coax a needed burp from Lady Mary Annabel and had contributed little to the discussion up to that point, introduced the thorny subject of the character of the perfect husband. "As I am unwed, I shall leave it to rest of you to enlighten me."

"Decisive without being overbearing."

"He must make me feel safe."

"Never raise a hand to me or my children."

"Temperate in his habits."

"Kind."

"Courteous."

"Faithful."

"Romantic."

Megge laughed. "A pretty word, Sybille, but what do you mean by it?"

"Oh, that's easy," Lady Sybille declared. "It was all written down by Master Capellanus at Queen Eleanor's Court of Love at Poitiers. Let me see:

"A lover turns pale in the presence of his beloved.

"When a lover suddenly catches sight of his beloved his heart beats fast.

"A man in love is always apprehensive.

"He whom the thought of love vexes eats and sleeps very little.

"A true lover considers nothing good except what he thinks will please his beloved, and

"A true lover is constantly and without intermission possessed by the thought of his beloved.

"That," she concluded with a flourish, "is what I mean by 'romantic.'"

"Sybille," said Lady Belinda, "we are talking here about husbands, not lovers."

"But it is the same thing, Belinda."

"It most certainly is not."

Clouds of confusion gathered in Lady Sybille's wide sky-blue eyes. "Is Frederick not my lover?"

"Of course he is," Megge interjected hastily before the older, worldlier women inadvertently trampled the girl's touching faith in the precepts of courtly love, though she could not have said why, exactly. Perhaps she had not entirely let go her girlish dreams after all.

"You surprise me, Megge," commented Lady Joan. "I thought you the most unsentimental and practical of us all. I have never heard you speak of love before."

Megge settled Mary Annabel against her shoulder and paced slowly about the room, patting her on the back that she might expel the gas from her tiny stomach. "I am not speaking of it now, Joan," she replied. "Master Capellanus does not write of love, although that is the word he uses; he writes of desire. This lover of his seems to me to be enjoying his discomfiture rather more than he should, and will consider it a price well paid when he finally embraces the object of his affections. One must wonder exactly whom it is he loves—his lady or himself.

"However," she added hastily catching sight of Lady Sybille's crestfallen look, "there may be very real affection on his part, and I am sure that there are marriages in which a man may be an affectionate lover as well as a husband. If Sybille believes she has been blessed with such a marriage, it is not for us to attempt to persuade her otherwise."

"Megge is quite right," Lady Orabella declared. "I considered myself so blessed, even if Humphrey is not exactly in the way of Master Capellanus's ideal. I am not sure I should like him quite so well if he were. A woman may consider herself fortunate if the husband chosen for her treats her with respect and meets his obligations to her and her children. If on occasion he can act the part of a lover, she is more fortunate still. But I believe that there is the woman who cannot and will not settle for less than true love, no matter how conscientious and affectionate her husband may prove to be."

"Well, good luck to her in finding such a man,"

said Lady Belinda, who had certainly not found one in her Charles.

"Perhaps you will find true love with this lord the king has selected for you, Megge," Lady Sybille chirped. "Do you think so?"

Megge laughed. "If such a thing exists at all, I am certain it would be the last place I would find it."

Lady Mary Annabel apparently agreed, as she clearly demonstrated by spitting up all over Megge's freshly laundered linen bliaut and dismissing the whole sorry subject by falling fast asleep.

Nor would Master Capellanus have considered Sir Olyver an exemplar of the ideal lover as he went about his business that day.

He retained his healthy complexion when he delivered the news to Megge that Edward would hold at Exeter, as the roads were impassable after the storm. His heart continued to beat strong and steady. As he was never apprehensive, even in the midst of battle, he could regard Megge with his usual composure. He had slept very well indeed and eaten heartily.

He could not, however, ignore the constant tightness in his groin when he thought about the passionate woman shuddering beneath him and the feel of her arms tight about his neck and her legs about his waist as she arched up against him and brought him to his explosive climax.

Nor the black moment when she should discover that she had gifted her virginity to her unknown betrothed, and thus deprived herself of the ultimate weapon in a woman's arsenal: her own ruin.

Chapter Thirty-Two

Edward of England, known as Longshanks on account of his impressive height and long legs, was a man of many parts, most of them so contradictory and perplexing that even his closest advisors were in a state of constant apprehension as to his probable reaction to a given circumstance. He was by turns forgiving and vindictive, flexible and obstinate, deeply religious and blasphemous, frugal and extravagant, unpretentious and insanely jealous of his royal dignity.

Fate had bestowed upon him the perfect mate in Eleanor of Castile, whom he had married when they were barely more than children, and would worship to his dying day. She alone provided the steadying influence that made of him by far the most effective King of England since the brilliant and contentious second Henry.

Edward had taken the cross in 1270 and departed Dover for the Holy Land to resurrect the faded glory of crusades past, to no effect whatsoever, as it turned out. He only returned to England the previous year to take the throne left vacant by the unlamented passing of his father, the third Henry.

As he was now deeply embroiled in another crusade closer to home—to bring the Welsh and Scots to heel—it had surprised everyone save his wife that he would quit London and make the long uncomfortable journey in the heat and humidity of high summer to the southwestern corner of his kingdom. It would have been no great matter to deal with the peculiar goings-on at Castle Rising simply by issuing a royal decree or by summoning the parties to London and reading them the royal riot act.

Edward's failings were many, but he was a good and loyal friend to those whom he loved and who served him well. That his old friend Lord Humphrey and Sir Olyver were players in this engaging little farce was more than sufficient incentive to lure him from the comforts and cares of Westminster.

And then there was his Megge, the bewildered little orphan with her startling blue eyes, keen mind, and mischievous ways, who had understood her duty and accepted with commendable dignity four betrothals and three marriages, though Edward knew it grieved her sorely. He loved her as a daughter and would see her settled once and for all with a man who would suit in every respect, though she might not believe it at first and would have to be dragged kicking and screaming to the altar.

His dear Eleanor had, in her gentle way, managed to sooth his initial displeasure and ruffled feathers upon receiving Megge's letter. He could scarcely believe his eyes when he read that she had taken possession of Castle Rising and was, in effect, attempting to extort concessions from Humphrey in order to take control of her fortune. Worse, she was making demands—worded ever so courteously, so cunningly, so very reasonably—of *him*, the King of England!

As if that wasn't vexatious enough, somehow she and a passel of equally misguided females had routed an entire garrison, scared them witless with some flumadiddle about fairies and derricks, and held their men folk to ransom by withholding their sexual favors.

It was all vastly entertaining and utterly fascinating.

Finally, there was Sir Walter, a snake in the grass if ever there was one. He posed no real danger to the Crown and Edward's ascendancy, not in the way of Simon de Montfort and his rebel barons eleven years earlier, but Edward disliked and distrusted him. He was forever skulking about looking for the main chance, hatching harebrained schemes, luring him into disastrous financial ventures such as the fiasco with those incestuous pox-ridden Milanese bankers.

Edward had arranged two advantageous marriages for Walter. Both wives had died young; if not as the result of direct abuse, then from emotional neglect and a perfectly understandable desire to remove themselves as far as possible from his unpleasant company.

Yes, the king thought as Bishop Odo droned on and on beside him at the high table of the bishop's palace at Exeter, a sojourn at Castle Rising would be an entertaining respite from the dreary affairs of state. Not to mention the fact that the fields and forests round about Castle Rising boasted some of the best hunting and hawking to be found in the kingdom.

"So you must see, Your Majesty," Odo concluded at

last, "that it is God Himself who commands us to undertake another crusade."

Edward had stopped listening to the bishop's harangue at least twenty minutes earlier. He had spent the time contemplating the excellent fare that might be expected at Castle Rising, with its ample supply of deep-water fish and abundant fresh game.

He tapped his long fingers upon the white linen cloth, and considered his reply. "Since you express yourself with such passion, Your Excellency, I expect you will want to be the first to demonstrate your own commitment with a generous contribution to the cause."

Bishop Odo nearly swallowed a fly that had been enjoying a leisurely meal in his bread trencher while he ranted on about accursed infidels, greedy Jews, lascivious women, nefarious gypsies, the arrogant French, the combative Welsh, the belligerent Scots, the primitive Irish, his shiftless tenants, his thieving servants, his spendthrift mistress, and his good-for-nothing-children. "As to that, sire, I will of course do what I can with the meager resources at my disposal," he allowed. "But now that I think on it, would it not be the nobler course to raise the funds by increasing taxes, tariffs, and tolls? Your subjects will rejoice at the opportunity to further so noble an undertaking."

"My subjects will hang me by the ballocks from Blackfriars' Bridge," Edward replied.

"Double the annual levy of service from your vassals?" the bishop ventured.

"And have another de Montfort at my throat?"

"Surely Her Majesty brought a substantial dowry . . . Er, perhaps not," Odo concluded hastily as the king stood abruptly, threw down his napkin, and strode from the hall.

"The Church must have some breeding program where they nurture these fools and hypocrites," he commented to his squire as he rode out to see for himself the condition of the roads. His baggage wagons would surely bog down in the mud, but there was no reason he could not ride on ahead to Castle Rising.

"Arrange for a messenger to ride to Lord Humphrey at the siege camp at Little Rising. We shall pen a letter informing him that we ride immediately. Then have the man continue on to the castle, where he will deliver our letter informing Lady Margaret to expect us. She need only prepare to receive us and six of our retainers. The rest of our entourage will set up camp nearby.

"By God, if I have to spend one more day in this provincial backwater eating swill unfit for swine and listening to that quacksalver I shall go mad."

Sir Walter stroked his chin, furrowed his brow, and worried the soft flesh on the inside of his left cheek with his teeth. For the first time since the brothers Alfieri departed this life for the warmer climes of eternal damnation, he might hold the advantage in his single-minded pursuit of Megge and her fortune. The problem he now faced was what to do with it.

By an amazing stroke of luck, one of his men had chanced upon the unconscious body of a man outfitted in the king's colors, who had somehow become unhorsed and knocked himself senseless when he struck the ground. In the saddlebag of his mount, which was grazing contentedly nearby, Walter's man discovered two letters bearing Edward's seal. He took a few minutes to rummage through the messenger's belongings in search of coin and to help himself to some wine from a leather flask before carrying his treasure back to Sir Walter.

Both letters were scrawled in Edward's hand and eschewed the usual formalities and flourishes.

Megge:
I come in two days' time with an entourage of six. You will hear me out and, I trust, realize that I have only your best interests at heart. You will no doubt recall that I am particularly fond of raw oysters in a cold yellow sauce of ginger and saffron.

Edward Rex

My friend:
Odo is an ass, and I will sleep in a ditch before I spend another night beneath his roof. I ride to Ermington. You may expect me in two days' time. Be warned, Humphrey: Walter will soon be sneaking about, if he isn't already, and up to his usual tricks. The man must be God's own fool to think I will tolerate any more of his nonsense, not to mention the wrath Olyver will visit upon him if he lays so much as a finger on his future wife.

Edward Rex

Shaking with rage, frustrated ambition, and humiliation, Sir Walter hurled his cup into the fire.

Olyver of Mannyngs had somehow weaseled his way into Edward's good graces and snagged the most sought-after heiress in the kingdom! That nobody. That upstart. That runt. A fifth son of no account, no better than a marauding mercenary, was to command one of the great fortunes in Christendom. Hold court in the great hall of one of the most magnificent castles ever built. Enjoy the privileged friendship and protection of his sovereign. Lie with Margaret de Languetot.

"God's own fool," Edward had called him.

Perhaps he was, thought Sir Walter, but as a fool has nothing to lose, he at least in the end might have the last laugh.

Chapter Thirty-Three

Edward might be every inch a king, but he took his rest like any other man. He snorted like a dyspeptic boar when he inhaled and wheezed like a dying donkey when he exhaled. He drooled, he grunted, he smacked his lips. He rolled this way and that, sprawled out on his back, flipped over onto his stomach. He muttered and moaned.

Ever conscious of his regal image, Edward would not have been pleased to learn that for the past half hour eight pairs of eyes had been following his every tic and turn. He might have slept on oblivious had not a delicate little cough alerted him to the presence of an intruder. His personal servant would never presume to enter the royal bedchamber without first tapping out a prearranged signal, lest the king seize the dagger he kept beneath his pillow and stab the poor man to the heart.

Feigning restless sleep, the king grasped the hilt of his dagger, rolled off the high bed, and crouched in a fighting stance.

Eight pairs of eyes widened at the fierceness of his visage; gawked at the wicked length of his blade; dropped to—and fastened on—the impressive display of the royal privities.

"Ladies," Lady Orabella ordered with extraordinary presence of mind, "close your eyes."

Two pairs of eyes snapped shut. Three narrowed to tiny slits. Three rolled back in their sockets as their owners crashed to the floor.

"God's ballocks," shouted the king—an appropriately worded expression of incredulity under the circumstances—as he gaped at the eight women arrayed in a semicircle around his bed.

A giantess in a soiled apron commanded the left flank. Crumpled on the floor at her feet lay a young girl, and beside her a lovely young woman with gently rounded belly and creamy skin, and another, monstrously pregnant, and not nearly so well favored. Seated as though in the place of honor was a pale, plump woman. Standing at her side was an elegantly attired, hawk-nosed woman, and next to her a sturdy square-jawed woman. At the right flank, like a matching bookend, loomed yet another giantess.

Given the fact that he was stark naked, it did not occur to the king to take offense that the five who were still conscious failed to pay him proper deference. Nothing in the canon of court etiquette could possibly pertain.

The door flew open. Edward's guards rushed in to lay down their lives for their sovereign.

"Out!"

Edward's guards staged a strategic retreat. The door slammed shut.

Silence.

"You are peeking, madam."

Gunny One bristled. "Am not. Your Majesty."

"And you, madam."

Lady Agnes sniffed her sniff.

"Perhaps you should assist your fallen comrades," Edward suggested.

"Won't do any good, you standing there with your parts blowing in the wind," Gunny One observed.

"How would you know I am still standing here with my parts blowing in the wind, madam, if you are not peeking?"

Lady Orabella, who was definitely not peeking, shifted in her chair. "Gunny, dear, I expect His Majesty is referring to Missy, Sybille, and possibly Clarice as well. Would you be so kind as to bring them round and fetch something for them to sit on? I am particularly concerned for Clarice."

"As well you should be, Lady Orabella," the king remarked. "We should not be of much use should she give birth on the floor of our bedchamber."

"If you would be so kind, Your Majesty, as to don some clothing, we can see everyone settled comfortably, conduct our business with you, and leave you in peace."

When a degree of normality had been restored to the scene, Edward seated himself in a high-backed chair and surveyed the odd little group before him. "I know you, of course, Lady Orabella, and you Lady Agnes. Who else do we have the honor to receive?"

"Gunnilda, sire."

"Gunreda, sire."

"Mistress Gilly, Your Majesty."

"Lady Sybille, wife of Sir Frederick of Wendover, sire."

"Lady Clarice, wife of Sir Gaston of Rigaud, Your Majesty."

"M-mm-mmm-mmmm-issy, your worship."

"Well, Lady Orabella, what is this business you wish to conduct with us?"

Lady Orabella folded her hands in her lap and took a deep breath. "It concerns Megge, sire. We come to you in the hope that you will hear our petition on her behalf."

"Does she know of this petition?"

"She does not."

"Proceed."

Lady Orabella paused to collect her thoughts. "We are the devoted friends and faithful servants of a resourceful, caring young woman who has given us the courage and the opportunity to demand a say in matters that most closely concern us. We are each and every one of us the better for her vision and forever in her debt, and we wish her happy."

Lady Orabella cleared her throat. "We understand that you wish her to marry yet again and may be considering my husband's brother, Sir Walter. Although we would not think of questioning your judgment, we should like to voice our objection to such a match."

"Hmmm. Have you some other candidate in mind?"

"No, sire, but we have drawn up a list of qualifications based on Megge's own stated preferences and our observations of what might give her the greatest chance of happiness."

Edward settled back in his chair. "This should be interesting."

Encouraged by the king's willingness to hear them

out, Lady Orabella drew a paper from a cleverly concealed pocket in the wide sleeve of her gown. "We have established three categories: Appearance, character, and suitability. Appearance because a woman wants to spend her life with a man who is not repugnant to her."

"Understandably."

"Character because she wants to respect him."

"We should hope so."

"And suitability because we are not unaware of her high station in life and the complexities of familial and political alliance."

"We presume Sir Walter does not meet these criteria."

"He does not," replied Lady Orabella.

A knock sounded at the door.

"Enter."

A servant bowed his way into the chamber. "Lady Margaret is below, sire, and asks if you will be free to receive her when she returns from her meeting with Sir Olyver." If he thought it odd that the king should be holding council with a group of women in his bedchamber he gave no hint of it.

"We will. You may go."

"Very good, sire."

"Lady Orabella, describe for us the perfect husband for Megge. Let us begin with his appearance."

"He must be tall, well-formed, and in good health," she began. "His hair will be fair, his eyes gray."

"Excuse me, Orabella, but Megge likes blue eyes," Lady Sybille interjected.

"Gray," Mistress Gilly declared. "She prefers gray."

"Blue, definitely blue."

261

"Gray."

"Let us say a bluish-gray or a grayish-blue," Edward suggested.

"Thank you, my lord," said Lady Orabella. "She does not like a pug nose, a low brow, a weak chin, or thin lips."

Edward steepled his fingers and nodded. "A strong, sculptured face, decisive mouth."

"She finds a strong, hard body particularly attractive."

"Does she indeed?"

"Elegance—though not of the foppish sort—and economy of motion."

"What about his, his, you know . . . ?" Missy blurted out. "I asked her but she wouldn't say."

"I should hope not," Lady Clarice exclaimed.

"But Long Ida thinks it's really important," Missy insisted. "She says—"

"Missy," Lady Orabella said grimly, "His Majesty is not interested in our views on that particular attribute."

"On the contrary," Edward murmured, "we are most curious."

Lady Orabella affected not to have heard the king's remark and quickly moved along to matters of character and suitability.

"Allow us to sum up the man you would have us find for Megge," Edward said when she had finished.

"He will be tall and extremely strong and—how shall I put it?—appropriately virile. A warrior or soldier, perhaps. He will have gray/blue eyes and long golden hair, but need not be handsome in the usual way. He will always hold his honor high and must command respect. He will be intelligent, perceptive, and shrewd. His station in life must be equal to her own, though his circumstances may not be. He must enjoy our friendship and esteem. He must agree to the joint administration of their estates and affairs. He will accord her the same respect she accords him. Have we painted a fair picture of the man, Lady Orabella?"

"I believe so, Your Majesty. If you have settled on Sir Walter, I beg you to reconsider. Megge deserves better."

The king smiled. "So she does."

"She asks only to be consulted in the matter. Always in the past she has bowed to your wishes. Will you not hear her out?"

"We will think on it. Now, as we have not yet bathed or broken our fast, you must excuse us."

"Thank you, Your Majesty."

"You there—Mistress Gunnilda, is it?—might you be the cook?"

"That I am, Your Majesty.

"We are particularly fond of raw oysters in a cold yellow sauce of ginger and saffron."

"Are you, now?"

"We are."

When the door closed behind the women, the king of England threw back his head laughed.

Chapter Thirty-Four

Sir Walter finished lacing his breeches and tossed a coin to the woman. She reeked of fish entrails, and he'd seen better skin on a plucked chicken, but she'd served the purpose. Besides, he hadn't had much choice. Megge had seen to that by bringing any woman a man might find even remotely tolerable behind the safety of the castle walls; and the Runt—for so he now thought of Olyver—had actually set patrols to ensure that those who remained in the village would not be accosted. Walter had been forced to ride several miles along the coast until he found an outlet for his lust, and his rage.

Just the memory of his meeting with Humphrey had him shaking in the saddle as he rode back toward Little Rising. He might have been ten again, and Humphrey a cocksure twelve, being chastised and bullied by an older brother who swaggered and strutted his consequence as the firstborn son and heir.

Although the braggart had become the buffoon, Walter had that morning been forced to sit through an interminable discourse on personal honor, family honor, duty, accountability, loyalty, morality, and common sense. Humphrey would be speaking with Edward, who had arrived unexpectedly the night before and was staying at the castle, about the incident in the cavern on the beach, and although Humphrey was satisfied that Megge had not been harmed—she had assured him she had accompanied Walter of her own free will—he could not help but suspect that Walter had been bent on compromising her. Edward would not be pleased to hear it.

"Tell me, brother," Sir Walter said when Humphrey's tirade had finally wound down, "what do you think Megge will say when she learns that Olyver is Edward's choice, and I presume, yours, since the king would not have settled on a fifth son without your intervention on his behalf?"

The earl regarded his smirking brother with narrowed eyes. "How come you to know that Olyver is Edward's choice?"

Sir Walter shrugged. "Oh, I don't *know*, of course, but it is not so very difficult to surmise. Why else would the great warrior waste his time on this foolishness, save there are spoils to be had?"

"Loyalty." Lord Humphrey snapped, "Something you appear to know nothing about. He is my man."

Sir Walter laughed. "You really are a fool, Humphrey. Olyver is nobody's man but his own."

"No, Walter, it is you who are the fool," Lord Humphrey shot back. "Do you think Edward will tolerate your nonsense here at Castle Rising? He has been more than patient with you over the years, with your fawning and scheming—yes, I know all about the Lombard bank fiasco—and it would not surprise me if he takes the lands I settled on you and banishes you from England."

Humphrey was right about one thing, Walter thought as he allowed his mount to drink at the Lis, Edward was just petty enough to do it. He might end up just another landless knight forced to sell his arm to whatever rampaging nobleman had need of men at the moment, and win for ransom what horse and arms he could in the tournament.

All because he was a second son. Had he been his father's heir he would have succeeded to the title, made his home in Flete Castle, had his pick of eligible wives. He would not have had to accept Humphrey's largesse and dance attendance on old King Henry and Edward. He would have been his own man.

As Sir Walter trotted on toward the paddock he happened to notice two men wearing Sir Olyver's colors on the far bank. They were seated out of the wind in a sheltered angle of the cliff at the base of an enormous rock fall. They appeared to be playing some dice game and to have settled in for the duration.

Why, he wondered, would Olyver station men there? He scrutinized the rock fall. If there was some way into the castle mount in the cliff he couldn't see it, but that didn't mean it wasn't there. Olyver must have discovered it and set a guard.

Walter smiled. As an exit is also an entrance, he might as well indulge in a bit of petty vengeance of his own before he lost all.

Chapter Thirty-Five

Megge stood with hands on hips in the middle of the great hall. Something odd was going on. What had begun as a search for Clarice to escort her to her meeting with her husband had unaccountably widened to one for Orabella, Agnes, Sybille, and both Gunnys. Even Missy, who usually trailed after her like a second shadow, was nowhere to be found. It was particularly vexing, as Sir Gaston had twice failed to appear for his appointment with Clarice, and Sir Olyver would probably be prodding him up the castle mount at the point of his sword at this very moment.

The venue for individual negotiations had been moved, as one could not expect the king of England to come and go through a postern door or the stable yard. The castle's main gate had been raised and the huge doors fastened back.

A strange siege, indeed, was Megge's ironic thought as she went in search of her shawl, which Missy had laid out on her bed with her usual meticulous care. There was Lord Humphrey whistling his way in and out each morning for his daily visit with Lady Orabella and the babes; the defending garrison blowing kisses from the walls; and the commander of the siege army lying with his counterpart.

Then the king of England had unexpectedly breezed in late the night before, greeted his refractory subject with a warm embrace and a fatherly pat upon the head, and taken himself off to bed. He had uttered not a single word of anger or reproach for having been dragged all the way to Devon to settle so trivial a matter when he had Welshmen and Scots to grind beneath his heel.

An observer might very well be to tempted to think this an entertainment of some sort, since the players seemed to be enjoying themselves entirely too much for the matter to be of any real consequence.

Under far different circumstances, were she that observer, Megge, too, would have found the whole thing amusing, if somewhat improbable. But she was not an observer. She was the chief player, and it had been her vision that persuaded these women to stand up for themselves, her ingenuity that had engineered this bold undertaking, and her serious responsibility to see that what had been promised was not only possible but accomplished. *That* was a matter of very real consequence.

And so it seemed it would be—for every woman but Megge herself. Nothing had been resolved yet, and the king's arrival to deal with the matter of her betrothal in person only emphasized that in the end he controlled her future as he always had and always would. At least Edward had dismissed Sir Walter's suit, but he had already chosen another, so her petition to be consulted had come too late. She could refuse, of course, as was her right as a widow, but as Sir Olyver had pointed out, Edward would have no difficulty getting round the provisions of the Great Charter.

As for her argument that a woman should have the right, if she so chose, to retain control of her own fortune within the bonds of matrimony or at least administer it jointly with her lord, she had only principle upon which to argue the point. Principle rarely stood against presumed privilege, especially when it was a woman who professed the principle and a man the privilege. She could but try, and she would begin when she met with the king in a few hours' time.

"My lady," someone called as she made her way over the drawbridge that spanned the deep dry moat toward the postern door in the north curtain wall. Little Robert from the stable yard trotted toward her.

"Yes, Robert?"

"I have a message for you, my lady. From the man."

"A message from a man? What man?"

"The man who gave me a penny, my lady. I never had a penny before."

"Did you recognize him? Might it have been Sir Olyver?"

"It wasn't the devil man, my lady. It was the other one."

"The other one? You mean Sir Walter?"

"Yes, my lady. He gave me a penny. He said I was to find you and give you this." Robert handed her a sealed note begrimed by small fingerprints.

"Thank you, Robert. You may go."

"My lady?"

"Yes, Robert?"

"Does Sir Olyver really eat little children and spit out their bones?"

Megge stuffed the letter into her pocket, anxious to be on her way. "He most certainly does not."

Robert frowned. "Is he a runt?"

"I don't understand."

"A runt is a weak little dog that nobody wants. Sometimes the bitch kills it, or it just dies because it's so puny."

"I know that, but what has it to do with Sir Olyver?"

"The man kept calling Sir Olyver a runt. He says he's going to teach the runt a lesson."

Megge could wait no longer. "I shouldn't worry about it, Robert. Off you go now, and thank you."

But she would worry. Walter was planning some treachery against Olyver, and it would be up to her to discover it. If he wished to meet with her again, which was the likely reason for the note, she must go. She had no time to read it now however as the hour had arrived for Sir Gaston to meet with his wife, and she would have to stall him until Clarice reappeared from wherever she had gotten to.

"Welcome, Sir Gaston," Megge said. "I am so pleased to see you here this morning. Clarice has been delayed, but she will be with you shortly."

For his part, Sir Gaston did not appear to be at all pleased to be there. Flanked on one side by a stern-faced Father Boniface and on the other by Sir Olyver, he sought to retain some shred of dignity by striking a righteous pose. He informed Megge that he and his wife were in perfect accord in all things, that he resented wasting his valuable time on such nonsense, and that he would so inform His Majesty at the earliest opportunity.

The opportunity to do so presented itself while he was still in the full throes of his indignation when the king himself strolled into view, arm in arm with Lady Clarice. "Ah, Sir Gaston, we see you have decided to hear your lady out at last. Excellent, excellent. You must be most grateful to Lady Margaret for affording you the opportunity to work out any little difficulties you and this charming lady at our side might have."

Sir Gaston was not in the least grateful, but he was no fool, either. "Aye, sire, that I am."

"We shall leave you to it then. Megge, my dear, we shall talk this evening. Meanwhile, it is a splendid day and we are off to hunt."

Laughing to himself, the king headed off in the direction of the stable yard. Father Boniface stationed himself within hailing distance should his assistance be required, his Bible, now heavily earmarked for every contingency, at the ready. Sir Olyver bowed to Megge and was gone.

Megge settled onto a bench out of the high summer sun but within sight of the postern door should Clarice have need of her. She pulled Sir Walter's note from her pocket.

Megge, I beg one last word with you. I cannot in good conscience allow you to continue in ignorance of your fate and the base betrayal that has been perpetrated upon you. Hear me so that I may leave Castle Rising with a clear conscience and some assurance that I have redeemed myself in your eyes. Time is of the essence; I must

speak with you before you meet with the king.
Send word by the stable boy.
I am, as ever, your humble servant.

Walter

Betrayal. What could Walter mean by it? Likely he sought to enlist her help in whatever mischief he planned for Sir Olyver and incite her curiosity to achieve his purpose. Still, a feeling of deep unease came over her, a suspicion that she had allowed some vital element of this business to escape her notice. She must be on her guard when she met with Sir Olyver and Lord Humphrey in an hour's time. If there were secrets, they lay with the two men who had conducted the siege of her castle with such nonchalance and easy accommodation. And if there was blame to be found it lay squarely with her, that she had allowed her instincts to be blunted by her fondness for one and her desire for the other.

No, she corrected herself as she set off down the road to the tent by the river: her love for the other.

Chapter Thirty-Six

Megge prided herself on having perfected at court the studied deportment and serene countenance necessary to maintain control in even the most awkward social situation. Nothing, however, could possibly equal the discomfiture of revisiting for the first time the place where two nights earlier she had come apart in Olyver's arms and watched with awe as he abandoned himself to his own wild release.

She managed to hide the faint blush that tinged her cheeks and be sure of her dignity, however, by sinking into a graceful curtsy and holding it somewhat longer than was absolutely necessary. By the time Lord Humphrey assisted her to her feet and they had exchanged the usual greetings, Megge felt firmly in control of herself and could look at Sir Olyver with a fair degree of equanimity.

He did not look in the least discomfited and regarded her in his usual attentive but noncommittal way. If their passionate time together held any special meaning for him, he showed no hint of it, nor had he during their two brief encounters since that night. Somehow his cool indifference made her ashamed of her own feelings toward him, and she resolved to set them aside, see this business concluded, and put him from her memory—and her heart—forever.

"Lady Margaret," began Sir Olyver, "I have as promised conveyed your proposal to Lord Humphrey that he honor the provisions of the Great Charter and restore your fortune and estates to your sole care and management. I have also apprised him of your offer to compensate him for his honorable administration of your properties while in his care and his kindness to you as your guardian. Since these matters lie between you and him, I will, if you wish, withdraw and leave you to speak in private."

"Nonsense, Olyver," said Lord Humphrey. "Megge and I should be glad of your good sense and counsel. There need be no secrets among us. Is that not so, Megge?"

Oh, but there were secrets, Megge thought. She would tread carefully. "Of course, my lord. I am certain Sir Olyver will continue to play an important and impartial role in these negotiations."

She smiled at Sir Olyver. "If you will allow me to correct you, sir, it was not so much in the way of a proposal as it was a demand. One does not negotiate a demand."

Sir Olyver regarded her thoughtfully. Apparently she continued to perceive him as an adversary despite their passionate encounter. Could he have misheard the words of love she had uttered over and over as she rode the rapture beneath him? Mistaken the shyly lowered eyes whenever they had come face to face since that night, the fleeting blush when she entered the tent? No, he had not. All the more reason, then, to sit back and take her measure.

"Of course, my lady. I misspoke."

Lord Humphrey cleared his throat. "Now, Megge, I am sure you know I bear you no grudge for inciting the women of my keep to this rash undertaking. I will even go so far as to say that some good may have come of it. And I am touched by your offer of access to your forest preserves and a half share in the revenues while I live and a smaller portion for my heirs. Unfortunately, I cannot accept compensation for something I cannot do."

"Cannot or will not, my lord?" Megge inquired.

"Both, my dear, and some of it I'm afraid I cannot explain at the moment. You will learn of it soon enough and you will understand."

Megge managed to still her anger. Secrets. "I see."

Sir Olyver shifted in his chair. "Perhaps, Humphrey, you can share with Lady Margaret your communication with the king regarding your brother."

Lord Humphrey perked up. "Ah yes, Walter. Well, you see, Megge, I did write to His Majesty regarding Walter's suit as soon as I learned of it."

"In support of it, I understand," said Megge. "You must have been disappointed to hear that he had chosen another."

Lord Humphrey's brows went up. "Where did you come by such an idea? Of course I did not support it. I begged him to dismiss it forthwith. Do you think I would countenance such a union, see you disparaged, your family name dishonored? Do you believe I care so little for you that I would see you forced to live with such a man?"

Megge stared down at her folded hands. Orabella had said almost the exact same words, and she was ashamed that she could be so blinded by her own interpretation of events, her own fear, that she had indeed thought this good man capable of such a thing.

"I am sorry, my lord. Pray forgive me."

The earl reached across the table and patted her hand. "There is nothing to forgive, my dear. It cannot be easy for you, this marriage business."

"It is not. Perhaps if you will tell me the name of the man Edward has chosen for me I will be better able to understand what lies in store for me and make my plans accordingly." Megge had no real expectation that Lord Humphrey would vouchsafe the information, but it was worth a try.

"I think it better that Edward himself," Lord Humphrey began, then broke off as he stared at Megge in horror. "Make plans? Surely you do not intend to disobey the king? He will have you in a convent and your fortune in his pocket before another day dawns."

"If His Majesty has settled upon a man I feel I cannot live with, I will certainly object, although I expect it will avail me little," Megge replied. "More important will be the man himself, whether he be open to my requirement that either I retain control of my fortune or that we share jointly in the administration of our estates. If he cannot see his way to it, then I will not have him."

Lord Humphrey mopped at his brow. "Good God, girl, what can you be thinking? Such a thing is unheard of. You will not find such a man in all Christendom. Will she, Olyver? Tell her."

Megge waited to hear what the great warrior would have to say on the matter. "Yes, my lord, pray do tell me."

Sir Olyver wondered at her tone of voice. It was no mere curiosity that prompted her interest in his answer. There was something of anger in it, suspicion, and an emotion he could not put a name to.

"Lord Humphrey is likely correct, my lady."

"There, you see, Megge! Olyver agrees."

Megge waited. Sir Olyver had more to say.

"However," Sir Olyver said with grave deliberation, "if Lady Margaret should be so fortunate as to find in Edward's choice a man whose love for her is greater than his own self-interest, she could have no possible reason to refuse him. Save some perversity in her nature," he added after a moment of reflection, "that she chooses neither to love nor be loved. In that case, it would be better if he did not love her but nevertheless bowed to her wishes. Therein would lie the perfect resolution, would it not, my lady?"

Megge looked at him steadily and did not reply. For some strange reason of his own, he wished to provoke her and she would not give him the satisfaction of knowing just how deep the cut had gone. Straight to her heart.

"Good heavens, Olyver," Lord Humphrey cried. "Have we not enough complication here without bringing love into it? Now, Megge, my dear, I fear we must leave the whole matter of restoring your fortune to you until you have spoken with the king. In any event, you must realize that I cannot sanction such an arrangement, as Edward would have to give his consent. But let me assure you, you can have no objection to the man he has chosen for you. In fact, you will be very pleased indeed. You can ask for none better. Can she, Olyver?"

Sir Olyver did not reply. He was watching Megge as she rose from her chair, adjusted her shawl, and prepared to depart.

"I thank you, gentlemen, for your time and courtesy. Lord Humphrey, you have my assurance that I shall always hold you in the greatest respect and thank God that you and Lady Orabella took me into your home. Sir Olyver, you have proved yourself a most capable intermediary, and I wish you every success in your future endeavors. Now, I beg you will excuse me as I have another engagement. Good day."

Lord Humphrey settled back in his chair. "Well, that didn't go too badly. Megge is a good sensible girl. And it's true, you know, she will be pleased when she learns you are to be her husband. She has feelings for you, Olyver, mark my words. I noticed a distinct blush upon her cheek when she arrived. You will bring her round in the end."

He would, thought Sir Olyver grimly, if he had to die to see it done, in which case Megge would once again find herself a widow, and the play would have to go on without him. Since he had no intention of making an untimely exit, he set his mind to the thorny problem of how a man might convince a woman that she is in love with him.

It did not occur to him that perhaps the first step would be to convince her that he is in love with her.

Chapter Thirty-Seven

"He's here, my lady."

Megge, who had been waiting for some minutes by the stable yard gate for Sir Walter to arrive, frowned down at Robert. "Who is here?"

"The man. He gave me another penny," Robert reported with a wide grin. "Now I got two pennies. He said as I should take you to him."

Not wishing to waste time questioning the child, Megge followed quickly. He trotted past the blacksmith's forge and the feed sheds, over the wide swath of beaten earth that constituted the outer bailey and across the drawbridge into the inner bailey. There he turned left and led her through a labyrinth of low-ceilinged guards' rooms in the inner wall to the very chamber that concealed the hidden stairway that led to the cavern below.

"He's in there, my lady."

"Thank you. And Robert, you shall have two more pennies if you promise me you will not mention my meeting with Sir Walter to anyone."

Robert's big brown eyes went wide. "Two more?"

"Three."

"*Three?* Then I'll have . . . I'll have . . ."

"Five. You will have five pennies, Robert."

The boy looked at her in awe. "Oh yes, my lady, I'll tell no one, I promise on my grandpa's grave."

"Good. Now off you go."

Megge paced around the small chamber trying to collect her thoughts before she knocked at the storage room door. It could be no accident that Sir Walter had chosen that room for their meeting. He must have discovered the entrance in the cliff face and made his way through the cavern to this spot.

Had he plans to abduct her, perhaps hold her for ransom? Or worse? Somehow Megge could not imagine him resorting to the ultimate solution to his problem, taking her by force and so compelling the king to sanction a marriage between them. Walter might be many things, but he was not a rapist. Or a fool. He could have no doubt that the king would slice his head from his body with his own sword should he attempt such a despicable thing.

Strangely enough, Megge felt a measure of pity for Sir Walter. He was not at all an agreeable man, but behind all the toadying and posturing and scheming, there dwelled an unhappy, embittered man who believed a mere twist of fate had denied him what rightly should have been his.

The door of the storeroom swung open. "Ah, Megge, I thought I heard you out here. Thank you for agreeing to see me. You cannot know how much it means to me. Come in, come in." Sir Walter pointed to an upended barrel where she should sit, and settled down on his own opposite her. He had arranged a little table between them with two wooden cups and a leather wine flask. A vertical arrow slit in the wall admitted just enough light to see by, though it did little to lessen the oppressive gloom of the place.

Megge did not wish to prolong this meeting a moment more than necessary. "What is this important matter you wish to discuss with me?"

Sir Walter poured a rich purple wine into her cup and handed it to her. "First, let us drink a toast, Megge." He raised his cup. "To our friendship, my lady. May you remember me with some kindness for the service I do you this day."

Walter was up to some terrible mischief, Megge realized. He could not entirely disguise the venom in his voice. "To friendship," she murmured and took a tiny sip. "Now, what is this service you wish to render me?"

Sir Walter set down his cup and assumed a grave countenance. "It is never easy to be the bearer of ill tidings, my dear. I should not do so now but for the sake of my conscience and my concern for your future happiness. I am now in possession of certain information that has been withheld from you concerning your new lord, not only his name but the devious way he has been introduced into your life without your knowing of it."

Megge blinked. "I know him?"

"You do. He has wormed his way into your confidence, if not your affections, and no doubt finds great amusement in your gullibility."

Megge set down her cup, folded her hands neatly in her lap, and lifted her chin. Walter need not speak another word. She knew. "That man is Sir Olyver."

"It is. I am so sorry, my dear."

"And Lord Humphrey is party to this?"

"Alas."

"And the king."

"But of course."

"Tell me, sir, how you came to be in this chamber."

If Walter was disappointed that his moment of triumph was to be delayed, he gave no sign of it. "Through the cavern, of course."

"Of course. And how came you to discover the entrance?"

Sir Walter affected surprise. "It is common knowledge."

"I see." Megge did see, all too well. Sir Olyver could have taken Castle Rising any time he wished. The entire siege had been a charade, a game.

"You may as well know it all," Sir Walter continued, relishing the moment. "You were promised to Sir Olyver before he and Humphrey ever left France. In exchange for lifting the siege of Castle Rising, he should claim his reward: you, Megge, the Lady Margaret de Languetot and all she possesses. I have my faults, Megge, but I would never toy with you in this manner. It verges on cruelty, in my opinion, and serves no purpose other than that it affords them amusement at your expense. Do you not agree?"

Megge could not move a muscle. "Yes."

"Well, I am very sorry for your sake, my dear. I wish there was some way I could help, but alas, it is beyond my power."

"On the contrary, Walter," Megge replied. "You have done everything in your power to thwart them in their purpose."

"Really, Megge, I—"

"Be silent, Walter. You have had your say. Now I will have mine.

"You come to me with this intelligence for the sole purpose of avenging yourself upon your brother and Sir Olyver. You assume by telling me that as I have been deceived, everything I have achieved here is an illusion. You assume that because men have indulged in their customary games of power and deception the battle is won and the cause lost."

Megge got to her feet and stared out through the narrow aperture at a group of shrieking children who were tossing a ball around and rolling in the dirt.

"You hope," she continued in a steady voice, "that by informing me that I have been an object of ridicule I will refuse to marry Sir Olyver though the king commands it, and suffer censure and perhaps the loss of all I hold dear?"

She whirled around. "You dare sit there and raise a toast to friendship? You expect me to believe that you are concerned for my future happiness? You alone are the object of your concern, Walter. If you cannot have what you want, you will not suffer others to have it. Rather than confront Sir Olyver, you would use me as your weapon against him."

"Megge, you cannot marry him! He is not worthy of you."

"That is for me to decide."

Sir Walter leaned back against the wall and rested his legs on another barrel. "Ah, so that is the way of it."

Megge said nothing.

"Are you in love with the great Sir Olyver, Megge?" he said softly. "Perhaps you have lain with him already, carry his child. Tell me, is he worth the price of your pride, your dignity, your high ideals? A fifth son, a mercenary, a man of no account. You will be quite a feather in his cap."

A distant memory stirred in Megge's mind. A snow-drift and strong arms and a man.

"I do not wear a cap, Lady Margaret."

"I beg your pardon?"

"I do not wear a cap, therefore I would have nowhere to put my feather."

"I am so very sorry, my lord."

"That I wear no cap and have no hope of a feather?"

"I don't know."

"Do not distress yourself, my lady. Your friend is quite right. A younger son must make his way in the world as best he can. It is the way of things. Farewell, Lady Margaret."

"Farewell, Sir Olyver. My lord?"

"My lady?"

"I hope you don't. Die in battle or perish from some vile malady."

Megge thought if she gave way to tears now, she might never stop crying. She longed only to end this terrible interview.

"Sir Olyver does not wear a cap," she said.

Sir Walter leaped to his feet. "Damn it, Megge, how can you make light of this? The man played you for a fool. He has known from the start that he would be lord of this place. He had no need to storm the walls or sneak in through the cavern to take possession. It was already his. You were already his. He used that buffoon of a brother of mine to reach for something he was never meant to possess."

"As would you."

"It is not the same thing," Sir Walter cried.

"Oh, but it is. You and Sir Olyver share a common bond. You are both younger sons."

"It isn't fair," he muttered.

"No, it is not. Any more than it is fair that I have so little control over my own life. But there it is, and we must all live with it as best we can. The difference between you and Sir Olyver is that he took what action he could to make a place for himself in the world. Whether one admires his methods or not, he has succeeded. But you, Walter, have allowed your anger to cripple you. You stand about expecting redress for the accident of your birth, and yet you resent it when it is given to you. Did not Edward arrange two advantageous marriages for you? Did not Lord Humphrey convey a respectable estate to you?"

Sir Walter slumped down onto a barrel and buried his head in his hands. "I am no better than a beggar waiting for someone to toss me a bone. How else was I to survive? I am no great warrior like Olyver. I can barely read and write. I have nothing to recommend me. Now I have lost it all. Edward will strip me of my estate if Humphrey does not do it first. I have no more now than I started with."

Megge moved through the gloom to his side and placed a hand on his shoulder. "It is not too late to learn to take control of your own life, Walter. It is never too late."

He looked like a beaten pup. "Where would I start, Megge?"

Megge poured a cup of wine and handed it to him, took one for herself, and sat down. "You could start at Avola, Walter. It is a sizeable estate in the kingdom of Sicily that might produce a very fine wine if it were properly managed. I am told the manor house is beautiful but in a state of sad neglect. It has been in my family for generations. As it is located in the independent kingdom of Sicily and was left to me by my great uncle, it is not subject to any authority but mine, and that includes Edward himself. I give it to you gladly."

"It is but another bone," Sir Walter muttered. "Wherein lies the difference?"

"The difference, Walter, is that it is not a bone but an opportunity. I will convey it into your hands free and clear, and have done with it. It will be up to you alone to make of it what you will. If you fail, you fail, and will have no one to blame but yourself. If you succeed, you succeed, and will at last understand your own worth. I pray that if God should bless you with sons you will see that each and every one of them has the opportunity to know his own."

"You would do this for me, Megge, even now, even knowing what I am?"

"Aye, Walter, I would. I believe that every man—and woman—should be given the opportunity to make of his life what he can."

"That is not the way of the world, Megge."

"No, it is not." She smiled. "But it could be." She raised her cup. "To friendship, my lord. May you remember me with some kindness for the service I do you this day."

Megge had been wrong. She could not cry forever. Eventually there were no more tears left to be shed.

She felt strangely calm now as she sat cross-legged in the wind-whipped grass atop a towering headland some miles from Castle Rising. Three hundred feet below, the sea hurled itself at the land; overhead, gulls swooped and screamed.

The occasional jingle of metal and creak of leather assured her that Lady Skye was grazing close by. Megge had run her flat out across the grasslands that swept clear to the edge of the cliffs, reveling in the power of the little palfrey's strong sure stride and the feel of sun and wind on her face and the heady freedom of knowing she could go anywhere and everywhere or nowhere as she chose. There had been no past and no future, only the moment.

But such a moment is gone all too soon, and Megge had now to confront the truths Walter had revealed to her. She reviewed the course of events step by painful step, and in the end knew that there was nothing to be gained from assigning blame to this or that person. All of them—Edward, Sir Walter, Lord Humphrey, Sir Olyver—had acted in accordance with their nature, their circumstances, and their understanding of the conventions by which a man must live.

All except Megge herself, and therein lay the problem and the reason things had gone so very wrong. Never once had she considered her own nature, what she, Megge—not Lady Margaret de Languetot, descendant of the Conqueror, heiress of the realm—needed most in her life; never had she looked into her own heart to discover what might bring her happiness.

What had she said to Lady Orabella that day in the ladies' solar at Flete? *Who better to know my own heart? No one, that's who!* But she hadn't known, not then. She hadn't even bothered to look. It had been so much easier to take action on behalf of Lady Margaret de Languetot: to occupy the precinct of Castle Rising and make it her home; issue her demands; and negotiate for the restoration of her fortune.

Those things were worth fighting for, and she could not regret that she had done it.

But now she had looked into her heart. She understood what she needed, what would bring her real happiness. She knew what she must do and exactly how she would go about it.

Chapter Thirty-Eight

Lady Orabella giggled. "We must practice often, my dear."

"Indeed we must," agreed Lord Humphrey as he settled his lady wife in his arms. "You see, it is as I said. There are ways to manage the business without another babe in ten months' time."

"Nine, Humphrey. Nine months' time."

"Oh. Well I expect you know more about it than I. In any event, I am glad to see that you have come round to my point of view."

Lady Orabella wisely changed the subject. "Humphrey, will you not tell me the name of the man Edward has chosen for Megge? It is so hard on her not knowing. It is hard on all of us for her sake. We want so much for her to be happy."

"And so she shall be," Humphrey assured her. "Edward knows what he is about. We need not question his judgment in the matter."

"That's exactly what we said to him," said Orabella, "but you know how he is, such a pragmatic man and really quite kind in his way but without, I fear, much understanding of a woman's heart. We were delighted, of course, that he was willing to hear our petition and agree to think on our suggestions."

Lord Humphrey disentangled himself from his wife's embrace, climbed out of the bed, and glared down at her. "We? Petition? Suggestions?"

Lady Orabella slipped from the bed, drew her shawl about her shoulders, and glared back. "We. Eight of us, although I fear Clarice and Sybille were not much help, fainting away like that. Little Missy just had to bring up the matter of size, which really was very embarrassing, although I don't think the king could very well object since he himself was standing there with his privities in plain view for all to see, and we all had to close our eyes—"

"Orabella," growled Lord Humphrey, "you will cease this babbling and explain what you are talking about. What have you done?"

Lady Orabella drew her plump self up to her full five feet. "I have *done* nothing that I or you need be ashamed of, husband. Megge deserves the very best kind of man. A group of us have decided that Sir Olyver is that man. We went to Edward to describe for him the perfect husband for Megge, right down to the color of his eyes and the cut of his clothes. Edward cannot possibly mistake the man we described to him. We pray that he will agree with us and reconsider the choice he has already made in favor of Sir Olyver. *That* is what I have done, husband, and I would do it again no matter what you say!"

Lady Orabella was rarely surprised by anything her husband did, so predictable was he. When he suddenly threw himself upon the bed and rolled this way and that and laughed until the tears ran down his cheeks, she could only think he must be suffering a seizure of some sort. She ran screaming into the passageway to summon assistance.

By the time help arrived, both the earl of Flete and his countess were wrapped in each other's arms, helpless with laughter, and not a word of sense could be had from them.

The little group huddled in the anteroom outside the august chamber where for generations the lords of Rising had ruled their people. They heard their pleas, passed judgment as to their innocence or guilt, adjudicated their disputes, and administered the king's laws. Some had done so with wisdom and compassion, some had not; but whatever their individual qualities and abilities may have been, their authority was absolute, even as the king's would be in the palace of Westminster.

As it so happened, the king himself sat in the lord's chair within at that very moment awaiting the arrival of Megge, who had gone out riding that afternoon and had yet to return. With him were Lord Humphrey and Sir Olyver.

"What did Robert say?" whispered Mistress Gilly.

"He said she was crying when she came to the stable."

"Megge was crying?"

Missy nodded. "And she didn't give him a penny."

"What has that to do with it?" demanded Lady Agnes.

Missy bristled. "How should I know? Mistress Gilly asked me what he said, and I said what he said."

"Now we mustn't lose our heads," Lady Orabella

counseled. "She's lost track of the time is all. I expect she's nervous. After all, she's about to learn who the king has chosen for her."

"He'd better choose that Sir Olyver," Gunny One growled, "or he'll be doing without his precious oysters in a cold yellow sauce of ginger and saffron and spooning up three-day-old gruel."

Mary rushed in. "She's coming! Long Ida saw her from the wall."

Missy wrung her hands. "Is she wearing her cloak? The wind—"

"Oh, be silent, child," Lady Agnes snapped.

"I'll just go and tell His Majesty that she's here." Lady Orabella bustled away.

Megge didn't seem in the least upset when a few minutes later she came hurrying down the hall, and if she'd been crying, her tears had long since dried. In fact, she looked remarkably well despite her dusty riding gown and windblown hair. Her skin glowed from the exhilarating ride along the headland, her eyes were bright.

"You look a fright," Lady Agnes scolded. "Megge, you have been riding astride again! You cannot think to meet with His Majesty dressed in that indecent gown. Split skirts. The very idea! And your hair!"

Missy, who made it her mission in life to be prepared when it came to matters of her lady's personal grooming, produced a wide-toothed silver comb and a garment whisk from some deep pocket. Lady Agnes snatched the whisk and began vigorously brushing dust and bits of grass from Megge's dark blue wool gown, while Missy teased the tangles from her long curls. Lady Sybille wiped away a smudge of dirt from

Megge's cheek with a moistened fingertip and smoothed her rich brown brows into perfect arcs.

"Bite your lips, Megge. They are not as rosy as they should be."

"Really, Sybille—"

"Bite."

Megge bit.

Orabella slipped out into anteroom. "Thank goodness you are here, Megge. You know better than to keep Edward waiting. Fortunately, Humphrey and Sir Olyver are keeping him company, else he would become testy, and one never knows with Edward when he is testy. Wherever have you been?" she fretted. "Oh, never mind, in you go. And Megge?"

"Yes, Orabella?"

"All will be well, my dear, you'll see."

Megge smiled down at her. "Yes, Orabella, I know."

Chapter Thirty-Nine

"Your Majesty." Megge sank into a graceful curtsy.

"It is about time, Megge," Edward growled.

"Pray forgive me, sire. I was exercising my horse, and rode rather farther than I had intended."

"With a groom, I hope."

"No, sire. I often ride out alone."

"Alone? That is most unwise, Megge, a young woman out and about in the wilds without proper escort."

"A man may ride out alone, sire," Megge pointed out.

Edward sighed. "You have not changed one whit since I left for the Holy Land, have you, my dear? It has been—what?—five years since I last saw you, and you are as contrary in your opinions as ever."

"I merely point out, sire, that—"

"Yes, yes. Let's not get into it now. We have far more important matters to discuss. Sir Olyver, if you will excuse us."

Megge had kept her eyes fixed firmly on the king

from the moment she entered the room, wary of what the sight of Olyver might cause her to do at this critical moment. She might be capable of anything: leap for his throat and rip it out with her bare hands, throw him to the floor and ravish him. She must, at all costs, maintain her composure, so she did not even deign to take notice of his courteous, "Your Majesty, Lord Humphrey, Lady Margaret" when he bowed and made his departure.

"For heaven's sake, sit down, Megge," Edward ordered. "You stand there as though I am about to pronounce a sentence of death upon you."

Megge settled down on a padded bench opposite the king and folded her hands in her lap. Edward had caused the lord's high seat to be moved from the dais upon which it usually stood and set near the hearth. He appeared very much at his ease with his long legs stretched out before him. Upon a table at his elbow stood a large silver flagon and small bowls of spiced nuts, gingered figs, and bites of yellow cheese cleverly cut in the shape of stars and flowers. A bowl of succulent fruits awaited the royal taste buds.

The king took up his flagon and drank deeply. "I have asked Humphrey to join us, Megge, as he is your legal guardian and an interested party in this rather odd situation we find ourselves in. As I am a latecomer to the scene, I should like to hear what each of you has to say about the events that bring a baron of the realm to lay siege to a castle full of women and children. You need not reiterate your demands, Megge. I seek simply to know the facts. I have already spoken with Sir Olyver, by the way. As you wish to be party to matters that most closely concern you—I must say you express yourself extremely well, Megge—you may begin."

A prisoner awaiting the hour when he will be led to the block, a traveler on a winter's night surrounded by a pack of ravening wolves, a naked soul trembling before the Throne of Judgment. Anything would be preferable, thought Sir Olyver, to spending this eternity under the unwavering scrutiny of the women of Castle Rising. Eventually, Lady Orabella had taken pity on him and led him to a bench in an alcove off the anteroom, where she chatted on about this and that and inquired after his family, none of whom it turned out he had seen in over a decade.

"It must be so very difficult," Lady Orabella remarked, "to be ever on the move."

Sir Olyver shrugged. "It is a way of life like any other, my lady. One becomes accustomed to it."

"I am sure one does," she replied. "Of course, a man wants children to carry on his name."

"He does."

"And a good wife to bear and nurture them. And a happy home to shelter them all."

"So I am told."

Lady Orabella paused to consider how to go on. "It is not so very difficult, once a man puts his mind to it."

Sir Olyver hid a smile. "A way of life like any other?"

Lady Orabella beamed up at him. "Exactly! Of course," she went on cautiously, "a man might hope for more in a wife than a mother for his children and a mistress for his hall."

"Possibly."

"He might hope for her love."

"He might."

"He might gift her with his."

"He might."

Lady Orabella heaved a sigh of relief and patted his hand. "All will be well then, my lord, you'll see."

Sir Olyver smiled down at her. "Yes, my lady, I know."

"I had the most extraordinary dream this morning," the king remarked while his squire went in search of Sir Olyver and Lady Orabella.

"Did you indeed, sire?" Megge said to be polite.

"I did. In the dream I awoke to find myself stark naked with my dagger in my hand in a bedchamber filled with strange women! What do you make of that, Megge?"

Megge searched for something to say. In just minutes Edward would tell her she must marry Sir Olyver of Mannyngs. She must prepare herself. "How very interesting," she managed. "Were they naked as well, my lord?"

Lord Humphrey laughed. "A good question, my dear. Well, Edward?"

The king affected disappointment. "Alas, they were not. It becomes even more interesting, Megge. It seems these ladies—I believe there were eight of them—were in some apprehension as to my sound judgment in a matter in which they held a particular interest. Since I am a reasonable man, even when I am standing naked before a crowd with my manly parts dangling down, I did not take offense and agreed to hear them out."

The king had Megge's full attention now. He popped a handful of sugared almonds into his mouth and munched. "Apparently, I had settled on a husband for a dear friend of theirs—that had occurred before the dream began—and they wished to acquaint me with the qualities in a husband they felt would ensure her happiness. The list was rather long, and I cannot remember the details—you know how dreams are—but I had a feeling, though I cannot say for sure, that they had a particular candidate in mind."

Megge's head snapped around. Lord Humphrey was sniggering behind his hand.

The king examined a small peach with a critical eye and returned it to the bowl. "I agreed to consider their suggestions."

Megge held her onto her composure by the slimmest thread. "And how did this dream end, sire?"

Edward shrugged. "I woke up at that point, so I have no idea. But I expect I would have decided to stay with the man I had selected. It is such a nuisance to have to change one's mind. Quite an extraordinary dream," he added as he reconsidered the peach and took a bite, "wouldn't you say, my dear?"

"Extraordinary," Megge heard herself agree, although what she really had in mind to say was unladylike in the extreme.

A knock sounded at the door, and the king's squire presented himself. "Lady Orabella and Sir Olyver, sire."

"Excellent, excellent," the king exclaimed. "Let us get on with this business. Please, Lady Orabella, make yourself comfortable. How are the babes? Might I tempt you with a gingered fig?"

Edward had learned early in life to use his imposing height and admirable physique to the best political effect. Accordingly, he stationed himself before the hearth, very much the monarch, very much the master of the moment, the focus of every eye.

"Megge, the time has come for you to marry," he declared. "I must confess that I cannot recall at the moment how many times I have said those same words to you in the past—"

"Five, sire," Megge supplied.

The king frowned. "Only five? I thought it more."

"Your father announced my first three betrothals."

"Ah yes, so he did. It is never easy to settle on a candidate," he continued, pacing back and forth with his hands clasped behind his back. "There are so many factors to take into consideration, and given your station in life you will agree that I have always taken great care to see that you were in no way disparaged."

"That is true, sire, and I am grateful for it," Megge said, wondering why the king was taking so long to get to the point. A warning bell at the edge of her awareness gave forth a tiny ping.

"As you have made it clear that you wish to play a part in the selection of your next husband I give you leave to do so now."

For a moment Megge was so taken aback that she could not credit what she had just heard. "Er, that is most gracious of you, Your Majesty."

Edward nodded. "It is, isn't it?"

Ping, ping, ping.

"I imagine over the years you have developed your own ideas as to the qualities you would most like to see in a husband?"

Megge might have been a mouse eyeing a bit of succulent pork set out just so in the middle of the trap, judging the likelihood that it could snatch up the morsel and be gone before the trap snapped shut. "I imagine I have, sire."

"Perhaps you have a particular man in mind?"

Clang! Snap!

This, thought Megge, was Edward through and through, perhaps the craftiest man to sit the throne of England since the second Henry.

"As I am your loyal subject, my liege," she said humbly, "I would never presume my own opinion could hold greater merit than your own."

The king resumed his seat, steepled his fingers, and regarded her thoughtfully. "Of course you would not," he murmured. "And as my loyal subject, you will no doubt wish to humor me and describe the man you would have as your husband."

Megge rose and took the spot before the hearth where the king had stood. She tucked her own hands behind her back just as he had done. She'd learned a few political tricks of her own in her twelve years at court.

"As you suspect, sire, I am no different from any other woman," she began, "when it comes to matters of the heart. As a girl I dreamed of a gallant knight who would rescue me from some terrible danger and kneel before me to swear his eternal love, though he might have to lay down his life for my sake."

A derisive "hmmph" came from the direction of Lord Humphrey, followed by a shushing sound from his lady.

"A girl cannot harbor such foolish dreams forever, of course," Megge continued, "and when I learned of Queen Eleanor's Court of Love at Poitiers they vanished like smoke. I read and re-read the inspired writings of that great poet, Master Capellanus, so many times that I could recite them by heart."

"Absolute hogwash," the king muttered.

Megge clasped her hands before her breast and allowed a look of rapture to steal over her countenance. "And then I discovered the *Roman de la Rose!* I cannot tell you, sire—I have not the words, though you flatter me that I express myself so very well—to describe the passionate emotions Master de Lorris's work aroused in me."

The king's eyes were narrow slits. "Megge—"

A tiny giggle, quickly muffled, was heard from Lady Orabella.

Megge clapped her hands and practically hopped up and down the way a child might when she has exciting news to tell. "And I have recently heard that a Master de Meun has taken up the story where Master de Lorris unfortunately had to leave off due to his untimely demise! I cannot wait to read it."

The king folded his arms across his chest, a sure sign of royal displeasure. "Your husband, Megge. You will describe him to us."

Megge realized she might have gone a bit too far. The affable "I" and "me" had been supplanted by the royal "we" and "us."

"Pray forgive me, Your Majesty. I allowed myself to get carried away."

"We are aware of that."

Megge knew the moment was at hand. She peeked into her heart one last time just to make sure. She was.

"There is no reason to describe him, Your Majesty, as he stands before you. Is it not fortuitous that he happens to be here among us?"

The flutter of a butterfly's wing could not have

been heard, so absolute was the shocked silence that settled over the room.

Megge stood demurely with hands folded before her, her eyes fixed expectantly on the king. She would have given anything to see the look on Sir Olyver's face, but felt it would ruin the dramatic impact of the moment. Besides, she might not like what she saw.

Edward finally bestirred himself. "We underestimated you, my dear."

"Have I displeased you, sire? Do you not wish me to choose as you have chosen?" Megge inquired with an anxious little smile.

The king's scowl was his only reply.

Lady Margaret de Languetot of Castle Rising turned to the man known as the Scourge of the Saracen, the Limb of Hell, the master of the siege, the most cunning warrior in all Christendom, and sank into an exquisite curtsy. She bowed her head.

"My lord Sir Olyver of Mannyngs, as His Most Gracious Majesty Edward of England has granted me leave to choose my own husband, I choose you. I pray you will accept my suit."

Chapter Forty

"I didn't, you know," the king remarked to Lord Humphrey some time later as they finished off the keg. "Grant her leave."

"Not in so many words, but you might just as well have handed it to her on a silver platter."

"I never saw it coming," Edward admitted.

Lord Humphrey thumped his old friend upon his royal back. "Don't be too hard on yourself, Edward. Neither, I'll wager, did Olyver."

"God help him, is all I can say."

But Sir Olyver *had* seen it coming, or most of it anyway.

He had watched with a kind of preternatural fascination as the gamekeeper threw open the cage door and gestured to the wary little fox that she was free to roam where she would. But it was a grateful little fox that settled onto its haunches at his feet and wagged a bushy tail, and the gamekeeper had smiled to himself as if he had known all along that she had nowhere else to go. Olyver had known, too, and had pitied the fox as she gazed around at the wide world for the last time.

The gamekeeper reached for her; she licked his hand. And then, in a blink of an eye she was no longer a grateful little fox, but a blur of dark fur and snapping jaws, a predator that had long ago marked its prey and was now whipping around and launching itself straight at the throat of an unwary gander.

He should have realized, Sir Olyver thought as he went in search of his betrothed; he should have seen the signs.

She had known. He couldn't say when Megge had learned that he was to be lord of Castle Rising, but he did know that Walter had a hand in the business. Walter would pay.

"Lady Megge? She might be in the nursery, my lord," the little maidservant said.

"And where is the nursery?"

"Well, it was in the southeast tower, my lord, but now it's not."

"Hmmm. That would mean it has been moved."

The girl nodded her agreement.

"And where might that be?"

"Somewhere else?" the girl ventured.

Sir Olyver gave it up and moved on. Eventually he spotted Missy trotting along with one of Megge's many cloaks over her arm. Where Missy went, there Megge was bound to be, and sure enough, a few minutes later he spotted her high atop the south wall. He waited until Missy had finished her fussing, and made his way up to the walkway through the damp dark spiral staircase built into the wall.

They had barely exchanged ten words since Edward had placed her small hand in his and given his sanction to their union. A nervous little priest named Jerome had bumbled his way through a rambling benediction that unaccountably included passages from the Song of Solomon, and women had popped out of every nook and cranny in the castle to giggle and gape at the soon-to-be lord of Rising. Sir Olyver had never felt so uncomfortable in his life.

"Good evening, my lady."

"Good evening, my lord."

Olyver was not surprised at her cool reception. He wasn't feeling all that warmly toward her, either.

They stood side by side watching the last tinge of rose in the sky fade to gray. "I commend you on your excellent performance," he remarked.

"I thank you, but it cannot possibly have been better than your own over the past few weeks," Megge replied.

Olyver turned his back on the dying light and leaned against the parapet. "I was not aware I was acting a part, my lady. Pray tell me how I have deceived you."

Megge walked several paces along the wall and turned to face him. "We agreed to negotiate under the Conventions of the Siege. I chose to speak for myself; you declared yourself to be Lord Humphrey's emissary and to speak on his behalf."

"That is so."

"We agreed that my dispute with the king had no part in the negotiations."

"We did."

"Perhaps it was foolish of me, but I interpreted certain of your remarks to mean that you yourself held no personal views as to the right or wrong of the matters under negotiation."

Sir Olyver shrugged. "I will allow that."

"How very kind of you, my lord. To continue, you claimed to have no stake in the outcome."

"There I must disagree. If you will recall our exchange of letters, you advised me to demand payment in advance from Lord Humphrey, and I replied that I should have exactly the payment I desired from the enterprise. The outcome of the negotiations had nothing to do with it."

The moment the words were out of his mouth, Olyver knew he could not have been more callous. In all his life he had never said anything quite so cruel to another human being. He remembered all too well the taunts he had endured as a child.

"Forgive me, Megge," he said softly. "That was uncalled for."

"Yes, it was. It is a pity you wear no cap, Olyver."

"I don't understand."

"As you wear no cap, you have nowhere to put your feather."

He remembered. "I am so sorry."

She turned back to the sea. "You need not apologize. I know what I am, what I have always been. I am known by many names: heiress, ward, chattel, payment, plunder, prize. Feather has rather a nice ring to it."

"Megge—"

She almost managed a little laugh. "Walter had it aright: You had no need to storm the walls of my castle, no need to take it by guile. It was already yours. I was already yours."

"He told you that?"

"Yes, he told me."

"Where did he come by this information?"

Megge shrugged. "He never said. He told me that even before you and Lord Humphrey left France, you demanded that I should be your reward for lifting the siege."

Olyver whirled around and kicked the granite wall. "That bastard!" Again. "That sniveling little coward!" And again. "That pitiful excuse for a man!"

Megge backed away.

"Did he touch you?" he shouted. "Did he, Megge? I'll kill the bastard. I swear by the cross that I will slit his throat and watch him drown in his own blood."

"Olyver, you must stop."

"What lies did he tell you, Megge?" Olyver raged. "Did he give you some sad story about being a second son and how unfair it was and how Humphrey got everything and he got nothing and everyone should pity him? Did he weep real tears? Did he warn you against me? Did he tell you what a runt I was? Did he? How my brothers beat me and belittled me and my father laughed at me? Did he tell you I am not worthy of you? Did he dare say that *he* is?"

"Stop this, Olyver," Megge commanded, "or I shall leave you here to rage until you can bear it no longer and hurl yourself onto the rocks. Be quiet, I say!"

Olyver slumped down against the wall and buried his head in his arms.

"That's better. Now I want you to listen to me and listen well. Walter did not touch me. He did not try to touch me. He came to me hoping to use me to revenge himself on you and his brother. He did not succeed."

Olyver climbed to his feet. "Where is he, Megge?"

"I don't know, and I would not tell you if I did."

"I will find him and I will kill him."

"Will you just listen to yourself?" she cried. "Who bears the greater share of the blame? The man who claims me as his prize or the man who tells me about it? Who causes me the greater pain and humiliation? *I* am the one betrayed, Olyver. *I* am the puppet on your string, the pawn, the object of your amusement, the prize. Shall I slit *your* throat and watch *you* drown in your own blood?"

"Please, Megge, I can take no more tonight. Let us be done. We will have the rest of our lives to debate the matter. This anger and resentment gets us nowhere."

"No, it does not." She leaned into him to rest her forehead against his chest, and let the tears come. "It is all so painful, so complicated, Olyver. I do not know where we are to begin."

His arms went around her and drew her close. "I do."

Chapter Forty-One

He came to her in the night.

Megge could not see him in the absolute blackness of the velvet-hung bed, not even the faintest outline of his powerful body. If his eyes spoke of his hunger she did not know it. Nor did she need to hear the words to know he would settle for nothing less than her total submission to his will and surrender to his need, for he came to her wrapped round with all his raw power and male arrogance and sanctioned ascendancy.

So he sought to take her according to his nature. And she challenged him and yielded and challenged him again according to hers.

In those dark hours, he was not a fifth son, a warrior, a deceiver. She was not an heiress, a crusader, a prize. There was no past for them, only the moment and the joining and the pleasure.

It was a good place to begin.

Chapter Forty-Two

For perhaps the first time in his life, Edward of England was not the focus of every eye, and certainly not the master of the moment. He was not even a monarch, but merely a corporeal obstruction that was in imminent danger of being mowed down and trampled into the ground.

He considered his options. He could put his trust in the fleetness of foot he had enjoyed as a younger man and try to make it out of the tunnel alive when the stampede began. Or he could execute a strategic retreat and reposition himself on the walkway above the barbican.

He wisely chose the barbican.

The women of Castle Rising had turned out in their all their finery, which might be anything from a richly trimmed velvet gown to a patched homespun tunic that had received its first laundering in a decade. They milled about in chattering, laughing confusion in the outer bailey until Megge appeared to try to marshal them into some sense of order.

Massed before the great doors of Castle Rising, the men of the siege camp stomped and snorted and all but foamed at the mouth, although they did keep to their ordered ranks under their commander's stern eye.

Father Jerome popped out of the chapel and trotted to the bailey end of the tunnel. Father Boniface positioned himself at the outer end.

Megge took up position before her troops, flanked by Orabella, Agnes, Sybille, Gilly, and the Gunnys; Olyver stood before his, with Lord Humphrey on one side and Sir Kay on the other.

It was, thought Edward, a cataclysm waiting to happen.

As nobody was going to listen to anything he might have to say anyhow, Edward had not bothered to prepare any remarks. He had, however, come up with a rather clever idea, if he had to say so himself.

A short blast of a trumpet signaled the start of the proceedings.

"Lords, ladies, faithful subjects. We are gathered here today to celebrate the lifting of the siege of Castle Rising!"

Cheers, whistles, applause.

"But first, let us have a benediction from Father Jerome and Father Boniface."

Boos, snarls, groans.

Father Jerome faced the ladies of Castle Rising.

"Hear the Word of God as entered into the Book of Ecclesiastes. "To everything there is a season and a time to every purpose under the heaven." He soldiered on until he came to "A time to embrace and a time to refrain from embracing," and stopped in mid-sentence.

311

"Is something wrong, Father Jerome?" Megge whispered.

"No. Yes. It is all so confusing." He searched the crowd for one special face. "God forgive me, my lady, but I cannot hold back any longer."

Megge frowned. "Hold back what?"

Father Jerome threw wide his arms and bellowed for all the world to hear, "I love you, Long Ida!"

The men outside the walls could have no idea why a great cheer went up from within the bailey, but as it seemed a good omen of the pleasures that awaited them, they cheered too.

Father Boniface glanced nervously at Sir Olyver and cleared his throat. "Hear me, my sons. Do evil. Do not do good. It is good to do evil. It is not evil to do evil. It is evil not to do evil. It is not good not to do evil. It is not evil not to do good. Good is not good. Evil is good. Amen."

Sir Olyver was still doubled over laughing when Edward gave the signal. The trumpets of rams' horn resounded over the walls of Castle Rising. The men of the siege army let out a great shout and stampeded through the tunnel toward the welcoming arms of their lovers.

"And the walls came tumbling down!" cried the king.

Father Jerome was snatched from the jaws of death by Long Ida and carried away to safety, but poor Father Boniface went down before the charge praying that he'd finally gotten it right.

Only a drift of dust over trampled grass, a bit of colored cloth here, a bauble there, bore witness to the pandemonium that reigned as the siege of Castle Rising was lifted. Women were snatched up and carried away to whatever closet, cupboard, or corner provided even a modicum of privacy. That it was not always the right woman brought on the inevitable altercation, but the exchange was soon made and the mad dash toward consummation resumed. Some couples managed to keep their wits about them and fled to the beach or the woods, but one or two lost their heads altogether and had to be hauled up off the ground and marched away to a more suitable venue at the point of Sir Olyver's sword.

"A most effective strategy, Megge," the king remarked as they strolled together through a neat garden of fragrant herbs. "Perhaps I shall withdraw this 'leave' I am supposed to have granted you and bring you up to Westminster to help plan my campaign against Llywelyn."

"I am honored, sire, but I decline."

He laughed. "Another fine strategy of yours, my dear. I bid you, you decline. I bid you again, you again decline. If I say yes, you say no. If I say no, you say yes."

Megge turned to him, serious now. "It was not always so, Your Majesty."

He patted her arm. "No, it was not; I do not forget."

They strolled on. "Although I hold to my royal prerogative never to have to explain and never to have to apologize, I will tell you, Megge, that there were times when I put my own political or financial interest above yours in finding you a suitable match. I am not proud of it, but it is the way of things."

"Please, sire, I would not have you apologize."

"Am I apologizing?" the king asked in surprise.

"Aye, you are."

"Oh. Well, that is all in the past now. The man I have chosen for you this time—"

"The man *I* have chosen, Your Majesty."

He glared down at her. "The man *we* have chosen . . ."

They were still sparring with one another when they reached the keep.

"What the devil is going on over there?" the king demanded.

"Oh God!" Megge took off running toward the steps that led up to the great hall. "Olyver, no!"

He didn't even hear her, so intent was his focus on the man beneath him.

"Lord Humphrey, stop him!" Megge cried. "This is madness."

Sir Walter lay on the ground with Olyver's knee on his chest and his dagger at his throat. "What do you here, Walter?" Olyver growled. "Perhaps you come here to die. If so, I will be glad to oblige you."

"I, I came to—"

"To do what? To take what is mine? Is that not what you do, Walter? Take what belongs to others? You cannot be bothered to go out and earn it for yourself. No, you sneak around like a thief, swoop in like a vulture—"

Megge stamped her foot. "That will be quite enough, Olyver."

He did not even look up at her. "Go into the hall, Megge."

"I most certainly will not."

"Humphrey, take her into the hall."

Megge bristled. "You will remember, Sir Olyver, that you are not lord of this keep yet. If you will not conduct yourself in a seemly manner, I must ask you to leave."

Lady Orabella appeared at the door of the hall. "Whatever is going on out here? Sir Olyver, what do you think you are about? You will hurt Walter kneeling upon him like that. Humphrey, why are you not taking some action? I am ashamed of you."

The king cleared his throat. "Sir Olyver, Sir Walter does not have the opportunity to explain his presence here with your dagger at his throat. We should like to hear what he has to say."

Olyver slammed his dagger into its sheath and rose to his feet. He did not extend his hand to help Walter up. He did not take his eyes from him for a single second.

Walter brushed the dust from his tunic, and with some dignity said, "I am here on business at Lady Margaret's invitation, Your Majesty. It will take but a minute."

"Indeed? What might that business be?"

Megge stepped in. "Pray excuse me, sire, but it is a private matter between Sir Walter and myself."

Edward glanced over at Sir Olyver. Walter was probably a dead man. "A private matter, is it? Very well. Five minutes, Walter, and then we should like a word with you in private ourself. Humphrey, you will join us."

Walter bowed. "As you wish, sire." Flanked by Megge and Lady Orabella, he disappeared into the keep.

"Stand down, Olyver," the king advised.

Without a word Olyver bowed to the king and stormed out of the castle.

"Olyver had better get that girl to the church door soon," Lord Humphrey remarked.

Edward laughed. "You don't seriously believe that will make a jot of difference, do you? Ah, there you are, Walter. Your business is quickly concluded. Megge, if you will excuse us?"

"Of course, sire." She turned to Walter. "God go with you, my friend."

"I will not fail you, Megge."

She smiled up at him. "You cannot fail me, Walter. You can only fail yourself."

Sir Walter of Avola tucked the deed to his future into his belt and went to his king and his older brother to ask their forgiveness.

"Lancelot, go up to the castle and see what is keeping Lady Megge. She should have joined the festivities long ago."

Lancelot scampered away.

"I have never understood it," the king remarked, "but women are always underfoot when you wish them elsewhere, and nowhere to be found when you summon them. Frankly, their lives are a mystery to me. What do they *do*? I ask myself."

The little maidservant Sir Olyver had encountered the day before trotted onto the bridge. "Your wine, Sir Olyver. And Gunny One wants me to tell you that she is ready to serve the oysters."

"Our oysters!" the king exclaimed.

The girl shook her head. "They are not your oysters, my lord. They are Sir Olyver's oysters."

"No, child, you do not understand. We asked for them most particularly."

The girl looked around. There was no one on the bridge except Sir Olyver and this lord. A great number of people were milling about in the light of the

316

giant bonfire in the meadow, but they were far away. Who was this other person the lord was referring to? "Perhaps you and your friend meant to ask for oysters," she suggested, "but you forgot."

Olyver stirred. "Sire, I think perhaps—"

Edward tried to remain calm. "Listen, child, these oysters are prepared in a cold yellow sauce of ginger and saffron, are they not?"

"Yes, my lord."

"There you have it! They are our oysters!"

"They are not!"

Edward leaned down and glared at her. "We. Want. Our. Oysters."

The girl glared back. "Well, you and your friend aren't going to *get* your oysters. You can't always have what you want, you know."

"We shall see about that," the king of England declared, and marched off toward the cook tent.

The girl looked up at Sir Olyver. "Shall I tell Gunny One you're ready for your oysters, my lord?"

He shrugged. "Why not?"

The girl trotted off, and Olyver was left alone on the bridge to brood. He had decided he would wait until this evening's celebration to speak to Megge. He had needed time to calm down, to think how best to handle her. He knew Walter was gone, but neither Humphrey nor the king would discuss the matter.

Lancelot reappeared. "I don't think Lady Megge is there, my lord."

"What do you mean she's not there?"

"I couldn't get in, so I can't be absolutely sure. The big gate is up, but the doors are closed. I tried the postern door and the stable doors, but they were locked. I didn't see any lights."

Olyver whirled around and stared up at the castle mount. "Get the king, Lord Humphrey, and Sir Kay. Tell the Gunnys I want them. Now."

Lancelot flew across the meadow, and in less than a minute everyone was staring up at Castle Rising and thinking the same thing: Something was very, very wrong.

Olyver barked out orders. "Kay, take some men and check the entrance to the cavern. Siward, take a party down to the beach. Have someone row around the promontory; see if there are lights anywhere. Where are the Gunnys? Good, there you are. Who would be up there? Not everyone came down for the celebration."

The women consulted together. "Megge told all the servants they could come down. The whole garrison is here, most of the children, too. That would leave Lady Orabella, who is only just out of childbed, and Lady Clarice, who is too close to her time to be out and about. There are the babes, of course, and Mistress Annie and the nursemaids."

"How many in all, would you say?" Olyver asked.

"Probably no more than twenty-five, my lord," Gunny Two said. "And Lady Megge, of course, if she's in there."

Sir Kay was back. "The entrance has been closed off, Olyver. The funnel is completely filled with rock. It will take a week to break it open."

Lord Humphrey paced back and forth. "We have to get in there, Olyver. Orabella and the babes may be in danger."

Sir Olyver turned to the king. "What do you think, sire? Should we scale the walls?"

"I think I should wait before taking any action and

see what develops, Olyver. Certainly the castle has not been attacked, or we would know of it."

By now a sizeable crowd had gathered by the river.

" 'Tis the Fay."

"Aye, the Fay."

"The Fay . . . the Fay . . . the Fay!"

"You will cease this flumadiddle at once," Lord Humphrey roared. "We are not savages who paint our bodies blue and dance naked beneath the moon. We are modern, civilized people. Only ignorant—"

"Look!" someone shouted.

Everyone looked.

"Listen!"

Everyone listened.

The crowd breathed in one long collective gasp of amazement.

"Mother of God!" said Lord Humphrey.

"We do not believe our eyes," the King of England admitted.

"Well played, Megge," murmured Sir Olyver.

Long after the sparks of blue and green fire had ceased to dance along the east-facing wall of Castle Rising and the last haunting echo of pipes faded away and the shimmering figure of silver could be seen no more, Olyver stood alone upon the bridge that spanned the River Lis. Sleeping bodies dotted the meadow, as the castle remained closed and dark. The king snored contentedly in Olyver's bed, having stormed the cook tent to lay claim to his oysters.

"She bids you come, my lord."

Olyver frowned down at the young boy who was tugging at the hem of his tunic. "Who?"

"She bids you come, my lord."

"Who is this lady and why does she bid me come?"

It had taken Robert all evening to memorize his one line. He was not prepared for this unexpected development. "She bids—"

"Yes, I know," Olyver said patiently, "she bids me come. But now you must tell me who this lady is."

Unable to depart from his prepared script, Robert abruptly changed the subject. "I got five pennies."

"Do you?"

Robert nodded.

"Hmmm. Well, I shall give you two more if you can tell me who this lady is."

"How many will I have then?"

"You will have seven pennies."

Robert considered that. "I want ten."

"Eight."

Robert shook his head. "Nine."

"Done."

"The fairy queen. She bids you come, my lord."

Chapter Forty-Three

"Good evening, my lord."

"Good evening," Olyver replied. "As we are betrothed, I should prefer you call me Olyver and I will call you Megge."

"And so we shall, my lord, but here there are protocols to be observed."

"Here?" Olyver looked about him, and only then noticed that the stool stood in its usual place before the entrance to the castle. No doubt in the darkness of the tunnel Megge sat on the padded bench.

"Ah, I see. Of course, my lady, you are quite correct. Respect for the dignity and station of one's opponent is the first rule of negotiation. One must not be too familiar."

"Pray take a seat," Megge said. "You will note that I have had the gate lifted."

"And why is that, my lady?"

"I would always have us deal in good faith."

"In that we are agreed," said Sir Olyver.

Megge smiled in the darkness. "Excellent. Before

we continue I should like to understand our respective roles. I speak only for myself. Do you continue to speak for Lord Humphrey?"

"Nay, my lady. I speak only for myself."

"And have you any expectation of reward, payment, or prize as a result of this negotiation?"

"Indeed not, my lady. I seek only that we are mutually satisfied."

Megge had to bite her lip to keep from laughing.

"Let me reiterate the main points we have discussed so far. Although we agreed that my dispute with Edward would not pertain, I am pleased to inform you that His Majesty did indeed grant me leave to choose my own husband. He has accepted my suit."

"I congratulate you, my lady, and wish you every happiness."

"Thank you, my lord. I have every expectation of being very happy indeed. To celebrate my betrothal, I have decided to grant Lord Humphrey access to my forest preserves irrespective of the outcome of this negotiation."

"That is most generous of you, my lady," said Olyver. "I believe that leaves only the matter of the restoration of your property to your sole authority. As I say, I do not speak for Lord Humphrey now, but as the matter is shortly to be resolved to your satisfaction, we need not discuss it."

"Resolved? To my satisfaction?" Megge hadn't expected this.

"Yes, my lady." Olyver could almost hear her thoughts scrambling around in her head.

"My lord," Megge said after a short silence, "the issue is not easily resolved at all as I am now betrothed; we have not only the king, Lord Humphrey, and myself to consider, but my betrothed who is soon to be my lord."

Olyver moved to the threshold of the tunnel. "I am sorry, my lady, but I have no influence with either the king or Lord Humphrey in this matter." He pulled a document from his belt that bore the earl's seal. "Lord Humphrey requested that I give you this."

So it was over, Megge thought sadly. The document would inform her that her property had been transferred to Olyver. Oh, she had known from the start that she probably fail, but somehow that did not lessen the shock now that she held the proof of it in her hands.

"Will you read it, my lady?"

Yes, she would. Perhaps seeing it in words would help her accept it. She took the document from Olyver and stepped out into the pale moonlight.

"B-but I don't understand," she said after she had read it. "There must be some mistake. Lord Humphrey has restored my properties to *me* and Edward has sanctioned it? No, that cannot be right." She read it again and passed it to Olyver.

"So it would appear, my lady."

"But what about you, Olyver?" she cried. "You will be lord in name only!"

He touched her cheek. "Megge, perhaps that is the way things must be. At least I will be your lord. I can ask for no more. I want only you."

She wrenched away from him. "No! It is not right. I would not have you walk in my shadow but at my side."

She snatched the document from him and made to tear it in half.

"Wait, Megge. Consider what you are doing. Is this not what you wanted?"

"Yes! But I was alone and thought I would always be alone because I would have to marry a man I did not love. But I have you now and I will never be alone. I have someone to love. If I must choose, it will be you." With that, she tore the paper in half and in half again and again.

"He bids me bring you this, my lady."

Megge spun around. "Robert?"

"He bids me bring you this, my lady."

"Who? Who, Robert?"

This time the boy was prepared. "He."

Megge took the document he held out. "Olyver, do you . . . ?

But Olyver wasn't there. And then neither was Robert.

Shaking her head in confusion, Megge sat on the stool.

Be it known to one and all:
That the houses, parks, fish preserves, ponds, mills, and everything pertaining to them, and the coin, plate, jewelry, personal and household effects formerly held in guardianship by Humphrey, Earl of Flete, for Margaret de Languetot of Rising are hereby conveyed to the lord and lady of Castle Rising, Sir Olyver and Lady Margaret, in the shire of Devon and under the stewardship of His Most Gracious Majesty Edward of England, that they may be held and administered jointly, and with due care that both may have an equal say in the matters that most closely concern them.

Signed by our hand this day, the 23 August in the year of our Lord, 1275.

Edward Rex
Humphrey, Earl of Flete

"Olyver of Mannyngs, you come out from wherever you are right now!"

Megge stamped her foot. "I know you're there."

"You must be mistaken, my lady," came a deep voice from the walkway above the barbican. "There is no one here by that name. Perhaps you have come to the wrong castle."

Megge settled her hands on her hips and glared up at the imposing figure above her. "Come down here at once."

"Alas, I cannot leave the wall unprotected, my lady, so you must come to me."

Megge marched through the tunnel, stomped up the wooden stairs to the walkway, and planted herself in front of him. "What," she demanded, poking the Scourge of the Saracen, the Limb of Hell, the most fearsome warrior in all Christendom in the chest, "if I had simply tucked the first document into my pocket and gone my merry way? Then where would you be?"

He smiled down at her. "I expect I should still be here on the wall, my lady."

Megge wanted to cry. "You would consent to such an arrangement? To be the lord of Rising in name only?"

"For you, my lady, only for you."

"Oh." She swallowed. "Well, that is very noble of you, my lord."

"It is, is it not?"

"You don't have to agree with me, you know," she replied huffily.

"I don't?" he asked in mock surprise. "Pray forgive me. I have heard that the lady of this place knows her own mind and brooks no opposition."

Megge decided a mischievous Olyver was going to take some getting used to. "You say that there is no one here by the name of Olyver of Mannyngs?"

"Nay, my lady, the lord of this place come the Sabbath will be one Olyver of Rising and his lady wife will be Megge. It is rumored she has vowed to be the most amenable of souls, who will never think to contradict her lord or question his judgment."

Megge scowled up at him. "Really, Olyver, I must protest!"

Olyver could not help but laugh as he pulled her to him and held her close to his heart, as he would forever.

"Megge, my love, I would expect nothing less of you."

GIRL on the RUN
JENNIE KLASSEL

Seventeen-year-old Lady Kaia is going to throw Lord Eben from the battlements if he calls her "little one" again. Men can be so thickheaded! But Kaia controls her destiny: She is headed to a distant land where women are educated and can marry the man of their choosing.

When Lord Eben finally catches up to Lady Kaia, he is confounded by the chaotic feelings she evokes in him. Why in heaven's name did he kiss her senseless? And when had his childhood playmate turned so desirable? As Kaia slips from his grasp once more, Eben realizes that to capture the lady will take more than wisdom. He will offer his heart—and hope she chooses to stop running and start loving.
